Patricia A. Bremmer

DEATH

FORESHADOWED

Elusive Clue

Series

Death Foreshadowed

Copyright © 2004

Patricia A. Bremmer

ISBN 0-9745884-2-3

For additional copies contact:

Windcall Enterprises
75345 Rd. 317
Venango, NE 69168

www.windcallenterprises.com

ACKNOWLEDGEMENTS

Many thanks to all that encouraged and helped me to create **"Death Foreshadowed"**.

Brandenn and Martin Bremmer, cover design and photography.

Debbie Karst, for her assistance in developing the character of Detective Karst.

Detective Glen Karst, used his expertise in his field to keep my crime scenes believable.

Jamie Swayzee, (The Comma Queen), for her assistance with editing.

Jennifer Donald, Spiritual Counselor and Teacher, for her input into the spiritual accuracy and editing.

Jack Sommars, screenplay writer, for all his comments, suggestions and criticisms.

To all of my readers that begged for more!

Chapter 1

The sound of a twig snapping underfoot broke the silence of that cold, November morning. Detective Karst paused to listen with all of his senses alert. He eased his way through the brush. It was impossible to walk unnoticed on the snow that crunched an icy sound beneath his boot. His eyes scanned the area ahead of him when suddenly, he heard the cracking sound of a gun blast. Detective Karst froze in his spot. He called out, "Do you think you hit him?"

Officer Smith answered, "I'm not sure. I'm going to release the dog, if he's wounded, he'll find him."

Karst hiked towards Smith's voice with shotgun poised, ready to fire.

"I didn't see a thing. How'd you find him?"

"I saw him over there, crouching down, making his way through the brush," replied Smith.

Moments later, they were joined by Lance, Smith's dog. He retrieved the pheasant Smith shot.

"That makes three for me, and none for you this morning," teased Smith.

"Yeah, Dave, I'm just getting warmed up."

Strolling along the edge of a cornfield not yet harvested, the swish of wings, and dry cornhusks alerted Glen to raise his shotgun dropping two birds with one shot. Lance ran ahead to retrieve the birds.

Glen glanced at Dave with a smile on his face. Not a word was spoken. Twenty minutes later, Glen dropped his last bird of the morning. Reaching their limit they returned to Dave's house for a steaming, hot cup of coffee, to remove the chill from their bones. Shelly greeting them at the door reminded them to clean their birds outdoors, not in her kitchen. Leaving the birds at the door, they entered the house. The fragrance of cinnamon rolls filled the room.

Shelly poured coffee while Dave passed a plate of cinnamon rolls to Glen, before helping himself to two of the steaming rolls, with melted icing.

Glen leaned back on his chair, pondering what life in a rural area has to offer.

"This is so peaceful. Do you have any idea how lucky you are?"

"Yep, I sure do. Since I left Denver, I've never looked back. I can honestly say I don't miss that rat race one bit. No more calls to jump out of bed in the middle of the night. The worst thing I have to deal with here, in the middle of the night, is a complaint about a barking dog."

"Boy, must be rough, and to think I passed up this job to let you have it," said Karst.

"Oh, come on, you know you'd never leave the city. You thrive on it all. I mean, we sure as hell don't have a SWAT team out here. What would you do for your adrenaline rush? My guess is, while you're there, you couldn't be happier. If I can drag you away once a year to go pheasant hunting, it's a damn miracle."

"Yeah, I guess you're right. Whenever I'm here, I have the same fantasy of moving here forever, but I think I'd be too fidgety after the first few weeks. I do like to be in the center of the action."

"Hey, are you guys gonna just sit there, and talk all morning, or are you gonna clean those birds, so I can fix them for supper?" teased Shelly.

"I don't want to miss the chance to have Shelly fix those birds, no one can cook them like she can," winked Glen as he got up to step outside to clean the pheasants.

"How's Shelly getting along out here, now that you guys have been here for a few years?" asked Glen.

"Better," answered Dave. "It was a little tough at first. She missed her friends, and the shopping. I think most of all she missed the restaurants and the movies. We've adapted though. Once a month, we drive to Fort Collins, or Denver, for a weekend of the city life. Makes it easier when we come back to the slow pace of this area. We've started going to the ball games. That's the biggest

3

event of the community. Shelly has a few clubs she's joined. She likes the church we go to."

"Well, that's the last one," said Karst wiping feathers and blood from his hands.

"Let's take these to Shelly, then I'll take you downtown with me," said Smith.

"Sounds good. Then you can show me what I've been missing."

Smith and Karst cruised main-street like the teenagers. Many people left their vehicles idling on this cold and snowy morning while they shopped the stores lining the small town street. Other residents rushed hurriedly down the sidewalks. The post office was one of the busiest stops of the morning. The local, coffee shop was filled with farmers passing time, telling stories, while waiting for the long winter days to pass until the first signs of spring, when they could return to the fields. Social life in the country remained strongly seasonal. Completing fall harvest, the community relaxed, focusing its attention on school sports. When their team made it to the state tournaments, nearly the entire town closed, allowing everyone to drive to the games. To a city person, it appeared as if one was stepping back in time.

Year after year, season after season, little change takes place.

Karst lowered his window to listen.

"What'd ya hear?" asked Smith.

"Nothing, that's just it. No honking horns, no sirens, only quiet sounds of people moving slowly through the town."

"Yeah, pretty great, huh?" laughed Smith. He pulled into a parking place in front of the drugstore allowing Karst a chance to soak it all in. Everyone who passed the two men, seated in the police cruiser, smiled and waved as they passed. Even the kids greeted them with smiles.

"I suppose you know all of these people."

"Not all of them, but most of them. Their routines are pretty predictable. You can find the same people day after day running the same errands, or taking walks. This is actually a touch of heaven, life is good here."

Smith experienced tough times while he was on the police force in Denver with Karst. Street violence took the lives of his two partners. Emotional recovery from that came slow for him. When you lose a partner you feel like you should've done more, it should've been you instead.

Smith himself had been shot twice. Nothing serious either time, but enough to give him a wake up call about the dangers of police work. Drugs played an integral part in the violence, along with gangs. In the past, most of the calls were domestic violence, robberies, and bar room brawls.

Now, officers are forced to explain to mothers their son or daughter was killed by a drive by shooting, a gang war, or simply for walking down the street at the wrong

5

time. Many of those young people were wholesome kids minding their own business.

When Smith woke up in his hospital room, recovering from his last gunshot wound, he discovered his partner was not so lucky. After his funeral Smith decided he couldn't take it any longer. He and Karst had been discussing a job that opened in a rural area in Eastern Colorado. Karst wasn't ready to leave the city, so Smith took the job.

Packing up his wife, Shelly, their two kids, Sean and Ann, the family relocated to Holyoke, Colorado. Fortunately, Sean and Ann were in middle school making the transition easier than dealing with peer pressure from high school. Being the new kid on the block is traditionally a difficult situation to be in.

"Come on," said Dave as he got out of his car.

Glen followed obediently, "Where are we going?"

"Thought we'd stop in at the coffee shop and see what's going on."

The attention of the regulars turned to the door every time the bell chimed as the door opened.

"Hey, Dave, thought you'd be out pheasant hunting this morning," said Larry, one of the local farmers.

"Back already, we had a good morning. We both got three. Of course hotshot here got his three with only two shots."

"All that fancy city police training you have, and you let this city slicker get the best of you?" teased Bob, another local farmer.

"Hell, this guy's not your typical city slicker gone hunting. He's on the SWAT team in Denver. We used to work together."

"Ain't there some law against a SWAT cop shooting poor defenseless birds?" teased Dan, yet another farmer killing time in the coffee shop on a Saturday morning.

The place burst into laughter. Dave and Glen sat in a booth. The waitress stopped by with a pot of coffee.

"The usual?"

She gave Glen the once over. It wasn't often they had nice looking strangers in town. Glen with his soft green eyes and light brown hair caught her attention. She watched as he walked towards the bathroom.

Tall and fit, no pot belly like many of the farmers, she sighed when she saw his wedding ring.

"Make that two," answered Dave.

She came back with two large jelly doughnuts.

"Dave, we just had cinnamon rolls. How do you have room for more?" asked Glen.

"It's all part of life in the country. I plan to put on about fifty pounds and enjoy every minute of it," said Dave as he patted his expanding middle. Dave had the same softness to his hazel eyes. His hair was a dirty blond, but with his expanding waistline he didn't turn heads like

7

Glen. "Homemade pastries are the best vice a person can have out here."

Glen took a bite of his jelly doughnut. He had to agree with Dave, they melted in your mouth in such a way that the customers of the corner doughnut shacks in Denver could only imagine.

"Are you guys going to the game tonight?" asked Larry

"That's the plan, unless Glen decides not to."

"Count me in, when in Rome ya know."

"Is your son gonna play tonight?" asked Larry.

"I hope so," responded Dave.

Dave scanned the room out of habit. Since it was hunting season, strangers were everywhere. This was a good year for hunting. The word spread quickly. There were more hunters in the area than the years before. Hunters were good business. They stayed in the motels, ate in the diners and shopped in the grocery stores. They were generally very easy to get along with and behaved themselves.

They kept the county population of stray dogs up. Many a hunting dog that the owner felt was well trained and primed for the hunt would take off in the direction of a bird never to return. The hunters would give up on their birds and use the rest of the weekend looking for their dogs. A week or so later a hungry pooch would show up at someone's farm and take up residence.

"Let's go by the station," suggested Dave.

Glen finished his coffee, nodded to the guys, then followed Dave out of the door. They crossed the street, got into the cruiser and drove the three blocks to the station.

Dave read his messages, made a few quick phone calls, and signed checks. Glen nosed around the office, reading a file here and there.

"You aren't kidding when you say it's pretty quiet around here. Looks like speeding tickets and summons work is the bulk of your duties. Don't you miss the excitement of homicide just a little?"

"I'm telling you, I'm a changed man after that last stretch in the hospital. I need to stay safe for my family. They're not ready to live life without me. Doesn't Debbie worry about you every time you step out the door?"

"Yeah, I guess, but she knew going into the marriage that was part of being a cop's wife," answered Glen. "Besides, I do everything possible to be sure not to make a widow out of her."

"Well, knowing what she was getting into still doesn't make it any easier. Shelly sleeps better now knowing nothing really dangerous happens around here."

"Sounds like you're trying to get me to slow down and follow your lead," commented Glen.

"When the time is right, I'll lead you into a more peaceful existence," said Dave slapping Glen on the back.

"Let's go get a bite to eat, it's lunchtime."

"You've gotta be kidding," moaned Glen.

"Oh come on, it's cold outside, gotta eat enough to keep ya warm."

"Yeah, but we're not bears storing up for a winter hibernation," reminded Glen.

The two had just gotten into the car to drive the three blocks back to the diner when a call came across the radio for Dave. "Hunters trespassing on the Olsen place."

"Got it," responded Dave.

"We're ready for some action now," teased Glen. "You sure we don't need the National Guard?"

Dave drove over to the Olsen farm. Mrs. Olsen answered the door.

"Those guys came by yesterday asking if they could hunt in our trees. We told them no. We even have signs posted. As you can see, they're out there as big as you please, looking for birds."

"We'll ask them to leave," promised Dave.
Dave and Glen parked on the road next to the hunter's pick-up truck. Dave stepped out of the car. Glen followed his lead. Dave was in uniform, but Glen was not. Glen reached into his pocket for his badge and hooked it to the waistband of his jeans. Dave reached his hand back inside the car and honked the horn. The hunters looked up then headed towards Dave and Glen.

Dave walked partway out to meet them.

"How's the hunting?" he asked.

"Not bad," replied the older of the two hunters.

"Might try hunting somewhere that doesn't have *No Hunting* signs posted, men."

"Gee, I guess we didn't see those signs. Sorry officer," answered the same man.

"You know if your eyesight's not good, and your hearing's bad, maybe you should go back to where you came from and skip the hunting trip all together," suggested Dave.

"There's nothing wrong with our eyesight or our hearing. I told you, we just missed the signs," replied the same man, a little more testy this time.

"According to Mrs. Olsen, her husband told you yesterday you couldn't hunt here. I just assumed you didn't hear him, like you didn't see these signs. I think you two should load up and leave this county. I don't want to see you hunting around here again. If I spot this pick-up again, I'll haul you in. Have a nice day."

Dave walked back to the car. Glen followed him.

"Sometimes I'd like to arrest guys like that just for insulting my intelligence," complained Dave.

"Gee Andy, you handled that real good," laughed Glen.

"So you think my life out here makes you think of Mayberry, huh? Someday you'll be begging me to take you on as Barney," Dave laughed back.

Before they could drive back into town for lunch another call came through. Someone had fallen through the ice on one of the ponds north of town.

11

When they arrived on the scene the ambulance, and a small crowd of people were already there. Seems a hunter's dog fell through the ice. He tried to save him and fell through himself. Both dog and hunter were fine, a little cold and shaken up, but fine.

"Now, let's go get that lunch before something else happens."

"Isn't this unusually busy for you?" asked Glen.

"Yeah, I'm just trying to show off for you."

After lunch they stopped by the station, then drove back to Dave's house. They spent the rest of the afternoon visiting about old times, and old cases. Glen brought Dave up to speed on some of the cases he was handling. The two worked well together. They were good friends, but had never been partners.

Dave did miss some of the detective work. He felt as if his brain was not being challenged with the lack of crimes in Holyoke. Fascinated, he listened to Glen describe the new forensic lab equipment.

Glen liked that type of detective work. If his investigation of a case required the use of the lab, he would hang around the lab as much as time would allow. He made good friends with the pathologist, and other members of the staff. Sometimes, he felt his cases might have gotten a little more priority because he was so well liked, and didn't mind helping out. He asked many questions. He wasn't trying to stroke the ego of the staff; he was sincerely interested in their work.

Sean and Ann listened to the stories for a little while. Sean was getting ready for the game. Ann was a cheerleader. Both kids were smart, good looking and respectable. Dave and Shelly did a good job with them. They made the right choice removing them from the public school system in Denver. They had many friends, but were not pressured into the drug and alcohol use at the local high school. No one wanted to get the cop's kids in trouble. The town was too small for that.

Shelly called the guys to the table for their pheasant feast. The kids didn't like to eat pheasant. They preferred to eat pizza in town with their friends before the game.

Shelly prepared the pheasant to perfection. Glen enjoyed it as always. Debbie was glad Glen didn't bring the plucked and bloody birds home for her to prepare, so all were happy.

Shelly cleared the table. It was time to drive to the gym for the game. Shelly and Dave always went together. Tonight he suggested they take separate vehicles, in case he received a call. He let the deputy off tonight to watch the game.

Dave and Glen waited in the parking lot for Shelly. People waved and nodded as they walked through the gym. Shelly's friends saved seats on the top row, the only place you could sit where you could lean against a wall. Sitting on bleachers for hours takes practice; most of the town people were seasoned veterans for ballgames.

13

The buzzer sounded, the game began. The gym was crowded. It was a big night for the local team. The sound of the crowd, the buzzing of the scoreboard, the smell of popcorn, reminded Glen of his days as a school athlete.

Glen and Debbie didn't have any kids of their own. They missed out on spending hours sitting on hard bleachers and baking for the cake sale at the game.

Tonight the school was trying to raise revenue for new uniforms. There was a wider assortment of food being served. There was a constant flow of spectators from the bleachers to the snack bar and back.

Just before half time, Dave suggested that he and Glen take a stroll outside to be sure there were no kids in the parking lot drinking. Of course, he knew there would be, and they knew he would be coming out, they just didn't know when. It was a cat and mouse game they played. It worked though, as it kept the drugs and alcohol down to a minimum, knowing they could get busted at any moment.

They made their rounds. They could see kids disappearing around cars as they walked. The smell of beer being poured out onto the ground filled the night air. The same kids would casually stroll past Dave and Glen to go inside to watch the game. You could be sure for the rest of the evening those that were spotted would remain clean as a whistle.

Glen thought the whole scene somewhat amusing.

14

The buzzer sounded signaling the end of the first half. Glen and Dave returned to the warm building. They visited with people in the hall. Dave bought a bag of popcorn, but Glen could not eat another bite.

They made their way back to their seats. Dave proudly waved at Ann on the gym floor performing a halftime cheer for the home team. He glanced down at the bench where the team was sitting. He gave a thumbs up to Sean.

The buzzer sounded again, the game resumed. With the third quarter barely underway, Tim, the star player from the home team fell to the floor. He must've stumbled on his shoestring. The crowd waited for him to get back up.

Dave said, "Wow, he must've gotten the wind knocked out of him."

The gym grew quiet. The ref and the coach went to Tim, as he remained motionless on the floor.

The crowd watched in silence.

"Is Doctor Foster here tonight?" the call came over the intercom system. "If Doctor Foster is here, please come down to the court."

Tim's parents found their way down the bleachers to the court to check on the condition of their son. The coach stopped them.

Dave and Glen jumped up to assist. It was obvious something was wrong. Dr. Foster was kneeling over Tim when the two officers arrived at his side. A crowd of athletes shielded the view from the bleachers. Dr. Foster began CPR. Glen assisted. Dave saw more people leaving their seats.

"Would everyone please remain seated. Dr. Foster has everything under control. I'm sure Tim will be just fine. We'll let everyone know as soon as we know what happened."

The EMT's arrived with a stretcher. Tim was not breathing. Inserting a tube down his throat allowed them to bag him until they could get to the hospital. The crowd appeared horrified; cheerleaders were crying. Tim's parents were escorted to the ambulance through the crowd. Whispers continued throughout the gym. Every eye was on Tim, and his parents as they left the floor. Fans were motionless, Tim's teammates were wiping tears away.

The team took a few minutes to regain their composure. The coach reassured everyone that Tim was in good hands, and everything would probably be fine.

"Well guys, are we ready to win this game for Tim?" asked the coach.

The boys looked at the coach, then at each other. One of the boys said, "For Tim!" as he slapped the hands of each team member.

The coach signaled to the ref that they were ready. The buzzer sounded, the players returned to the court to continue the game.

Most of the spectators stayed. Shelly left the game, she wanted to be sure Tim was really okay. At the hospital she could visit with Dave.

The remainder of Tim's family members, as well as close friends of Tim's parents, appeared at the hospital to offer moral support.

When the ambulance arrived at the hospital. Everyone rushed at top speed. In the emergency examination room, Dr. Foster and his staff tried desperately to revive Tim, but were unsuccessful.

Dave and Glen stepped into the room to gather news for Tim's parents. His parents Rose and Ed paced the hall outside of the room. Rose tried to be brave. Ed kept telling her Tim was a strong, young boy. Whatever happened out there on the court, could not keep him down.

Dave looked at Tim's limp gray body on the table. A sight he and Glen had experienced too many times before. Dr. Foster's eyes caught Dave's. He shook his head.

"Let's call it," he said.

"Eight forty-seven p.m.," replied the nurse.

Dave sank down onto a round stool with wheels in the corner of the room. He knew what he had to do next. He so dreaded telling the parents with Dr. Foster.

Glen watched from across the room. Instantly, aware of the gravity of the situation, he went to his old friend, putting his hand on his shoulder.

17

"Can I help? Would you like me to tell the parents?"

No, that's okay. Dr. Foster and I will do it. I'm sure they'd rather hear it from us," answered Dave.

Dr. Foster, the nurses, the EMT crew, and the two officers stayed in the room for a moment of silence to regain their composure before meeting with Tim's parents.

Dr. Foster stepped out of the exam room with Dave at his heels. Tim's parents looked pleadingly at Dr. Foster.

"So Doc, what happened? Is he going to be alright?" asked Tim's father.

Before he had a chance to answer, Tim's mother looked into Dave's eyes. He could not hide the pain.

"No! No! Tim! Please God, not Tim," she sobbed.

Her husband looked at her, wondering how she knew anything, when no one had spoken. He looked back to the doctor.

"I'm sorry Ed, he didn't make it. We did everything we could, he seemed to have died almost before he hit the floor."

"But...what happened? He was such a healthy kid? Was it his heart?"

"At this point, I don't have an answer for you. After the autopsy we should know more."

"There's not going to be an autopsy. You're not going to cut into my son!" screamed Rose.

"Now, honey, maybe Doc's right. We should try to find out what happened."

"I said no one is cutting Tim up. That's not going to bring him back. He died and we'll bury him with respect. He's not getting butchered to answer some questions when that won't bring him back."

"I guess there'll be no autopsy then," said Ed.

"I want to see Tim now," said Rose.

Dr. Foster led Rose and Ed into the examination room to view their son's lifeless body. Once in the same room with Tim something came over his mother. She was terribly distraught, but she had this strong sense of Tim's presence in the room; a peaceful presence. She looked at the body that once encased the soul of her son. It was nothing more than a shell now; Tim was no longer connected to it.

She felt the pain a mother feels when she loses a child, the sick wrenching pain deep in the pit of her stomach. She wanted to vomit, but then that haunting feeling that he was in a better place kept her from losing control.

Rose and her son were extremely close. She had the feeling that Tim was trying to reach out to her, to tell her he was okay. Or was she just trying to cope in any way she could, by imagining the feeling. Either way, it gave her a small shred of comfort in an otherwise devastating situation.

Chapter 2

The tent over the grave flapped loudly in the wind. The people attending were huddled closely together. Men and women were dressed in their Sunday clothes, not offering much comfort from the cold. The wind cut through the fabric, causing a burning sensation on the flesh.

Nearly everyone who knew Tim was there. The students from his school were released from classes to attend his funeral. When an older person dies from a lingering illness there is sadness mixed with relief, the suffering has ended. But when it is a child, no one seems to be able to accept it. The death of a young person appears to be without purpose. There is no sense of relief, only pain to the friends and family members left behind.

Pastor Bob gave the graveside service. He rushed through it more quickly than he wanted as he saw the discomfort the weather had on the group gathered around the gravesite.

With his closing words he extended an invitation for all those present to return to the church for a dinner.

It is customary for the ladies of the church to provide a meal for the family and friends of the deceased. The church was packed with people forming a line to fill their plates. Drinks were poured and set out at a separate table. A second table was kept supplied with desserts.

At first the room, although filled with so many people, was very quiet. As people ate their meals, walking back and forth for drinks and desserts, the conversation grew louder. Even Tim's parents were socializing with their friends.

Soon the conversation at the tables changed from Tim to the price of grain and new farm equipment. For those that were not immediate family, it was just another social get-together. The young people were the first to leave. They knew they did not have to return to school. They broke off into groups, disappearing to each other's homes to spend the rest of their free day having fun.

The group dwindled down from a few hundred to thirty or forty of Tim's family members and closest friends of his parents. The ladies from the kitchen were gathering the plates and putting away the food. The drinks and desserts were left out a while longer so the remaining people could help themselves.

Pastor Bob walked among the group shaking hands and introducing himself to people who did not attend his church. While Pastor Bob was visiting with Tim's parents someone called out, "Oh my God, Lyle! Are you okay?"

21

Everyone stopped to look up. Lyle's wife, Carol, ran across the room to her husband who had just fallen to the floor, spilling his hot coffee on his way down.

Lyle a large man, weighing two hundred and fifty pounds, five foot nine inches tall was lying on his side in a heap. At fifty-two years old he was terribly out of shape. His wife Carol was the same age and in much the same condition.

A crowd gathered around Lyle. Dave was upstairs in the church lobby visiting with people when Shelly ran to him. One of the ladies from the kitchen called 911.

Dr. Foster had just stepped out of the church. Dave knowing he was leaving ran out to stop him. Together they raced back into the church. Carol had opened Lyle's snuggly fitting suit jacket and loosened his necktie.

"He just fell over without warning," she said to Dr. Foster as he bent down to feel for a pulse.

"Please step back," he asked the group gently as he began CPR. Dave helped.

Lyle was not responding. It seemed like eternity to Carol before the EMTs arrived with the ambulance and a stretcher for Lyle. A tube was inserted down Lyle's throat and he was being bagged as they wheeled him out to the ambulance. Carol rode with him. Dr. Foster continued to do chest compressions while one of the EMTs kept the rhythm of the air bag going.

22

Once the ambulance arrived at the hospital Lyle was rushed to the emergency examination room. Try as they might, the crew with Dr. Foster could not revive Lyle.

"What happened?" asked one of the nurses.

"I'm not quite sure, a heart attack would be my guess. He's overweight and he smokes. He was in last week with the flu. I think there was far too much stress for his heart to handle."

"Damn," said Dr. Foster. "Let's call it."

"Two thirteen, p.m." said the nurse.

Carol, pacing the hall with Lyle's brother, looked up when Dr. Foster came out to speak with her.

"Well Doc?" she asked with pleading eyes.

"I'm so sorry Carol, he didn't make it. I'm pretty sure it was his heart. That bout of the flu he had last week, coupled with his smoking, being overweight, and the stress of the day was just too much for him. I'm sure he went quickly. If I had to guess, I'd say his heart just stopped instantly without warning. Did he give you any indications he wasn't feeling well before he fell?"

"He was having a little difficulty breathing, but then again he'd been sick and his breathing did become labored easily, so I didn't give it much thought," replied Carol, feeling badly for not watching him more closely.

"Would you like us to perform an autopsy to be absolutely certain it was his heart?"

"I'm not sure. I don't know what to do? What should I do?" she asked.

23

It was finally hitting her. This was not just an illness; Lyle had not just passed out. Lyle was dead. She knew he hadn't lived a very healthy life. She hadn't expected him to live to a ripe old age of ninety, but she was not prepared for him to go so soon and so suddenly. Her own symptoms of feeling weak and faint became apparent.

Lyle's brother helped her to a chair. A nurse left to retrieve a glass of water.

"What should I do?" she asked his brother Dick. "Who should we call? We've got to make arrangements. Should we do an autopsy?"

"Just calm down. You don't have to make those decisions this very minute. I'll call the kids and let them know. We'll get together with them and go from there," he said.

Dick's wife stepped outside the hospital into her car. She began calling Lyle's kids. She told them they would be taking Carol home with them and they could reach her there.

Dick said, "Thanks for everything, Doc", as he shook hands with Dr. Foster. He knew that Doc felt badly for not saving Lyle. When you live in a small town and you're the small town doctor, you become socially involved with many of the people in the community, making it extremely difficult when you can't save the life of one of their loved ones. The residents of the town have so much faith in your abilities, you are the only one that can help.

24

When there is nothing you can do, it is difficult to face them.

"I'm so sorry, Dick, I really am. I'll call John at the mortuary and have him come get Lyle. Let me know if you should decide to do the autopsy before too much longer. Okay?"

"Sure Doc, we'll visit with his kids and let you know as soon as possible."

Dick and his wife walked Carol to their car. They took her to their home while they waited for Lyle's two sons to drive over. When the boys arrived, Dick gave them some time alone with their mother before he took them aside to ask about the autopsy.

The two boys looked at each other, then at their Uncle Dick.

"I don't know, what should we do?" asked Pete, the older of the two boys. "Is that something Mom would have to pay for?"

"Yeah, she'd have to cover the expense. Doc thinks it was a heart attack. If you want to know for sure, he'll need to do the autopsy, but if you feel okay with his diagnosis, then there's really no reason to do one."

"Let's not put Mom through the agony and the expense then," said Pete. His brother nodded.

Dick called Dr. Foster to tell him the family made the decision not to have an autopsy. Then Dick offered to help the boys make plans for the funeral. How ironic it was to go to a funeral today only to leave to plan another.

Back in Denver Detective Karst was busy running down leads about a missing child. Samantha Egerts, a cute, little, blond girl, had been missing since the evening before. Samantha belonged to a nice family in the Littleton area. She left her friend's house to walk home around seven p.m. the night before. This normally safe neighborhood beckoned for kids and dogs to happily play in the street on their bikes and skateboards. Samantha's walks back and forth to her friends' homes were a common occurrence.

The neighborhood reacted in an uproar. Nothing like this had ever happened before. No child, nor even a dog, had ever been reported missing from this sleepy neighborhood.

Detective Karst rang the bell to Samantha's house. He and Thompson waited on the step for someone to answer. They pulled up their coat collars to protect themselves from the cold wind blowing circles around them as they stood at the door.

Samantha's aunt came to the door.

"Hello, my name is Detective Glen Karst and this is Detective Thompson. We'd like to ask you a few questions about Samantha if we could."

"I'm Sam's aunt, Kathy, please come in. Her parents are in the living room."

She escorted Karst and Thompson to join them. Sam's dad looked up.

"Any luck? Did you find her?"

"No sir, we haven't got anything for you at the moment. We need to ask you some questions, if we may," answered Karst.

"Shouldn't you be out looking for her?" asked Sam's mother.

It was obvious by the panic in her voice, that her nerves were frayed.

"Can you tell me the last time you saw Samantha?" asked Karst.

"We've been through all this already," responded Sam's dad. He wasn't in much better shape than her mother.

"I know, and I apologize for putting you through this again, but I have my own questions I need answered and I'd rather hear the answers from you, if you can just bear with me."

"We saw Sam yesterday morning at breakfast. She ran out the door to join her friends who she walked to school with," answered her father.

"Did she arrive at school as scheduled?" asked Karst.

"Yes, we checked with her friends and they said she was in class all day. She walked home with her friend Sharon and had supper with her. They were working on some science project, so they went there directly from school."

"What time did she leave Sharon's house?"

27

"At seven o'clock. She has to be home by seven thirty on school nights."

"Was she walking home alone?"

"We live four blocks from Sharon's house. The two girls left the house together. Sharon walked two blocks with Samantha, then they parted and each walked two blocks alone. They've been doing this for a few years now. They've never been bothered by anyone. Everyone in the neighborhood sort of keeps their eyes open and observant when there are kids out and about. Everyone knows everyone's kids, their cars, and their dogs."

"Did anyone see Sharon while she was walking alone?"

"Yes, we called all of the neighbors. A few of them watched the girls say good-bye."

"I'd like the names of those people also, if you would, before we leave," requested Karst.

Samantha's mother walked over to her desk to write down the names, addresses and phone numbers of her neighbors for the detectives.

"It was pretty cold and dark last night. Would she have accepted a ride with someone to get in out of the cold?"

" I suppose I should've just driven over and picked her up. If only I would've just picked her up," sniffed her father. He was to losing the control he had during the beginning of the questioning.

"Sir, please don't blame yourself. If the girls had been walking back and forth for years you would have had no reason to do anything different last evening," said Thompson, trying to reassure her father.

"Would she have accepted a ride with anyone last night?" asked Karst again.

"No, she would not accept a ride from strangers. She knew better."

"But would she accept a ride from someone she knew?"

Her father looked across the room at Samantha's mother for an answer.

She walked over to join them.

"I suppose if it was someone she knew from the neighborhood she might, but she only had a couple of blocks to walk."

"We're sending our men door to door to ask everyone if they saw her, or a strange car, or anyone's car for that matter, shortly after seven last night," asked Thompson.

"I have a few more routine questions to ask, so please don't be offended by them. I must ask. How were you and Samantha getting along? Had there been an argument, say yesterday morning before she left for school?"

"Surely, you don't think she ran away? She's only ten. Where would a ten year old go?"

"No, I'm not saying she ran away. I'm just trying to cover all the angles here."

"No, we didn't have any arguments with her. She's a great kid. She's so responsible. We've always been able to trust her completely. If she says she's going to be somewhere at a certain time we can be sure she'll be there. That's what has us so puzzled, she'd never done anything to cause us to worry. I don't think she'd start now."

"So there's no chance she went to a slumber party or anywhere that you may have forgotten you discussed?"

"Not on a school night. Besides, she didn't show up for school and all of her friends were there," said her mother.

"Does she have a boyfriend?" asked Karst.

"You've got to be kidding," replied her father a little angry. "She's only ten, she has no business with a boyfriend. Our little girl is not that kind of a girl. She's a good girl."

Thompson and Karst exchanged glances.

"Let's say she told you she had a boyfriend, how would you react?" asked Karst.

"I'm not sure, I mean she's way too young. I guess I'd tell her she was too young and we couldn't allow it."

"Are you aware sir, that most kids her age at school have puppy love romances? They exchange letters and phone calls. Generally, it's nothing very serious until a couple more years have passed. So it would not be

30

uncommon for Samantha to have a secret boyfriend that you and your wife were totally unaware of."

Samantha's father looked shocked that his ten-year-old little girl could have a boyfriend. For the first time in his life he felt his daughter might have a private life that did not include him.

"Does she have a diary or journal that you are aware of?"

Samantha's mother said, "I bought her a diary a year ago. She keeps it in her room."

"Have you ever skimmed through it?" asked Thompson.

"No. I guess I thought all of the entries would be innocent."

"May we take a look in her room?" asked Karst.

"Sure, right this way."

Samantha's mother led them down the hall to Sam's room. Teddy bears and dolls filled the room. There were posters on the walls and ribbons hanging from her mirror. There was no sign of makeup in the assortment of lip-glosses on her dresser.

Searching her drawers, her mother found the diary. She handed it to the detectives. Thompson thumbed through it.

"Can I have the most recent school picture you have of her?" asked Karst.

"I gave one to the policeman that came by earlier, but I have more copies." She left the room to retrieve another photo.

"Looks like this little girl did have a crush on some boys at school. Her diary reads pretty tame though. She lists the number of times in a day she saw Mr. Wonderful and whether or not he saw her. Looks like each romance lasted about a week or so and they rarely spoke to each other," said Thompson.

Her mother returned with the picture.

"Did you find anything?" she asked.

"Looks like you have a sweet, innocent, little girl. There's an assortment of crushes on different boys. No real interaction with any of them, just normal ten year old girl stuff."

Thompson returned the diary to the mother. She looked through it herself.

Thompson glanced around the room.

"Does your daughter own a computer?"

"No, but she uses ours whenever she wants to."

"Does she have an email account?"

"Of course, what kid doesn't anymore?"

"Can we take a look at her email log?"

Sam's mom walked them to their office and turned on the computer for them. Samantha did not have a password and apparently had nothing to hide from her parents. The extent of discussions about boys with her

32

friends was just as tame as the diary. This little girl was a real sweetie.

Karst and Thompson left with a new understanding of Samantha.

"I don't like the feel of this case," said Thompson.

"I know what you mean. This little girl wouldn't do anything wrong on her own. My guess is she's been abducted. I'd hate to be in her parent's shoes. If we can't find her they'll be destroyed."

They returned to the station to read through all the reports from the officers scouring the neighborhood interviewing all the neighbors and their kids.

Not one lead on this tough case. It was as if she vanished into thin air within two blocks of her house. With each passing day, the chance of finding her alive would grow dimmer. Moving quickly is the best way to find her, but with no leads, there was not much to check out.

Pastor Bob for the second time that week faced his friends and neighbors on a cold winter's day to bury another member of the community. Tim's death was a shock to the community, but someone Lyle's age and in poor shape, was not the same shock. Sadness set the mood. The group was invited to join the family for a dinner at the church. The crowd today was much smaller than for Tim's funeral. The young people from the school did not attend. This funeral was more typical for the size of the community.

Carol remembered just a few days before she and Lyle were in the same church basement eating the same food for Tim's funeral. Not much change in the small, rural community.

The next day was Saturday; there was a new ball game to attend. Life quickly returned to normal for all but the closest of friends and family members after a death.

Dave and Shelly went to the game to watch their kids perform. Dave's mind wandered back to last game when Tim dropped to the floor. He glanced around the gymnasium, people were yelling, cheers were being sung. The teams were hard at it trying to steal the ball and sink a basket.

How insignificant lives really are in the scheme of the universe, thought Dave. Today someone will be born; someone will die, just like the seasons. New life begins and winter brings death. It is all nothing more than the cycle of life. One can only hope during his or her lifetime to grow and expand with knowledge. How sad to go through life never reaching for the unknown or having questions as to one's existence.

Dave left Shelly's side to make his rounds of the parking lot. Half time was approaching and the lines were beginning to form at the concession stands. Once again, there were many home cooked goodies prepared for the uniform fund. Most people attending the games were very happy to purchase food items and donate to the fund. It was a win-win situation for all.

It's funny though, no one penciled in the amount of time or the cost of the ingredients that went into making the donated food. Many times families were just buying their own food back. Seems like an odd way to make money, but it felt less painful than reaching into your pocket to make the same cash donation that the food cost to prepare.

Dave stepped back inside the building, brushing the snow from his shoulders and stamping his feet on the gray mat by the door before walking down the school corridor. No kids outside that night, far too cold and snowy.

Dave was searching the crowd for Shelly to see if she wanted something to eat. Suddenly, a scream rang from the girl's bathroom.

"Help! Somebody, help us! We need help in here!" screamed a high school girl, holding the door open.

Parents and teachers raced down the hall towards the bathroom. A small group shoved their way past the girl holding the door to see what the problem was.

Sheila, a high school freshman, lay on the floor unconscious. One of the mothers was a nurse. She felt for a pulse.

"Call 911," she yelled.

She checked for a cleared air passage then began CPR. Soon a crowd encompassed the nurse and Sheila. She did not respond. Her friends in the bathroom started to cry. One of the mothers ushered the girls out of the

35

bathroom and told them to clear the halls so the EMT's could get through.

Dave rushed in. He observed the young student with pale, graying, skin lying on the floor.

"Is she breathing?" he asked.

The nurse administering CPR shook her head as she rose up to take breath.

Dave took off his jacket, kneeling down to give her a break, he took over the CPR.

"Where's the EMTs?" screamed the nurse, as she ran to the door to look down the hall.

She was exhausted and frightened. Although she's been trained in CPR, as had all the hospital staff, this was the first time she had to actually perform it on someone. Not being in the safe setting of the hospital added to the feeling of helplessness.

She saw the EMT's running towards her now, with their stretcher. She showed them the way while she filled them in on the details.

That night Dr. Foster did not attend the game. He was called at home to meet the ambulance at the hospital. The halls were lined with spectators as the stretcher carried Sheila out of the building.

"Not again," said one of the parents.

Dave followed the stretcher out of the door. Shelly followed closely behind carrying Dave's jacket. She drove their car to the hospital. She stood against the wall in a corner watching as Sheila's parents arrived. Dave came out of the ER to greet them. Dr. Foster and his team were too busy working on Sheila to leave the room.

"Dr. Foster is with her now," he said to the frantic parents as they met him in the hall.

"I need to go in with her," said Sheila's mother shoving her way past Dave.

He caught her in his arms.

"Why don't you let Doc finish checking her out. He'll let you know as soon as he knows something. It's not a good idea to distract anyone in there when they're trying to do their job," suggested Dave.

He had a sick feeling in his stomach. His instincts told him it was not good. He left Denver to get away from having to deal with the pain and the suffering parents went through when he had to tell them they just lost a child. In the three years since he had been in Holyoke he only had to tell parents once that their child had died and that was in a car accident on a gravel road. In just one week two of the town's children might be gone.

He'd hoped he was wrong about Sheila. He hoped Dr. Foster could bring her back. He continued to hold Sheila's mother in his arms while she sobbed. Her father paced the hall. One by one more people appeared in the hallway of the hospital, some to offer their support, others curious as to what had happened.

Shelly continued to hide in the shadows. She could feel the pain the family was going through. She remembered the times she was in their situation wondering whether or not Dave was going to make it after his gun shot wounds. She fought the thoughts of what she would do if it was one of her kids laying in there on the table fighting for her life. A tear rolled down her cheek, then another. She tried to choke back the tears, but the sad energy from the scene she observed kept the tears flowing.

She disappeared into a bathroom to gather her composure. When she returned watched Dr. Foster as he was talking with the family. Dave was standing with the parents. She studied the group hoping to see a sign of relief on someone's face. Then she saw Sheila's mother nearly collapse to the floor. Her father staggered to the wall for support. Dave was holding her mother up.

Shelly stopped where she was. She leaned against the wall. She could not take another step forward. She could not muster up the strength to give to the parents. She was emotionally exhausted herself. She waited in the hall until the parents disappeared into the examination room to see their daughter's body. She stepped quietly down the hall, hoping no one would notice her. She laid Dave's jacket in plain sight on a chair near the door, knowing that he would notice it. She slipped out of the door and raced to her car. Once inside, she burst into tears. She drove herself home crying all the way.

Dr. Foster stepped back from the table allowing the parents all the space they needed to mourn their daughter. They stroked her hair and kissed her gently.

They told her how much they loved her. They wept over her body while the nurses and staff slipped out of the room. Only Dr. Foster remained. Dave waited outside in the hall.

He found his jacket on the chair. His eyes searched the halls for a sign of Shelly, but she never surfaced. He was sure she couldn't handle this and went home. He sat in the chair his jacket had been laid on. He tipped his head back against the wall. He was spent. Thoughts of last week and Tim came to mind. Then he thought of Lyle. He remembered CPR on Tim didn't work. His heart must've stopped beating before he hit the floor was the comment he remembered Dr. Foster making.

He listened as he heard Sheila's father begin to speak.

"Can you tell us what happened?"

"To be honest, I'm not sure. The stories I got from the ambulance crew and the nurse that did CPR on her was that she didn't respond to anything. She wasn't breathing and there was no pulse. No one saw her fall to the floor. Some girls found her just laying there when they went into the bathroom. Does she have any history of asthma?"

"No, she's never had any problems with anything like that. She's always been really healthy," answered her mother.

"How about this flu that's been going around?"

"Nope, nothing. She hasn't complained about anything."

"Doc, do you think it could be drugs? I mean, I don't think she's been taking drugs or anything but then you know the parents are the last to know about these things," asked her father.

"I know my daughter and she doesn't take drugs," snapped her mother.

"Well, I guess drugs should not be ruled out. She has been in perfect health and then it appears that her heart stopped," said Dr. Foster.

Dave sat straight up in his chair. Her heart stopped. Tim's heart stopped. Lyle's heart stopped. Three people die in just one week. All three people die of unknown causes. Doc tells all three families that their hearts just stopped. Is this a coincidence? Is Doc missing something? If these people had been in a city hospital would they be alive today? Is Doc not capable of handling emergencies? Wild thoughts raced through Dave's mind.

He felt bad questioning Doc's abilities. He tried to remember each case in greater detail. He felt a little better when he realized there was someone close by to administer CPR nearly immediately in each case. Not one of them responded to the attempts at CPR. His instincts as a cop told him not to brush these cases off as a coincidence.

Chapter 3

It was early Sunday morning in Denver. "Aren't you going to get ready for church?" Debbie asked.

Glen looked up at Debbie. She was dressed for church while he sat unshaven at his desk going over the files for Samantha Egerts, the little girl who was missing. Glen's eyes scanned Debbie's body. He never tired of looking at his beautiful blond wife. Each time he looked at her it was as if he was seeing her for the first time. He really loved his wife and wished they could spend more time together. Maybe Dave had the right idea, moving to a rural community that allowed him more family time.

"I'm not going today. I need to work on this case. Time means everything to this little girl."

"Why does that not surprise me?"

Debbie walked over to Glen and sat on his lap. She stroked his hair and kissed him.

"I'll stay home with you. Maybe we can talk about it and something will come to you."

She returned to their bedroom to change into jeans and a sweater. She made another pot of coffee before joining Glen at his desk. He gathered up the papers so they could sit in front of the fireplace while they talked. She followed him to the fireplace where she put the coffee mugs down and fluffed the pillows behind her before she sat down.

Glen began, "We have this sweet little girl from a great neighborhood and a wonderful family. She vanished into thin air. She was walking alone two blocks to her house after leaving a friend's house. No one saw anything unusual. Many neighbors reported seeing her and her friend say good-bye and walk in opposite directions. No one mentioned seeing her after that."

"What's the neighborhood like? Are there lots of trees or bushes?" asked Debbie.

"I saw some large pine trees and yes, there were hedgerows going around a corner that she had to walk past. Every inch of the area has been gone over by our crime scene guys."

"Could they have missed something?"

"Anything's possible but these guys are good. I'm sure if there was something to find they'd have found it. There's really no sense in going back and looking myself. I mean, what could I possibly find that they didn't. It's been a few days. Whatever they missed might not be there. The snow may have covered it up, or the wind might have blown it away..."

Debbie got up in the middle of Glen's sentence. She went to the hall closet to retrieve their coats.

"Hey, what are you doing?"

"Come on, let's go take a look ourselves. I can tell you are trying to convince yourself there is no need for you to go look, but deep inside you feel the need to check it out."

Glen jumped up, glad to have permission to act on his inner feelings, "You're right, different eyes see different things."

He didn't want it to appear he didn't trust the crime scene investigators. He trusted them totally; he wanted to check for himself.

They traveled across town to Littleton. Glen drove slowly down the streets in Samantha's neighborhood. He stopped in front of her friend's house. He pointed out the direction the girls walked together. He cruised along following their course. He stopped again where the girls had parted ways to begin their walk alone.

People in the neighborhood were sweeping the snow from their sidewalks and cars. Many were getting ready to leave for church services. All of them stopped and stared at the car containing Glen Karst and his wife Debbie.

"Look at those people, nothing gets past them. This is the ultimate in community watch neighborhoods. My guess is they are even more guarded now that Samantha has disappeared. Someone will probably call in our car and plates," said Glen.

"Can you blame them? I'd be doing the same thing."

43

They continued down the street. Samantha had to walk around a corner up ahead. Her location was not visible from her friend's house or the path that her friend would've taken to go back home. Samantha would be walking the last block out of view of her friend.

"If someone had a car parked around the corner, her friend and the people on this part of the block wouldn't have been able to see it," Glen pointed out.

"Do you think someone could have been in those bushes and grabbed her as she walked around the corner?"

"Maybe," responded Glen. "The people around the corner would have to be the ones that saw her walking home and no one did. Only the people before she rounded the corner saw her. Something happened to that little girl one block from her house, after she rounded that corner."

Glen was glad Debbie encouraged him to come back to the scene. He felt he was gaining a better scenario about the incident. He drove the car slowly past the corner, studying the bushes for a spot where someone could hide. There appeared to be many spots where a person could remain invisible to the people in the neighborhood, especially since it was dark when she disappeared.

He followed the curve of the road and finished the drive to Samantha's house. Glen pulled into her parent's driveway to turn his car around. Together he and Debbie sat in the car studying the view of the corner from that vantage point.

There was a small section that was not visible from her parent's house or her friend's house, a blind spot for the neighborhood watch. Glen was convinced it was in those few feet of sidewalk that this little girl had been abducted.

He and Debbie drove closer to the corner and parked the car. Together they got out to walk around. Glen hid in the bushes and had Debbie walk past him on the sidewalk. He was able to reach out and grab her.

They searched the spot where Glen had been hiding for anything that could confirm his theory. They came up empty. A theory was all he had. There was no way to prove it. There were no witnesses, no signs of a struggle, not a single bit of evidence lay on the ground or clung to a branch in the bush. They were back to square one with a good theory, but no proof.

Glen and Debbie drove home.

His thoughts turned to his good friend in Holyoke. He thought how peaceful his life is this morning. He and his wife were probably at their church in their peaceful little town where nothing ever happens. He wasn't stressing on a Sunday morning about the disappearance of a little girl with not one lead. He called Dave.

Glen had planned to leave a message just to tell him he was thinking about him and to return his call. Much to his surprise Dave answered the phone.

"Dave? Glen, what are you doing home? I thought you'd be in church this morning."

"Wish I was, but too much is going on here, I stayed home to think. I sent Shelly on with the kids. I needed to be alone."

"Why? What's up?"

"I wish I knew. I can't decide if there's a problem here or if it's all just a coincidence and I'm overreacting."

"You're not typically one to overreact, what's going on?"

"Remember the night you were here and that kid dropped dead at the ballgame?"

"Yeah, did you find something out about that?"

"Not exactly, his parents didn't want to have an autopsy done, so the case is closed. But then at his funeral another person just dropped over in the same manner."

"Another kid?"

"No, a guy in his fifties that was in bad health and overweight. He just fell over in the church basement after the dinner."

"I know it's quiet in your town and two deaths in less than a week can be a big deal, but if this guy wasn't very healthy I fail to see the connection."

"Well, I didn't think there was one until last night, when a high school girl was found collapsed in the girl's bathroom. She didn't make it either."

"Any idea what she died from?"

46

"Nope, nothing conclusive. Doc said her heart must've stopped. That's the same thing he said about the other two. So Glen we're talking about three people dead in one week, all from their hearts stopping. Two of them were kids. I'm afraid there might be a connection."

"That's really weird. Had any of them been ill?"

"Neither of the kids, but the old guy had the flu last week."

"If you leave him out of the equation, say he did die because of his health, then you've got to wonder why two high school kids would be dead in the same week."

"That's what I thought. I haven't said anything to anyone here yet. I'm sure the town's gonna be talking about it soon."

"How well did these kids know each other?"

"I'm not sure. What are you getting at?"

"If he died from some heart thing like athletes do occasionally, could she have been suicidal from his death. Were they dating or anything like that?"

"Well, if it's a suicide, we won't know until the autopsy gets done. There was no note or any signs that would indicate suicide."

"How well do you know these kids? Could we be dealing with some bad drugs being passed around the school?"

"Anything's possible. They seem to be clean cut kids but when it comes to kids and drugs nothing surprises me."

47

"If there's anything I can do to help, just let me know."

"That'd be great. I'd like to make you my confidant in this mess until I'm certain there's something to investigate. I hate to speak out of turn and cause an uproar in the town. People here are very quick to jump to conclusions and panic. Say, did you call for anything important?"

"No, not really. I'd been thinking about you and your peaceful existence. I was a little jealous. I'm working on this case about this little girl that vanished. I don't have good feelings about it. Time's slipping away and you know what that means."

"Gee, sorry Glen, I know how cases with kids seem to really eat away at you. Any leads?"

"No, that's just it, we have nothing to go on. No one saw a thing and this is in one of those neighborhoods where everyone knows everyone else's business and nothing slips past them."

"Did the crime scene people come up with anything?"

"Nope, when I say no lead, I mean no lead at all on this one."

"Well, I wish you luck, if there's anything I can do..."

"Hell no, sounds like you have your hands full right where you're at, but thanks for the offer. I guess I'd better go. Debbie has lunch on the table. Say hi to everyone for me and remember, if you need anything, just say the word."

"Thanks Glen, good luck, and give Debbie a hug from me. Bye."

"Bye."

Glen put the phone down. He thought about the ball game and the boy that had collapsed. He wondered if Dave would find the deaths connected. Then he walked to the table to join Debbie for lunch.

"How's Dave doing?" asked Debbie.

"The strangest things may be happening in his small town."

Glen told Debbie all of the details over lunch. It was a nice temporary diversion for him. He needed to clear his mind about little Samantha.

He and Debbie resumed discussion about Samantha during dessert. Debbie bought a cheesecake for Glen, his favorite; she knew he was having a rough weekend.

They discussed motives, there were none. Everyone in the neighborhood got along nicely. Her parents knew of no one who would want to hurt her, or them, by taking her. All they could come up with was the worst-case scenario, a child molester.

The next morning Karst was in his office with Thompson discussing Samantha's case. He told Thompson about going back to the crime scene. He explained the lay of the bushes allowing someone to stand in them unnoticed waiting for his prey. He could have been waiting for anyone, a boy, a girl or a woman to attack. They agreed that it might have been nothing more than Samantha being in the wrong place at the wrong time. There was nothing to indicate that he stalked her. Of course, there was nothing to indicate anything. The two skilled detectives and Samantha's parents were totally frustrated.

Later that morning they were called into their sergeant's office. When they walked in he said, "Close that door behind ya."

Seated across the desk from their sarge was a woman in a purple suit.

"Gentleman, I'd like you to meet Jennifer Parker."

Miss Parker rose to meet the two detectives.
Glen reached his hand out to her, "Hello, I'm Detective Glen Karst and this is Detective Jim Thompson."

She shook the hands of both men. She cradled their hands in hers, longer than a typical handshake. Both men were aware of this.

Sarge began, "Miss Parker has graciously come forward to help us with your case involving the disappearance of Samantha."

Both men looked immediately at Miss Parker.

"Did you see something that might help us?" asked Thompson.

"Well, sort of," she began.

Sarge cut her off, "Miss Parker is a psychic, gentlemen."

Karst and Thompson shot glances at each other. They wanted to leave the room as soon as they could come up with a good enough excuse to allow them to do so.

"Miss Parker has come at the request of Samantha's mother. Seems she read a book written by Miss Parker about psychic connections to missing and dead people."

The guys could tell by the tone of their sergeant's voice that he was being kind while being extremely skeptical.

"Maybe you should take her to your office and see what she may have for you."

They were trapped. They could leave the office quickly as planned but they weren't leaving alone.

Glen gave a *you've got to be kidding* look at his sergeant. He smiled back. Then went back to reading the papers on his desk.

Miss Parker rose to leave with the two men.

Glen, the gentleman as always, opened the door for her.

"Right this way, Miss Parker."

"Please, call me Jennifer. Miss Parker is too formal, especially if we're going to be working together on this case. First names are so much better, don't you agree?"

"Most definitely," responded Thompson with a patronizing tone to his voice. "My name is Jim and this is Glen. Glen is the primary on this case, so you will be working almost exclusively with him. He'll keep me informed on the progress the two of you are making. It was really nice meeting you. I'm sure I'll see you around the office here. You'll be in great hands with Glen here."

Thompson disappeared as quickly as he could, leaving Glen and Jennifer standing in his office.

"Have a seat Jennifer. Can I get you anything? Some coffee or tea? How about a doughnut? I'm sure there's a box of them floating around the office somewhere."

"No, thank you. I don't eat sugar. A nice cup of herbal tea would be wonderful though."

"Sure, tea. Coming right up." Glen left the office. He went to the coffee table to look for tea. There were only plain tea bags.

"Hey, anyone got any herbal tea?" he asked in a low tone to the officers seated nearest the table.

One of the women officers opened her desk drawer exposing an assortment of herbal teas. She handed several different varieties to Glen. He thanked her profusely and returned to his office with a hot cup of water and an assortment of tea bags.

"Aren't you going to join me?"

"I have a cold cup of coffee here to finish."

"I think you'll find you work better and your mind would be clearer with a nice red herbal tea."

"Actually, when I drink something I don't like, it angers me and that clouds my mind," said Glen.

He kept thinking up ways to get even with Thompson for running out on him. He walked back to the coffee table and returned with a hot cup of coffee for himself.

"About Samantha's case, how do you feel you can assist us?"

"I'm not sure that I can. Her mother asked me to come by to work with you."

"Okay, how do we work together on this then? Do you want me to tell you what we have so far? Normally, I wouldn't share the information with anyone at this point in the investigation, but under the circumstances I suppose I can tell you we have no leads. We have nothing to share with you."

"May I see a picture of Samantha? You do have that, don't you?"

"Sure, of course, here."

Glen opened the file on his desk, removed Samantha's photo and handed it to her. Jennifer took the photo. She stared at it for a long time. She clasped it in her hands and closed her eyes. Glen watched her all the while trying to not burst into laughter. After years of being a cop, he'd be home early every evening, if looking at someone's picture was all it took to solve a crime.

"Nothing, I feel nothing, I see nothing."

"Well, it was worth a try. Thanks so much for coming in. If anything comes to you later on, please don't hesitate to come by and tell us what you know," said Glen, as he stood to open the door.

"Do you have any personal belongings of the girl?"

"No, just this photo her mother gave us when we were questioning them the day after her disappearance."

"I think it might be easier for me if I had something that belonged to the girl. Can we go to her parent's home now?"

"I'd really love to accommodate you, but I'm swamped here, and I just can't leave. Tell you what. When I get a chance I'll swing by her house to pick something up. I'll call you when I have something."

She stood and left his office. She knew he didn't believe in her or her abilities. She was not surprised. Many people did not understand nor believe in psychic powers. Jennifer knew that most people have psychic abilities to varying degrees, but in this culture people are taught to ignore them. They are brushed aside as coincidence or women's intuition.

There are times in everyone's life when they have been thinking of someone, the phone rings, and it turns out to be that very person who is calling. At other times a person has a premonition or a dream about something and it comes true. These are psychic powers at work. If

54

the ability is not nurtured it is easily lost and explained away. Many people own pets who have a psychic connection to them. The animal knows when the owner is about to come home, even though animals have no ability to tell time.

Jennifer was not offended by Glen's lack of understanding. She confronts that on a daily basis. People are afraid of the unknown. She went back to her home and called Samantha's mother. She explained her need for something that belonged to Samantha asking her to take it to the police station for Detective Karst. She instructed her to call her as soon as she deposited the item with Detective Karst.

Jennifer drove back to the police station and waited for the call on her cell phone from Samantha's mother.

The drop had been made and the call came through. Jennifer left her car to go back to Detective Karst's office to continue her work. He was surprised to see her standing at his door.

"May I come in?"

"Uh, sure, come in. Is there something I can help you with?"

"No, I'm here to help you. May I have the item Samantha's mother brought to you?"

Glen looked up at her with a wry smile on his face. He handed her a stuffed animal that Samantha slept with.

"But how did you know?"

55

He was beginning to wonder if she did have some psychic powers after all. How else would she have just appeared at his door minutes after the mother dropped off the teddy bear?

She smiled at him.

"No, it's not what you're thinking. I went home and called Samantha's mother and asked her to bring something to you. I instructed her to call me when she did, so I could meet with you as soon as it was delivered. I was parked outside, she called on my cell phone."

"Oh hell, I just thought you were showing off," he said, a little sarcastically. He assumed she would do just that.

He watched her with the stuffed animal. Running her fingers through the fur she played with the plaid bow tied around its neck. She sniffed the perfume that Samantha had sprayed on the little brown bear. Seated in the chair with the bear sitting on her lap with both hands around it. She sat there not saying a word.

Glen sat across from her watching her intently. He was so distraught over the disappearance of this girl that he hoped there was something to this psychic stuff. He'd heard of many psychics helping on cases, gaining national coverage. He'd never worked with one nor knew anyone that had. He wanted to believe it, at least for this moment, for the sake of Samantha.

Jennifer smiled as she opened her eyes. She looked at Glen.

"Thank you."

"For what?" he asked.

"For believing in me. I could feel your energy mix with mine and that of Samantha's, once I felt the power of your desire, things were more clear for me. You know that two heads are better than one. Twice the energy makes readings more powerful."

"I don't get it. What happened? What are you talking about?"

"I was getting weak readings from the bear mixed with a few strong ones. I couldn't feel anything definite, then I felt you hoping I would find something. Your strong feelings mixed with mine gave me a more clear picture. Samantha is alive. She is frightened, but unharmed and very much alive."

"Are you sure? How can you know that? I only wish you were right."

"I am right. There is no doubt in my mind."

"Where is she? What happened to her?"

"I'm not sure. I saw darkness and could smell pine...no some other type of evergreen...maybe juniper bushes. It was cold; she was feeling cold, then fear, extreme fear. I think she was outdoors in the cold; it must've been dark. Someone grabbed her, or frightened her. But I am convinced she is alive."

Glen was now taking a keen interest.

"Do you know where Samantha lives?"

"No, I knew that she disappeared from her neighborhood, so I purposely did not want to go there until you wanted to take me. I had to be able to tell you what I could feel *without* being there. Then I could tell you what I feel while being at the scene. I had to let you know that I am for real. Was I close? Were the bushes that I mentioned in her neighborhood?"

"Yes, you're right. She disappeared on a cold night in the dark. When I went back to the scene, I discovered a short stretch of the sidewalk that was not visible from much of the neighborhood. That stretch of sidewalk is lined with some type of evergreen bushes. I stepped into them myself. My theory is that someone was hiding in the bushes waiting for a victim, then reached out and grabbed her."

"I agree with your theory, Detective Karst."

Glen stood and paced around the room. He ran his hand through his hair. How could this be? How could this woman have the same theory as mine? She's never been there, no one gave her any details and this theory is mine. There is no proof, just the theory. Is she for real?

Glen fought the urge to become excited. If this woman is for real, then little Samantha is still alive and unharmed. Joy quickly spread through Glen's body. He felt exhilarated at the prospect the little girl was still alive after so many days. But there was the logical part of him that was fighting his feeling of elation.

"Come on," said Glen.

Jennifer stood to follow him. He grabbed his coat, escorting her quickly through the maze of desks out to his car. Glen started the engine.

"Where are we going?"

"You tell me."

Jennifer was a little angry. She felt like he was testing her. Psychic ability is not something that can be turned on and off at a whim, unless a person is extremely disciplined, and even then it is difficult. She was not up to a test.

"I'm going to drive you to her neighborhood. Just tell me if you can feel anything, anything at all that can lead us to her."

Jennifer relaxed. She could tell by the sound of Glen's voice that he believed her. He was not testing her. He wanted to work with her. As he approached the neighborhood, he drove more slowly.

"Don't tell me anything. Just let me feel it."

He agreed.

As they followed the curve around the corner, Jennifer said, "Stop."

She stepped out of the car.

"This is the spot. I can feel fear here on this spot."

She was standing very near the spot that Debbie had been standing when Glen grabbed her from the bushes. Jennifer stood on the spot, first facing one direction and then the other. She turned to Glen.

"She came from that direction and was walking towards her house in this direction. Am I correct?"

"Yes, you've got it just the way we were told. Her friend's house is down the street there almost three blocks. Glen pointed towards her friend's house. Her house is down this way about another block."

"I can tell you little Samantha was grabbed and pulled into the bushes here."

"Okay, if someone grabbed her here and pulled her into the bushes, how did he get her out of here without being seen?" asked Glen.

"I'm not quite sure. I feel a bag of some sort and something with wheels."

"A car. Did someone drive her away in a car?"

"No, I don't feel an engine. I'm sorry, I wish I could be of more help."

"That's okay, you're doing great. Just relax. We know she was picked up here, right where I thought it had happened. We think she's still alive, but we just don't know where she is, or how she was taken there."

Glen and Jennifer walked back to the car. Glen drove her back to her car at the station. She was very quiet. She seemed tired after her afternoon with Glen. He sensed she felt badly because she could help him no further.

He dropped her at her car and thanked her.

"If anything else comes to you, please don't hesitate to call me."

She waved goodbye to him, turned, and got into her car. He stayed in the parking lot until she drove away. With both hands on the steering wheel, he let out a deep sigh and then leaned his head back to think about the events of the day.

When Glen arrived at home Debbie had supper ready for him.

She could tell immediately by the look on his face that something happened that day.

"What?" she asked.

"What do you mean? What?"

"Something happened today. Didn't it?"

"Yep, I met with a psychic."

Debbie laughed, "You and a psychic, boy that's an odd couple."

"But Debbie, she knew. She knew about the cold, dark, night. She knew about the bushes. She knew Samantha was afraid of her abductor and she says Samantha is still alive."

"Oh my God, Glen, is she for real? Do you think that little girl could still be alive?"

"You have no idea how badly I want to believe her. I've never had any experience with this stuff but there's a part of me deep down inside that believes her. I took her to the scene and she knew which direction she had walked from and which direction she was walking to. She took me to the spot on the sidewalk where I grabbed you. But understand, I'm not ruling out the possibility that she put this together from the info she got from the parents. I'm not sure what purpose that would serve."

"Okay, so where did she tell you she is now?"

"That's just it, she doesn't know."

"Are you going to work with her tomorrow? What do the other guys say?"

"No one knows. I haven't said anything to anyone yet. I need time for all of this to sink in. She agreed with my theory. We just don't know how he got her out of the neighborhood. She said there was no car. She said there was a bag of some sort and something with wheels, but no car. I can't imagine how no one saw anything."

"It was dark and those bushes were pretty thick. Do you think he kept her there until everyone went to sleep that night then took her away."

"I suppose that's possible, but it was pretty cold. I'm not sure how long he or Samantha could last sitting in bushes on a cold night."

"Was there any other way out of the bushes, besides the street?"

"I'm not sure, I guess just through yards. I'm going back over there around seven to see what it all looks like at night."

They finished their supper. When the time drew nearer to seven, Glen and Debbie drove back to the spot where Samantha had been abducted.

They parked the car and walked to the bushes. They climbed inside. It was obvious the bushes had been there for many years. There were signs that kids may have played in them, using them for forts. Glen remembered playing in bushes like these in his neighborhood.

The area behind the bushes, on the yard side, was not lighted by the streetlights. They walked through the bushes coming out onto the yard. They walked through the lawn between two large houses. There were no lights on between the houses, probably so they wouldn't shine into the bedroom windows. They were able to walk through the side yards and into the backyards of two other houses, then to the sidewalk on the street. They stopped and looked back. The entire distance was unlighted.

Someone could have grabbed the little girl, knocked her out, put her into some type of bag, maybe even a sleeping bag. Then she could've been loaded into a wagon or wheelbarrow and pushed through the unlighted yards to the street, where a car may have been parked.

Glen felt a rush of adrenaline. He knew he was on to something. The girl no longer vanished into thin air; she was carried, or wheeled into the darkness along the path that they had just walked.

Chapter 4

The phone rang at Dave's desk.

"Sheriff's office, this is Dave Smith."

"Hi Dave, this is Doc Foster. I think I have a problem."

"Why, what's wrong?"

"Sheila's parents don't want us to do an autopsy. Her dad is for it but her mother says no. Her dad wants to rule out drugs."

"I'm sorry Doc, but we have to have that autopsy report. We can't let this one slip by, not after Tim and Lyle's deaths."

"I don't see what Tim and Lyle's deaths have to do with Sheila. I understand you guys wanting the autopsy because there was no apparent cause of death. Tim's death though, was nothing more than one of those freak athletic accidents, and Lyle was not a healthy man. Sheila's death is much more of a curiosity."

"Well, you're probably right, but I need to do my job and that's to rule out any foul play."

"So what am I supposed to do about her parents? I can't force them to sign autopsy papers."

"No, you can't, but if they refuse we're going to have to override that decision and order one ourselves. The county will have to pay for it. This is ruled a suspicious death and we need answers."

"I suggest you go talk to her parents then. I'll go ahead and order the autopsy."

Dave hung up the phone dreading the task ahead of him. It was terrible the family lost their daughter. The parents stood divided about an autopsy. Now he had to tell them they had no choice.

He drove to their house. Many cars were parked on the street in front of their house, family members he suspected.

Dave stepped out of his car adjusting his gun belt, then his hat. He drew in a deep breath as he walked up the sidewalk to the door. Before he could ring the bell the door opened. Susan, a friend of the family opened the door.

"Hi Dave, come on in. Everyone's in the kitchen. Pretty sad story, huh?"

"Yeah, it's pretty rough losing a kid."

He followed her into the kitchen. He removed his hat as he shook hands with Sheila's father. He walked over to her mother who remained seated and put his hand gently on her shoulder.

"I'm so sorry for your loss."

Her mother responded, "Thank you."

Sheila's father handed him a cup of coffee.

"Can we speak in private?" asked Dave.

"Sure, let's go into the living room."

The two men left the group gathered in the kitchen to have their chat.

"What can I do for you?"

Dave hesitated for a moment. He took a sip of his coffee.

"What did you decide about the autopsy?"

"Well, we decided against it."

"Don't you want to know her cause of death?"

"I certainly do, but my wife and I can't agree on it."

Dave took another sip of his coffee. He glanced around the room. His eyes focused on the bookshelf filled with trophies.

"Sheila was quite the athlete wasn't she?"

"She sure was. She really loved her sports, but I don't think you came here to talk about Sheila's trophies. So, what's on your mind?"

"I'm not quite sure how to tell you this, but we are going to have to insist that there be an autopsy. Her death has been ruled a suspicious death and we have to follow through to learn the cause."

"I don't understand. We're her parents, don't we have to give permission for that?"

"Well, ordinarily yes, but in a circumstance like this we have the ability to override your decision. We

66

hoped you would want this for yourself and we wouldn't have to insist."

"You mean to tell me, as parents we have no right? Your office can just step in and demand we do this?"

"I'm afraid so."

"Why in the hell are you picking on Sheila? You didn't force Tim's parents to perform an autopsy. Was it because he was the star of the team and you didn't want to drag his name through the mud, but you don't mind finding fault with Sheila?"

Dave patted him on the back.

"No one is trying to find fault with Sheila. We lost two kids in the same week. We just have to rule out any sort of foul play. I heard from Doc that you wanted to rule out drugs yourself. I'm not saying that Sheila took drugs, but what if someone gave her something. You'd want to know wouldn't you?"

"Foul play, in Holyoke? You've got to be kidding! That's absurd. Why would anyone want to hurt Sheila? She was a very popular girl. Everyone liked her. I think you're nuts."

"Do you think someone wanted to hurt our little girl?" questioned Sheila's mother as she entered the room.

"We're not sure. We hope not, but we have to know," answered Dave.

"He says we have to let them do the autopsy on Sheila. He said we have no say in the matter. By law we have to let them," said her father.

"Is that true?" she asked turning back to Dave.

"Yes, ma'am, I'm afraid so."

"Well, then do what you have to do, but I think I'd like you to leave now," she said, with tears in her eyes.

"Yes, ma'am."

Dave put his hat on and let himself out of the door quickly. When he reached his car he started it immediately and drove away. He wanted to remove himself from the view of the family as fast as he could. He drove to the clinic.

In the small waiting room, there were a half dozen or so people waiting to see Doc Foster. He was the only doctor in the town. He walked over to the receptionist.

"Do you have an appointment?" she asked as she scanned her appointment book.

"No, I need to talk to Doc."

"Take a seat and I'll call you when he's free. He's with a patient right now."

Dave took a seat. Two children playing across the room looked up and saw the sheriff dressed in his uniform. They stopped playing and ran to their mother's side. They leaned into her for comfort while they watched Dave with large eyes. It made him sad that some kids look at law enforcement as the bad guys. How will they ever seek help if they are afraid?

He smiled at the two kids as he opened a package of gum. He popped one stick into his mouth. They watched. He offered them a stick. They looked up at their mother. She nodded. Slowly they walked over, snatched the gum and returned quickly to their mother's side. The look on their faces softened, as did the gum in their mouth. Soon they were back to playing with the toys, while chewing their gum.

A nurse called Dave in to visit with Doctor Foster.

"I stopped by Sheila's parent's house. I explained the need for the autopsy. They're not gonna fight us but they sure weren't too happy. They asked me to leave."

"I'm not surprised. Her mother was dead set against it. I went ahead and set it up. We should get some results back within a week or two."

"Good. Thanks Doc. I can't decide if it would be better to find something or not."

"I hear ya, Dave. It would be nice to know what really happened, but let's hope it's nothing ugly or illegal."

Dave stood, put on his hat and shook hands with Doc before leaving.

Dave kept a low profile the rest of the week. He was sure the town would be buzzing about how cruel he was forcing the parents to cut up their daughter against their wishes. He was not looking forward to facing most of the town at her funeral on Wednesday.

Pastor Bob did not preside over this funeral. Sheila and her family were not members of his church. Pastor Steve was performing the service. The weather that day was much more pleasant for a winter's day. The wind was not blowing and the sun shone brightly on everyone at the cemetery.

Dave and Shelly stood at the back of the crowd. He was just doing his job ordering the autopsy, but he felt guilty just the same. Shelly insisted they attend the dinner at the church since this was their church. Dave agreed, reluctantly.

Sheila's father walked up to Dave extending his hand.

"I'm sorry about the other day. We've had some time to talk about it and realize you're just doing your job. I hope there are no hard feelings."

Dave was relieved to shake hands and be forgiven.

"Nope, no hard feelings. I'm just glad you understand why I had to do this."

Larry, one of the local farmers, coaxed Dave away for a private talk.

"So, what in the hell is going on? What do you think happened? Is it true you think someone killed this girl?"

"Now, I didn't say that. This is just a routine procedure when someone young dies so suddenly with no apparent reason. Let's not jump to conclusions here. I'm sure we'll discover some medical reason for her death, not foul play."

Soon, other men, and a few women surrounded the two men, hoping to get a tidbit of gossip about the reason the autopsy was ordered. Dave remained calm trying to dispel any further gossip. His goal was to convince everyone it was strictly routine. Many of them seemed disappointed.

Dave made eye contact with Shelly through the crowd. He let her know he wanted to leave. When she met him at the door they slipped away before anyone else could confront Dave.

"I suppose it got pretty rough for you in there," said Shelly.

"You guessed it. The size of the crowd that turns out when a child dies is overwhelming. I sure didn't want to get cornered by the entire group."

"Looks like they closed the school this time. I saw all the teachers including the coaches at this one. I think it's beginning to wear a little on the kids losing two classmates in one week," she said.

"I'll just be glad when we get the reports back from Denver. Hopefully, they'll not find anything to cause concern and our sleepy little town can return to normal."

A few days passed since Detective Karst told Thompson about his discovery at the scene. He explained what Jennifer Parker had told him about the visits he and Debbie made to the area where Samantha was last seen. The crime scene investigators made another sweep of the area following the path the assailant might have taken between the houses in the dark.

Detectives Karst and Thompson went back to the neighborhood to question everyone again, this time about

71

someone pulling a wagon or pushing a wheelbarrow. No one had anything to add. Karst asked everyone to check garages and garden sheds to see if anything was missing. Everything seemed to be in order, but one of the neighbors did mention his garden wagon, although it was in the shed, it was not in the exact spot where he usually kept it.

"Do you keep this shed locked?" asked Thompson.

"Nope, the person that does my lawn has free access to it for all of my tools. No one ever bothers anything in this neighborhood. As a matter of fact, all of my neighbors and I swap tools back and forth frequently. Sometimes when I need something I have to make a few calls before I can locate who might have borrowed it."

"So is it possible one of your neighbors borrowed your wagon?" asked Karst.

"I suppose it's possible, but why would anyone want it this time of year. No one is doing lawn work. Especially with all the snow we've been getting."

Karst looked around the inside of the tool shed. He noticed a tarp over some peat moss bags in the corner.

"Is this tarp the way you left it?" he asked.

"Gee, I don't know. I just toss it over the bags. I really didn't pay any attention to it."

Karst called the team inside and asked them to check the tarp and the wagon thoroughly.

"When was the last time you were in here?" asked Karst.

"I don't know, last week? I guess I took the snow blower out of here."

"Was the wagon in its proper place then?" quizzed Karst.

"I couldn't tell you. I wouldn't have noticed anything today except you guys were asking about it. What's this all about anyway? Does this have anything to do with the disappearance of Samantha?"

"We're just being thorough."

"Don't go getting any ideas about me, or my family. We've already been questioned and we weren't home that night. We've already been cleared."

"No one's accusing anyone of anything. We're just checking things out," replied Karst wishing he would go away now and let them do their work.

"Someone give Jennifer Parker a call. Here's her number," said Karst as he handed a slip of paper to one of the officers at the scene.

"What should I tell her?"

"Just ask her if she can come right over. Tell her we'll send a car over for her if she'd like."

"What the hell do you want her here for?" asked Thompson. "Surely you're not buying into any of that shit, are you?"

"I'll do whatever it takes to find that little girl, even if it sounds absurd. I'd rather save her life than save face."

"Suit yourself," said Thompson not wanting any part of the psychic.

The crew finished their work and was packing up to leave when a cruiser pulled up with Jennifer Parker inside. She stepped out of the car as Glen approached.

"Find something?" she asked.

"We're not sure. I thought I'd like your input on something." He walked her along the path where he thought Samantha had been taken. He didn't say a word.

Not far along the path she stopped. She stood still, closed her eyes, then spoke to Glen.

"She was here. She was on this spot. She went that way."

Jennifer pointed towards the houses ahead and the tool shed. She walked ahead of Glen.

"I know she's been here. She was not afraid though. She was in peace. Actually, I don't feel her being aware of being here. I think she might have been drugged or passed out or something."

She walked towards the shed. She was here. She touched the wagon. This is the object with wheels that I spoke of earlier. I believe someone drugged her and kept her inside this shed. She turned to the tarp. She placed her hand on it.

"This is what she was wrapped in."

Karst checked with the crew before they pulled away to be sure they dusted the wagon for fingerprints when they were checking the entire shed. They assured him they had.

Jennifer turned to Glen.

"He's a young man, in his late twenties, blond hair, kinda scruffy looking. I can see him with her. Now I can see Samantha. She's in a small room. There's a light bulb hanging from the ceiling. She has a cot in the room with an army blanket on it. She's not alone. There's another little girl in there with her. She has red hair."

"Quick, make a call and see if we have any other missing kids," yelled Karst to one of the officers standing by.

The young officer ran back to Karst breathless.

"Yes, they just released an Amber alert about another little girl, nine years old with red hair. She disappeared early this morning on her way to school."

Thompson took off his hat and ran his fingers through his hair.

"Holy shit! Glen, either this broad is for real, or she's the one that nabbed these kids, and is playing mind games with us. What do you know about her?"

"She's cool, I had her checked out. I'm ashamed to say I had the same thoughts earlier. Now we have to find these two girls."

They walked back to Jennifer.

"Can you give us anything else? Any feeling or vision of where they might be?"

75

"No, I'm sorry. I can't," she said with a tear in her eye.

"That's okay. You've given us a lot to go on. We'll get those prints run and see if anyone comes up that matches your description. We're gonna get this guy, I can feel it."

Jennifer looked up at him. She took his hand and walked away with him.

"Go with it, Detective Karst. You feel you're going to get this guy. You're connecting with him. Concentrate, you have the power within you. Just use it."

"I'm afraid I can't do what you do. You're gifted that way. I just can't do it."

She held both of Glen's hands in hers. She closed her eyes and suggested he do the same.

"What do you see?"

"Nothing," he responded.

"Try again, what do you see?"

Glen closed his eyes and tried to let his mind go blank.

"I can't see the girls, I can't see the guy. I can't see anything."

"You must see something, no matter how ridiculous, think. What do you see?"

"Railroad tracks, I see railroad tracks." He pulled his hands away.

"See I told you I can't see anything that would help the girls. I like trains, that's probably why I saw railroad tracks. This is silly. We've got to find the girls."

"That's okay, it'll come to you when you need it."

"I'm going downtown to see if they've come up with anything from here. Would you like me to take you home?"

"Sure, that would be great."

As Detective Karst was driving Jennifer to her home he was feeling a little foolish. He was beginning to believe her until she started trying to find the power within him. He lost much faith in her.

They were just a few blocks from her home when she turned to him and said, "They are okay now."

At that moment a call came across the radio for Karst. They had just picked up the two little girls. Their kidnapper had released them unharmed.

"That's the best news I've heard in a long time," said Karst into his radio. "Where did you find them?"

"Someone called in a report about two little girls playing on the railroad tracks. The caller thought it was too dangerous. She thought we should pick them up before they were injured," said the dispatcher on the radio.

Glen turned to Jennifer. Her face was aglow with a huge smile. She knew Glen possessed a stronger power within than the average person. She knew he credited his ability to be a good detective with a gut instinct, but she knew he had an unconscious control of his psychic powers.

"I'll be damned. I did know something didn't I?"

Jennifer nodded.

"Would you like to ride along to meet the girls and call the families?"

"You bet, I wouldn't miss it for the world."

Together they drove downtown to meet the girls and their families. It was a joyous reunion for all.

The girls told the same story. They were walking when someone reached out and grabbed them. He put a cloth over their faces. They went to sleep. When they woke up they were in this scary room. Samantha was alone for most of the time before the other little girl was put in with her.

The man fed them and brought them toys. He never harmed them in any way. They could hear him on a phone. Somebody wanted them, but then changed his mind. They could hear him arguing with whomever he was talking to on the phone. Then he came in to get the girls. He always wore a stocking hat whenever he came into their room, or took them out blindfolded to use the bathroom.

He blindfolded them one last time after the phone call. He took them to his car and drove for a while, then stopped. He took them out and stood them on the railroad tracks. He told them to wait until he drove away then to take off the blindfolds. He told them if they

78

followed the railroad tracks it would take them home. They obeyed his every demand, and then the police car picked them up. Their stories matched perfectly. They were two lucky little girls.

The parents took their girls home. Glen drove Jennifer home. He was going to sleep that night for the first time since Samantha had been abducted. He called Debbie from his cell phone to tell her it was over. She was relieved as well.

Glen walked Jennifer to her door. He shook her hand.

"Thank you for everything. I hope we can work together again some time. Maybe you can help us locate this bozo that nabbed the girls."

"You will do fine without me. The prints you took will lead you to your man. But we will meet again. Next time you will come to me. You'll come on behalf of a friend. Promise me until that time you will no longer brush off your feelings and intuition as a coincidence, but you will see it for what it is and try to develop it."

"Sure, I'll give it a try. Hell, I might even read your books."

"I'll have them sent to your office."

Jennifer stepped into her house. Glen walked to his car. He stopped at the door and looked back at the house. He felt some connection to her. Although they just met on this case, he had this feeling that he knew her from somewhere else. He was about to brush the feeling off when he remembered his promise to her. He kept the thought with him instead.

When Glen walked in his house Debbie met him at the door.

"Dave wants you to call him as soon as you can. I told him to call your cell. I told him the girl was found. He said he didn't want to bother you until you were finished for the night."

"I wonder what he wants?"

Glen changed clothes. Debbie brought him his supper. He called Dave as soon as he'd finished eating.

"Dave, what's up? Debbie said you called."

"Hey, old man, congratulations on your case. I'm really happy for you. Debbie said this guy nabbed two kids and they're both fine. That's great. What are the odds in this day and age?"

"Boy, that's the truth. I tell ya we had our doubts in the beginning, but then this psychic told us the kid was still alive, that gave us some hope."

"No shit? You worked with a psychic? Was she for real?"

"Yeah, I think she was. Actually, she was pretty cool. I expected someone really weird but she seemed, well, normal. She was just in touch with things that we can't seem to grasp. I learned a lot from her. I also learned to give those people, the real ones anyway, a lot of respect."

"Good for you, but I don't think I'd be that open minded."

"So what's up with your deaths in a small town? Kinda sounds like a good book title."

"That's what I'm calling about. The body was sent to Denver to Arapahoe County for testing. Can you nose around a bit and see what you can find out. I'm impatient. I hate to wait for the entire report. I just thought if you had the time you could find out as things were happening and keep me posted. You did say you wanted to help and all. So I thought I'd call in the favor, stated Dave."

"Of course, I'll help if I can. You don't have to beg. I'm not sure how much I can find out or if I can find out anything any faster than you can, but I'll poke around to see what I can find," said Glen.

"That'd be great. Today we had her funeral. The parents were anxious to get her back from Denver to go ahead with the arrangements. I had to override their decision about the autopsy. I felt like a heel. I even got cornered at the funeral today. Some people think I'm hiding something from them. The sooner I can find out what she died from the better."

"Since these girls have been found I'll take some time tomorrow and stop by pathology to see what I can find out."

"Well, Glen, I'm gonna let you go. I'm sure you're ready for some sleep. It's been a long week for you. We'll talk again soon."

"You've got that right. I feel like I could sleep for the next three days. I'll call you in a couple of days to let you know what I've found out."

Glen took a long hot shower then climbed into bed with Debbie. He made love to her, then fell into a deep sleep.

Dave was also in a deep sleep when the phone rang.

It was the dispatcher.

"Dave, I think you'd better head over to the hospital. We had a 911 call. Lee's taking his wife, Sheri, in. It's probably nothing serious, but you did say you wanted to be called day or night if someone called in. So I hope you won't hold this against me in the morning."

"Heavens no. Thanks for the call. I'll go over to the hospital."

Dave quickly dressed in his uniform.

Shelly asked, "What's going on? Where are you going?"

"Just go back to sleep. Lee's taking Sheri to the hospital. He called 911. An ambulance is going to meet them part way on the gravel road since they live so far from town. I'm going to meet them at the hospital. I won't be long. Go back to sleep."

He kissed Shelly good-bye and went to the hospital to wait for the ambulance.

He and Doc visited while they waited.

A nurse came in and said, "They're almost here." Everyone jumped into action. The emergency room began to fill with nurses. The stretcher carrying Sheri was brought in with Lee close behind. He left his truck on the road to ride in the ambulance with her. She was being bagged as they wheeled her past Dave.

He waited outside in the hall while Lee explained the story to Doc. Dave stood close enough to listen to the entire story.

"We were asleep when she woke me. She said she was having trouble breathing. It was as if her chest was tight or something. She could barely speak. I called 911 and carried her out to my pickup. I laid her in the backseat and drove like a bat out of hell until I saw the ambulance. None too soon either. I couldn't hear her gasping in the backseat any longer. They said she still had a pulse."

Doc motioned with his head to a nurse. She knew to escort Lee out of the room.

"No, that's okay, I want to stay with her."

"We need to work on her and it would be better if you waited in the hall."

Reluctantly he agreed. Dave brought him a cup of coffee. Lee repeated the story to Dave.

"Has she been feeling ill?"

"Nope, she's been fine. I'm the one that's had this damn flu, but she's been fine."

In the emergency room Doc and his staff worked feverously on Sheri, but they could not save her.

Doc, trembling, with sweat beaded on his forehead, said to the nurse, "Call it."

"Two-thirteen a.m."

"Ask Dave to step in here a minute would ya," Doc said to a nurse.

He walked to the corner of the room. He slid down onto a stool. Dave joined him.

"She didn't make it, huh, Doc?"

"No she didn't. Dave this is like a carbon copy of the rest. They are just not responding at all. I'm stumped. I feel like I'm losing my touch. How can I face this town? They rely on me to keep their families healthy. What am I supposed to say to Lee?"

"I'll go out with you."

Doc stood up taking a deep breath, as he walked past the table where Sheri's body lay. He didn't look at her; he didn't speak to the nurses. He just walked numbly past all.

Lee looked up from the chair where he was sitting. He was sipping his coffee, thumbing through a magazine. He was comfortable knowing Sheri had made it to the hospital and all would be fine.

Doc walked up to him. He put his hand on his shoulder.

"I'm sorry. We did all we could."

Lee looked up in disbelief.

"What do ya mean, you did all you could? Are you telling me she didn't make it?"

Dave spoke up, "That's right Lee, they did everything they could, but they couldn't revive her."

Lee could not speak. He didn't move a muscle. He just stared at the wall ahead of him. He was so unprepared for the death of his wife of twenty-five years. There was nothing to prepare him for this day. She was in perfect health.

Dave took Doc aside. "I'm not sure how he's going to feel about an autopsy, but I must insist again. Do you understand? This makes four people now in a very short amount of time."

Dave walked away and went home. He paced around his house for an hour or so. He watched the clock. He needed to call Glen. He couldn't stand it any longer. He made the call.

A groggy Glen answered the phone.

"Yeah?"

"Glen, it's Dave. I need your help, old buddy. We've got another body."

"No shit!" Glen was wide-awake now. "Tell ya what. I've got some vacation time coming. Let me take a few days. I'm coming out. I'll see if I can get away tomorrow."

The next morning Glen cleared his calendar with his sergeant. He packed before he left the house. He called Debbie to tell her he was definitely going; drove the three hours to meet his long-time friend.

Chapter 5

Glen drove through the town slowly. He watched the people attending to business as though nothing had happened. As far as they were concerned nothing had happened. Most of the town had not yet heard of Sheri's death. Gossip had already started about the two teenagers.

There was speculation about drugs. People were quick to point fingers and blame. Since Tim was the star athlete no one wanted to believe he was involved in something he shouldn't be. Sheila caught most of the blame. She and Tim had gone out once. Now everyone assumed she was the one messing around with drugs, convincing poor innocent Tim to experiment. Served her right that she would die after killing poor Tim.

In every store, at the post office, at the café, and even in church, whispers were beginning. What would the gossip change to when the town discovers the death of Sheri?

The parking lot at the courthouse near Dave's office was nearly full. Glen was a bit surprised. He parked his car then went inside to search for Dave. He walked into his office. Dave and all of his officers were in a meeting. Glen peeked into the room, then backed out to wait until they were finished.

"Glen, come on in. This conversation should include you," called Dave.

"Guys, this is Detective Glen Karst from the Denver PD. I called him this morning to apprise him of our situation here. He's been filled in on all of the details. Glen and I used to work homicide together when I was in Denver. He was at the ball game with me when Tim died. He's volunteered his time to come here to brainstorm with us."

Glen took a seat to listen to what they had to say. The other officers nodded to Glen.

One officer said, "Tell us about Sheri."

"Not much to tell yet. Lee said she woke up having difficulty breathing. It got so bad she could barely talk. He called for an ambulance to meet him half way. The EMT's attempted CPR on the trip. Doc took over when they arrived at the hospital. He just couldn't save her. Her heart appeared to have just stopped beating. His guess was a heart attack."

"Any past history of heart problems?" asked Glen.

"None. Her husband, Lee, said she was very healthy until this one and only episode," responded Dave.

Another younger officer watched Glen, then said, "Dave do you think we have something going on here? You obviously brought Glen here for a reason. These cases, do you think they're connected?"

"I hope not. I hope we're dealing with nothing here but one big nasty coincidence. I'm just not willing to sit back and wait for another death before I move on some sort of investigation. Sheila and Sheri were required to have autopsies, we'll see what the test results show."

"Are you going to contact CBI soon?" asked Glen.

"I suppose I should, but I would really like to have something to give them first. I thought we should wait for the autopsy report to come back on Sheila. If they find something we'll contact them before we get the results back on Sheri," explained Dave.

"Don't you think we can handle this ourselves?" asked the same young officer.

It was obvious that this was potentially the most exciting thing to happen to this small town from a law enforcement point of view. The young rookie was anxious for something to sink his teeth into other than the typical small town crime they'd been dealing with. He was not anxious to turn it over to the Colorado Bureau of Investigation. He wanted to give it a try on a local level first.

"No, I don't think we can handle this ourselves. As a matter of fact, I know we can't handle this one ourselves. We're just not equipped. We don't have any of the equipment we need to conduct a thorough investigation. Hell, we can't even do the fingerprints here. We need these guys to help out."

"That's right," said Glen. "I've worked with them over the years. They're not gonna come in here and ramrod everything. They'll do what needs to be done. They're not gonna bully any of you around. They have a job to do and they are damn good at what they do. But I'm with Dave here, let's hope there's nothing to these deaths and we won't have to call them in."

A third officer that had been sitting quietly in the corner observing and listening to everything that was being said commented, "Who would want to kill all of these people? What could he have to gain by killing a couple of kids and two older people? I don't think there's a case here. I think we could be overreacting on this. My God, this is Holyoke, Colorado. This is not the home of some serial killer."

"No one said anything about a serial killer. Let's not get that gossip started. That's all we need. We'd never get a moment's rest here or at home. This town would panic," scolded Dave.

Dave looked at his watch.

"It's about lunchtime. Why don't two of you head home? I'll need one of you to stay on for the day shift as scheduled. Life as usual, remember? We'll get together in the morning to finish this discussion. Glen and I are going to put our heads together this afternoon. We'll decide which course of action to take."

"What do we tell people when they ask?" questioned the young officer.

"Nothing. Tell them nothing. Just a coincidence, that's all. Information we discuss here had better not get around town. If it does, I'll know one of you leaked and when I find out who, he'll be out of a job," said Dave.

He grabbed his hat and coat and left the room with Glen following closely behind.

"You were a little tough there, weren't you old buddy?"

"No, not in the least. You have to understand small towns, Glen."

He went on to explain, nothing truly exciting ever happens. When you read the paper there's just not much news. That's why small towns are so noted for gossip. People have to make their own news. A few stories get spread around; as they move through the community they get embellished a bit. Generally, the story gets dropped only to be replaced by another. It's almost a form of entertainment. Most of the time no harm is done. The story gets exposed as blown out of proportion. Sometimes people with thin skins get pretty hurt by it all. Occasionally, a family might even move away because they can't take the gossip.

"I guess I never thought about it that way. I understand now why you don't want any leaks. I can't imagine someone pointing a finger at an innocent person and causing his life to be so unbearable that he has to leave town, especially when there was no connection to the crime."

Glen stood at Dave's car. He looked down the street three blocks to the café.

"Would you like to walk instead?"

"Are you insinuating I need the exercise," laughed Dave patting his stomach.

"I've been sitting for over three hours driving here. I didn't run this morning. I feel like I need the exercise," explained Glen.

"I need to keep the car with me in case I get a call. If you'd like to walk or jog over, I'll drive and get a booth for us."

Glen started jogging in place. That was his answer to Dave. Dave got into the car and drove away. Glen jogged around the parking lot a couple of laps before he started down the sidewalk to the café.

He checked out the residents of the town. Everyone who could see him, watched him. A jogger on their main street in town was not a typical sight. His instincts were up. He didn't think the deaths were coincidental. Then he thought maybe he was jumping the gun a bit. Suddenly, he thought of Jennifer Parker, the psychic he worked with on Samantha's case. She told him not to brush off those feelings and thoughts so easily. If he felt there was something more to this case than meets the eye, he should go with it.

When Glen arrived at the café he saw Dave still sitting in his car. He climbed in with him.

"Something wrong?"

"No. Look inside. The place is packed. I'm going to get the third degree as soon as I step in there. I thought if we go in together I'd be less apt to get cornered for questioning."

"Okay, let's go. I'm hungry."

The two old friends went into the café to find an empty booth. Dave was right. The place was filled. Glen was surprised. A couple of guys gave up their booth for the two.

"Hey Dave, sit here. We'll join these guys," said one of the men as he sat at a table with a couple of neighbors.

The entire café stopped talking to watch and listen to Dave and Glen.

Larry, one of the local farmers, said, "Hey, aren't you that pheasant killing SWAT guy that was out here a couple of weeks ago? Are you here for more birds?"

That question put Glen on the spot.

"Naw, it's just hard to stay away from a peaceful little town like this once you find it. Besides where else in the world can a guy get a slice of pie like they make here?"

That caused laughter to ring through the café. Still no one went back to his usual conversation. They mumbled a bit back and forth then finally a brave soul came forward.

"So Dave, what's the scoop with Sheri? We heard she died last night."

"Yeah, too bad isn't it. Doc says she had a heart attack," answered Dave.

Larry joined the conversation.

"Say Dave, don't you think it's odd that we've had four people die in such a short amount of time? Maybe there's something in our water supply. Maybe the whole town's gonna die."

The waitress walked past Larry; she knocked his ball cap down over his eyes.

"Don't say things like that. Are you nuts?"

Dave and Glen ordered the daily special, meatloaf. They ate quickly so they could leave before the questions became too serious.

"Let's go to my place where we can talk," suggested Dave.

When they arrived at Dave's house no one was home. The kids were in school and Shelly was working part time at the grocery store. She needed something to keep her busy. She hated sitting around the house all day. She was a great housekeeper, but that only took a couple of hours in the morning. Now that the kids didn't need her as much she wanted something to fill her days.

Dave grabbed a couple cups of coffee for them. He led Glen into his office.

94

"Okay, tell me what you think is going on," said Glen.

"No you first. You're on the outside looking in."

"Well, from the outside looking in I don't really see anything that would cause me to be suspicious except for the number of deaths in such a short time. The girl would be my most suspicious death. The ball player can be explained away. So can the two older people, but the girl has me a little curious."

"Yeah, me too. God Glen, I hope there's nothing here. I'm not sure this town would be able to handle it. I'm sure it would ruin it forever. It's like stepping to a Norman Rockwell painting. Kids are always playing in the streets, riding bikes and skating. No one has to lock their doors or worry about serious crimes. That's one of the things that drew me to this community. I'd hate to see it change."

"I can understand that completely, but change is inevitable. Even for small town America."

"Yeah, I guess you're right. But if something's going on, why did it have to happen on my watch?"

"Fate? Maybe you're the best one to handle it and the townspeople should be happy to have your experience working for them."

"I've looked at the preliminary findings from the autopsy report on the girl. It does appear her heart stopped. There was no sign of heart disease or any other type of degenerating disease. Her arteries, valves, everything looked good. This girl was in perfect health from a medical point of view. The last thing to rule out would be some type of chemical in her system. We're still waiting for the report from toxicology."

"That can take a couple of weeks."

"I know."

"Well, let's go over the facts so far."

"Okay, Tim dropped at the ballgame. Doc thought his heart gave out. No autopsy was performed. Then we have Lyle, he died at the church dinner following Tim's funeral. He'd been sick. He was overweight and not in good health. Then we have Sheila, freshman girl, perfect health. The autopsy report hasn't found anything conclusive. Finally, we have Sheri. She had trouble breathing and supposedly died of a heart attack. That was Saturday night. They'll be performing an autopsy today."

Glen reached across the desk for a pad of paper. He drew a chart containing the names of the victims, the day of their death, the apparent cause of death and the location of death.

"This is a little curious."

"What?" asked Dave.

"Well, check this out. Both kids died at the school on Saturday nights. Sheri died on Saturday, well she started to, but was pronounced dead on Sunday morning."

"I thought about that already. But how does that tie in with Lyle?"

Glen cleared away papers from Dave's desk to expose a desk pad calendar. It still had September on it. He pulled up the sheets until he reached November. He checked the date that the other victim had died.

"He died on Wednesday. Does that mean anything to you?"

"Wednesday, huh? Well, Wednesdays are big church nights here. I couldn't tell you if either of them attend church events on those nights."

"Yeah, but Lyle here died at the church in the early afternoon. Not at a church event in the evening."

"True, that doesn't really make a connection."

"You know Dave, if we were in Denver looking at this same chart, what would we see?"

Dave took the chart from Glen. He studied it as if he were back on the homicide team in Denver.

He said, "If these people were in the same neighborhood or area, and they all died on Saturday. I'd say there could be a coincidence. Maybe even a serial killer. But I'd also look at the cause of death and not get too excited. People die of heart attacks every day. There is just nothing here to assume foul play."

"Exactly what I was thinking. I'm afraid we may be making more of this than there really is, just because they are happening in a small town."

"Damn, I wish those reports would come in. I hate the wait. If this was all a coincidence then we should have nothing to worry about. If we're wrong and something is up, then we could lose another innocent victim this week."

"Tell ya what. I'll stick around until Thursday. If nothing happens I'll head back to Denver. If, God forbid, something does happen I'll try my damnedest to help you figure it out."

"Thanks Glen, I knew I could count on you. In the mean time, let's try to nose around a little without causing any suspicion or alarm, and see if we can connect the two older vics."

Most of the afternoon seemed to slip away from them. They put away their notes when Dave's daughter Ann walked in to say hello to Glen.

"Hi, Mr. Karst, are you back to do some more hunting?"

"You can call me Glen. No, I'm just back for a visit."

"It's nice to see you again."

Ann turned to walk out of the room. Glen jumped up to follow her out of the door. Dave shot him a glance of surprise. Glen looked back at him and motioned for him to stay put.

"Say Ann, do you have a minute?"

Startled she turned around to see Glen standing behind her.

"Sure Mr. er... Glen. What can I help you with?"

"I'd just like to visit with you about the kids at school if that's okay with you?"

"Sure. What do you want to know?"

Glen escorted her to the livingroom out of earshot of her father.

"Just between you and me, I promise I won't tell your dad anything you don't want me to."

She stared at him nervously.

"What can you tell me about Tim before he died?"

"I don't know. What are you wanting to know?"

"I know there's drugs at the school. There are drugs at every school. If you or any of your friends are into drugs, I promise I won't tell your dad, but I need to know if Tim was a user."

"I don't think so. Coach is pretty tough about that kind of thing. He doesn't want any of his players to use or drink while in training. He comes down pretty hard on them. I heard him yelling at someone in the locker room when I was walking down the hall past the door. He was really mad. I don't think anyone would have the guts to do drugs for fear he'd find out."

"Are you sure? Are you absolutely sure? I know a lot goes on behind the teachers' and coaches' backs and I would never let anyone know where I got my information from."

"I didn't know Tim very well. He was a senior so we didn't hang out together, but the talk around the school is that he was clean."

"Any idea who was getting yelled at by the coach the day you overheard the lecture?"

99

"No. Sorry. He's so different than our old coach. Coach Jones, he's a real grouch. Coach Callister was really nice. I didn't want to get caught outside the door when he sounded mad, so I left right away."

"No, that's okay. You're doing great. What about Sheila? Could she have been on drugs?"

"I heard she tried some pot once. I don't think she liked it. At least, that's what she told everyone."

"Do you know if Sheila or Tim had any one at school that really disliked them?"

"No, they were both pretty popular. At least Tim was. Sheila was popular in her own small group. She was kind of plain looking and the guys were not really chasing her or anything, but she seemed really nice. I used to have her in a few classes and we sat together during some study halls. I don't think she ever did anything that would cause anyone to not like her."

Glen took a deep breath. He was not getting anything he could use. Not even the slightest lead on who to talk to.

"You don't think someone tried to hurt either of them do you?" asked Ann with panic in her voice.

"No, honey, I'm sure that's not the case. I just wanted to rule everything out. I just hate to see something happen to a couple of kids. I thought, maybe, if someone was dealing some bad drugs we need to stop it before someone else gets hurt. I didn't mean to alarm you. Don't say anything about our conversation to any of your

100

friends. Your dad tells me stories get started pretty quickly and I don't want anyone pointing a finger where he shouldn't. Can you promise me that?"

"Sure, I guess. I won't say anything if you don't want me to."

"Thanks, I won't interrogate you anymore."

She smiled at Glen then went to her room.

Glen returned to Dave who remained seated at his desk wondering what Glen had been up to.

"What was that all about?"

"I just thought if I asked Ann some questions about the two kids without you being within earshot she might be willing to tell me something she wouldn't want you to know."

"Well, did it work? Did she know anything we can use?"

"Nope, not a thing."

"I didn't think so. I'm pretty close to my kids. I'm sure if one of them learned something they thought I should know, they'd come forward with it pretty quickly."

"So where do we go from here?"

"Tell you what, there's a soup and pie supper tonight, put on by the cheerleaders, to raise money to go to camp. Most of the town turns out. Let's go and nose around a bit. What'd ya say?"

"A soup and pie supper. I'm game, whatever that is."

Later when Shelly and Sean came home the entire group made plans to drive over to the school building for the meal. Glen was impressed with the size of the crowd. Dave was not kidding about most of the town turning out. The food was pretty good as well. Glen had two pieces of cheesecake for dessert.

His eyes continually scanned the crowd. Everyone seemed so wholesome and down to earth. Even the kids looked more clean cut as a whole, then the kids the same age from the city. He was more convinced then ever they were barking up the wrong tree thinking the deaths could be foul play.

Dave weaved his way in and out of the crowd. Slapping people on the back, visiting a little here and a little there. He looked like a hummingbird searching for nectar. Glen stayed with Shelly while Dave worked the crowd.

After about an hour he returned to the table. The two kids had already left to hang out with their friends. Glen looked at Dave. He couldn't read his face.

"Let's make a sweep of the parking lot," he said to Glen.

"Okay."

Their leaving freed Shelly to mingle with her friends instead of babysitting Glen. Glen was beginning to understand the routine. The kids go out to drink. Dave makes a sweep of the parking lot. They dump the beer, then casually walk inside, just like at the ball games. They walked around the lot where the smell of beer started to fill the air. Kids were getting into cars to leave. Others were walking quickly towards the door to the gym.

Dave and Glen turned to walk back inside when the screech of car tires caught their attention. They heard a scream, followed by another.

Dave yelled to Glen, "Come on!"

But Glen was already running.

They ran to the other side of the building. A small group of kids had already gathered around a car. Everyone's eyes were fixed at the ground behind the car. As they approached they heard one girl on the phone calling 911.

A pair of girls ran up to Dave and Glen. "Help! Jane's been hurt. She's not moving."

Dave and Glen raced even faster the last few yards. The crowd opened allowing them full vision. Jane, a red haired woman from the local drugstore, lay motionless on the pavement. Glen felt for a pulse. There was none.

"What happened?" asked Dave.

"I'm not sure," said the young man who was driving the car. I pulled around the corner here to leave the lot and I felt my tires roll over something. I stopped to see what it was. I didn't mean to hit her. I didn't even see her. I don't know where she came from. I didn't see her. I really didn't see her."

The boy was trembling. His girlfriend, a passenger in his car said, "That's right. I was with him. I don't know where she came from. I didn't see her either. I felt the same thing he did. We thought maybe there was a log or tree branch or something on the ground."

Glen examined the woman. Dave was prepared to assist him with CPR. He watched Glen, surprised that he wasn't preparing for CPR. Glen looked up at Dave. He shook his head. The ambulance and EMT's arrived. Glen stood back so they could examine her.

Dave and Glen strolled a few feet away from the crowd.

"This woman has been dead for a little while. Her body temperature has already dropped. She couldn't have died from being hit by this car a few moments ago. I think she was already dead lying on the ground and these kids were probably making the corner a little faster than they should and didn't see her until they ran over her."

Glen and Dave stood by watching them take the body away in the ambulance. One of Dave's officers arrived on the scene. Dave told him to take all the kids inside and ask them if they have anything to add to the story that the driver had already given.

Returning to Shelly they informed her of the situation. Quickly, they departed to the hospital to meet Doc.

Dave watched Doc as he examined Jane. He pronounced her DOA. He phoned the mortuary and then her husband.

"Well?" asked Dave.

"I can't tell you anything. She was obviously dead before the car hit her. Because of the damage done running over her with both the front and rear tires I can't tell if she'd been hit by a different car earlier or what caused her death."

Dave, Glen and Doc walked into a private room.

"Doc, this makes five. Do you think there's any connection here with the other four?"

"I wish I could give you an answer, but I can't. Ordinarily, I'd say no, but under the present circumstances. I'd have to say I'm suspicious."

Dave took off his hat and ran his fingers through his hair. Glen could tell he was distraught.

"Another death. Another could be accidental death. Could be another damned heart attack. Nothing tells me it's a homicide except my gut. I can't go jumping the gun on my gut feeling."

At that moment Glen thought of Jennifer Parker.

"Yes you can. If your gut tells you this is connected then it's connected. That woman psychic I worked with said we tend to ignore those gut feelings too often when they can actually be our subconscious minds telling us the truth about a situation."

"Oh hell Glen, don't give me that psychic shit right now. I have a real problem here."

"All I'm telling you is go with your instincts, trust them. Let's handle this like a homicide, because deep down, that's what you believe it is."

Doc excused himself from the room.

"I'm gonna have to go talk to her family. You guys know where to find me if you need me."

Dave nodded to Doc as he left the room. He looked over at Glen.

"So you really think we have a homicide here? Do you think it's just this case? Do you think we're dealing with a hit and run? Maybe some scared kids who don't want to come forward?"

"Possible, that's definitely possible. But five deaths in less then two weeks in a town that maybe has seven or eight unusual deaths in a year. I don't think this case is an isolated one."

"Let's go back to the school and see if my guys have gathered any more leads for us."

Glen looked down the hall towards the family as Doc was telling them what happened. They were distraught as to be expected. If someone is behind these murders, he has to be stopped, and soon. Whoever it might be was heartlessly trying to kill as many people as quickly as he could before getting caught, or leaving of town.

Once back at the school Dave took one of his officers aside. He and Glen listened to his story. There was nothing new. No one saw or heard anything new.

One man walked up to Dave.

"What in the hell is going on around here? Are you doing anything to try to figure out why so many people are suddenly coming up dead? Aren't you going to do anything to those kids that ran her down? What kind of law do we have in this town anyway?"

"We're working on it. Don't worry about those kids. We'll handle them. We're doing our job. These things just take time. We're still waiting for the autopsy results before we have anything concrete to go on. Please, just be patient. We'll let all of you know as soon as there's something to tell."

The man walked away. Suddenly ten others were around him trying to find out what Dave had told him.

"I have a feeling this is just about to get ugly," said Dave.

Shelly walked over to join them.

"Let's get out of here," she said.

On the way home she told them about all the women questioning her. They were accusing Dave of not doing his job.

"Looks like the town folk are finally beginning to wonder the same things we are," commented Glen.

Glen and Dave disappeared into Dave's office as soon as they arrived at his house.

Shelly brought them each a cup of coffee. She also brought in a pump thermos filled with enough coffee to keep them going on what she thought was about to become a long night.

After she had the men situated she phoned around town looking for her kids. When she reached each of them at a friend's house, she instructed them to stay put until she arrived to pick them up.

First she picked up Sean, then Ann. She told them what happened. She warned them things might get a little rough at school. Some of the parents were accusing their dad of not doing his job. She also told them if they wanted to skip school the next day she would understand. Then she dropped the bomb on them that she wanted them home every day after school until they had a better idea of what was going on.

Both kids knew by the tone of her voice that there was no need to argue. They disappeared into their rooms as soon as they entered the house.

Shelly looked in on the two guys to see if they needed anything else before she went off to bed. They assured her they could take care of themselves.

Glen had added Jane to the chart. She was not an older person, she was not a teenager, it was not a Wednesday, and it was not a Saturday.

"Is there a connection?" he asked.

"No one saw her go down, that's like Sheila. It happened on school grounds. That's the same as Sheila and Tim."

Glen looked up at Dave.

"It's time, my friend."

"I know, I know."

Dave dialed the number for CBI.

Chapter 6

Early Tuesday morning Dave and Glen were seated in his office explaining to the deputies what they were about to do.

"I called CBI. Someone should be arriving this morning. They'll be here to help. I want each and every one of you to treat them with respect and not hold back any details. They are working with us. We are not working for them and they are not working for us. We are all in this together. Is that clear?" pressed Dave.

The group did not particularly like being treated like a bunch of kids, especially in front of Detective Karst.

Dave knew they were all extremely inexperienced with homicide. He hoped they would follow his instructions to the letter and keep a tight lip. He remembered what it was like to be a rookie on a homicide team. You always hoped to be the one to find that one clue, that one piece of evidence that would crack the case and make a name for yourself. He expected his men to feel the same way. He hoped he could stay one step ahead of them to prevent any mistakes.

"That's it for now. I'd like all of you back here around eleven to meet the men from CBI."

The group filed out of the door. Once out in the hall they felt free to complain about Dave. They felt confident they could handle it themselves.

"Well, what's your plan, Glen?"

"I told you if there were any more deaths I was staying on. I guess I'd better call my office to take some vacation time. Then I'll call Debbie and have her pack some extra clothes and meet me in Sterling. That'll save me driving all the way back to Denver to pick up my things."

"You know Debbie is welcome to come stay with us for awhile as well. We have plenty of room."

"I know, but she has her work and the dogs to take care of. I'll pass on your invitation, but I'm sure she's going to prefer to stay home."

"I really appreciate you taking time off to help out. I'm sure I could work well with CBI but it makes it easier to hash things out with you."

"What are you planning to tell them when they get here? Do you think we're dealing with a homicide or two?"

"You know my instincts tell me yes, but there just doesn't seem to be enough evidence to put anything together that would suggest connected homicides. Actually, I'm slightly nervous about calling them, in case I'm jumping to conclusions."

"No, Dave, you're doing the right thing. Relax, if there's something to find they'll help. If there's nothing no one will say you over reacted. I think everyone in town will be pleased that you are making every effort to solve these deaths once and for all."

"I hope you're right."

There was a gentle tap on the door. The dispatcher opened the door and escorted Martin Harmon in from CBI.

Dave and Glen rose to their feet.

"Welcome to our little town here. My name is Dave Smith. I'm the sheriff. This is Detective Glen Karst from the Denver PD."

Martin shook hands with each of them.

"My name is Martin Harmon, I'm with CBI. I hear you might be having some suspicious deaths going on."

He turned to Glen.

"Denver PD, huh? I'm surprised they sent someone from your department clear out here. That's a little out of the ordinary, isn't it?"

Glen responded, "Normally it would be, but Dave and I are old buddies. Dave used to work homicide with me in Denver before he moved out here. I'm on some vacation time to offer any assistance I can."

"Can I get you a cup of coffee?" asked Dave.

"That would be great," replied Martin.

111

Dave poured a cup of coffee for Martin, then topped off Glen's cup and his own. He set the box of doughnuts on the desk and a stack of napkins.

"Thanks," said Martin. "I had an early morning, this sure helps."

He eyed the doughnuts as well. He had left Denver without breakfast. He grabbed a jelly-filled powdered doughnut then took a seat in front of Dave's desk.

Glen made himself comfortable across the small room on the window ledge. He wanted to give the impression that Dave was in total control and he was just there to help when and if needed. He by no means wanted Martin to treat him as if he were in control because he was from Denver rather than this small town.

Martin began, "Tell me what you have."

Dave said, "We have five deaths in less than two weeks. I know that's not unusual in the city, but it strays far from the norm for Holyoke. The first death was a teenage boy. He died during a ball game."

Martin was taking notes. "What did the autopsy report say?"

"There was none. His mother refused to allow it. We didn't see any need to push it. Kids across the nation die periodically during ballgames. Typically, there's some undetected heart problem that surfaces during the stress of the game. I've even heard of kids getting hit in the chest with a ball at just the right spot with enough force to stop the heart."

"Yeah, I've heard the same thing. Was there any history of illness or heart problems with this boy or anyone in his family?"

"Nope, none, according to his family."

"Did anyone attempt CPR at the scene?"

"Dr. Foster, our town doctor, was at the game. He immediately started CPR on Tim. When the EMTs arrived they ran a tube down his throat and bagged him all the way to the hospital. He didn't respond."

Martin continued to write. "Did this Doctor Foster have any ideas what might have happened?"

"He assumed his heart just stopped."

"Okay, who's next?"

"Next, we have Lyle, an older gentleman. He died in the church basement at a dinner following the funeral for Tim. He'd been sick with the flu. He wasn't in the greatest shape. He was overweight and smoked. He complained about having difficulty breathing then collapsed onto the floor. His wife went to his side immediately. She loosened his tie and tried to make him comfortable. Dr. Foster attended the funeral so he was still on the premises when Lyle went down. He attempted CPR, but again, there was no response."

"And what did the autopsy say about Lyle?"

"Well, there wasn't one. His wife and boys decided against it. They knew he wasn't in the best of health and Doc had already told them he suspected it was his heart. He felt the bout of the flu he had the week before coupled

113

with the stress of the funeral and his overall bad health was all too much for his heart to handle."

"Is it customary out here for no one to request autopsies?"

"Most people don't request one unless they feel they need to know without a shadow of a doubt what caused the death. Typically, if we have an older person or a car accident, an autopsy is not done. Most of the time, when someone dies from a long time illness in the hospital, the family foregoes an autopsy. They are mostly done when it is a young person or a totally mysterious death."

"Do you have many young people or mysterious deaths?"

"Not until recently. That's why I've called you in on this."

"Okay, that's two deaths tell me about the others."

"Next, we have another highschool kid. This time a girl named Sheila. She was found passed out on the floor in the girl's bathroom at the high school. One of the parents close by was a nurse. She began CPR until the EMTs arrived. The story is pretty much the same as with Tim."

"No autopsy done again?"

"No, this time I had to override the parents decision against an autopsy. I ordered one myself."

"What did the results tell you?"

114

"The preliminary results showed nothing. The girl was in perfect health. We are still waiting for the results of the toxicology report."

"Did Dr. Foster decide this one was heart related as well?"

"Yes, he did."

"Okay, next."

"Then we have Sheri. She was an older woman in her fifties. She woke during the night experiencing difficulty breathing. Her husband called for an ambulance to meet him on the gravel road to save time. He put her in the backseat of his pickup and drove to meet the ambulance."

"Why didn't he just wait for the ambulance to come to him?"

"That's not uncommon out here. They live about twenty-five miles from town. It's the fastest way to get medical assistance. By the time he met the ambulance he was worried she was not breathing at all. Her gasping had just stopped. He was relieved to turn her over to the EMTs."

"What happened next?"

"Well, when the EMTs took over they said she still had a pulse. Doc and his crew worked on her but like the others she didn't respond."

"Another bad heart?"

"Don't know yet. The autopsy report is not in yet."

"And the last one?"

"That would be Jane. Her situation is entirely different."

"In what way?"

"Well, Glen and I were in the parking lot at the highschool last night. We heard tires screech and kids screaming. We ran to the scene. Jane's body lay on the ground. A couple of kids in a car had run over her."

"You mean they didn't even see her? Or is this a case of bad blood between students?"

"No, it was nothing like that. They didn't see her."

Glen stood up from his perch on the windowsill.

He added to the conversation. "I was the first one that went to her. I'm convinced she was down before those kids ran over her. Her body temperature had already dropped. I think those kids were making the turn too quickly and were definitely not focused or expecting anything or anyone to be in their path. I know it took them by total surprise."

"What did Doctor Foster have to say?" asked Martin.

"He said he couldn't tell by the damage done to her body if she had been hit by a car previously or had..."

Before he could finish Martin piped up with, "Or if she had died of a heart attack and the kids ran over a dead body."

"Sounds bad, doesn't it?" agreed Dave.

"So, who is this Doctor Foster anyway? Has he been around here for a while? Is he a new young doctor or does he know his stuff?"

"Doc's been around here for a number of years. He's never had to deal with this sort of situation before. He's under a lot of stress from it all. The town is talking about him and his ability to save lives under emergency situations."

"I can imagine," said Martin.

"Will there be an autopsy done on this last person," he checked his notes, "Jane?"

"Yes, sir that's the plan," answered Dave.

"What's next Martin? Where do we go from here?" questioned Glen.

"I guess the next step is to check the status on those reports. I'd also like you take me to each place of death."

"Do you have any more questions for us?" asked Dave.

"Oh, I'm sure I will once we begin to dig a bit. Shall we leave?"

Glen looked at his watch. It was nearly eleven.

"Maybe we should wait until after lunch. Dave, your deputies are due here in just a few minutes to meet Martin, remember?"

"Oh, that's right. I totally forgot. I told my men to come by and meet the crew from CBI so you could use them in any capacity you see fit. Then we can grab a bite to eat at the café before we examine the scenes. That is, if that's okay with you?"

"Sounds great to me. I don't think another hour or two is going to matter since the crime scenes are already cold. I just want to get pictures for my notes."

Dave's phone rang. He took the call.

Glen excused himself as he left the room to call his office and Debbie.

Martin finished writing his notes.

Glen walked back to Dave's office, followed by the deputies reporting for their eleven o'clock meeting.

Dave quickly introduced everyone to Martin. Martin shook hands with each of them. He jotted their names and phone numbers down in his notebook so he could reach any one of them if he needed them.

Dave thanked them for coming. When they left, the three men drove to the café for lunch.

The café was crowded as usual. Silence fell upon the room when the three men entered. Whispers were heard from across the room as they were seated in their booth. No one spoke to Dave or Glen. All eyes were upon Martin.

"I wonder who that guy is?" whispered Larry.

Bob whispered back, "I was talking to Terry this morning. He said they all had a meeting at the courthouse and that Dave was bringing in the big shots from Denver. He said he and the rest of the deputies are being forced to turn over the investigation to him. He was pretty pissed about it."

"So who exactly are the 'big shots'?"

"Colorado Bureau of Investigation. Sort of like the FBI for Colorado."

"Wow, that means this must be bigger than Dave is letting on. I was suspicious when that SWAT guy showed up again. I wonder what is really going on here?"

"I don't know, but I agree with you. I think Dave's hiding something from us."

"So what do you think? Can there be some disease or something in our community? Maybe that flu is not really the flu. Maybe it's one of those deadly diseases like they had in China or Africa? How do we know this guy is really from the CBI? Maybe he's from the CDC."

"What's CDC?"

"You know, the Center for Disease Control. When there's something really bad going on they call for them. Everyone knows they don't want the town to know because they are afraid of some panic or something."

"You know what? Two of them deaths happened in the school building. I think I'm gonna pull my kids out of there until we know what's going on," said Bob.

Bob got up to leave. Larry downed his drink and followed quickly behind. They both went by the school building and pulled their kids out. Bob's wife was upset with him for frightening the kids. She was sure Dave would not take any risks with the kids if there was something they should be concerned about, especially since his kids were at the school. She drove the kids back to school.

After she dropped her kids off she drove over to Larry's house to visit with his wife. She was in a panic. After the two women talked, Larry's kids were returned to school as well.

No one at the café talked to Dave and the two men he was with. Glen nodded his head at a couple of the guys in the café, trying to be sociable. It was obvious the mood was not as friendly as in the past. Martin didn't pick up on the silence and lack of friendly behavior. That was more typical in Denver where he was from.

After lunch Martin was ready to start his investigation. The three men drove to the school building. They walked into the gymnasium where Tim had died. The room was eerily quiet. Together Dave and Glen relived that night for Martin. Nothing unusual jumped out at him.

Next they went to the girl's bathroom where Sheila had been found. Class was in session so the bathroom was empty. Martin looked around the room. There was nothing to help them out. The room had already been cleaned by the janitor, as had the gymnasium and the locker room.

They went by the church. It was locked. Dave went next door to knock on the pastor's door. When Pastor Bob came to the door, Dave explained why they were there. Pastor Bob escorted the three officers into the church and down to the basement where the dinner had been held.

Martin looked around the room. He went into the kitchen.

"Where did the food come from that was served that day?"

"The ladies from the church prepare the meals when there's a funeral," responded Pastor Bob.

"I'd like a list of names of the women that prepared the meal for that day if it would not be too much trouble," requested Martin.

"You don't think the food had anything to do with Lyle's heart attack do you?" asked Pastor Bob.

"I'm just covering all my bases," replied Martin.

"I doubt if it was the food," said Dave. "There were a couple hundred people and no one else got sick or had any problems."

"Good point," agreed Martin. "No rush on that list, Bob."

Glen was very quiet that day. He didn't want to intrude plus he really had nothing to add. He had never been in the church basement before. He and Dave had already been down this same course of questioning at Dave's house when they were searching for any shred of evidence to connect the deaths.

Martin thanked Pastor Bob and they left.

Dave called Lee, Sheri's husband, to see if he was home. He was. They drove out to visit with him. His house was full of family assisting with funeral arrangements.

"Lee, this is Officer Martin Harmon, from the Colorado Bureau of Investigation. He'd like to ask you a few questions about Sheri."

"Sure, I'll answer the best I can."

He led them into the kitchen so they could be alone.

"Has your wife ever experienced any heart problems before that night?"

"Nope, she's been the healthiest of all of us."

"Was she on any medications?"

"No, like I said she was the most healthy one in our family."

"Did your wife drink?"

"Sheri? Hell no. Look, she didn't drink, she didn't do drugs, and she wasn't on any medication. She watched what she ate and she exercised. She was in great shape. She's never sick. I'm mean, she was never sick."

"Were you with her all day?"

"No, I was in town that day."

"Do you have any idea what she ate that day?"

"No, the usual I guess. I wasn't home for lunch. She was fine when she left to go to the church that night."

"Did she seem okay when she came home that night?"

"Yeah, sure. She seemed fine. She came home after the kids went to bed. She stayed to help clean up after the church meeting. She brought a couple of pieces of pie home. We had coffee and ate the pie then went to bed."

"Did both you and Sheri eat the pie?"

"Yeah. No wait a minute. She didn't eat hers. She put it into the refrigerator for her lunch the next day."

Lee looked at the refrigerator across the room. Tears welled up in his eyes. Sheri had made plans for a day she was never going to see. He was going to miss his wife terribly.

Glen walked over to the refrigerator. He opened the door. The refrigerator was packed with cold cuts, and casseroles from neighbors and friends. There was an assortment of cream pies inside, with fruit pies and cakes on the counter.

"Which of these pies did Sheri bring home with her?" asked Glen.

Lee walked over to the refrigerator. He looked inside. He moved the contents around on the shelves.

"It's not here. It was just one piece of blueberry pie on a paper plate. I don't like blueberry so I ate the slice of cherry pie that she brought home."

"Where do you suppose that blueberry pie slice is?" asked Glen.

"I don't know. Someone here probably ate it."

Martin continued with his questions for Lee.

123

Glen was haunted by that piece of pie. He listened to the conversation for a little while longer. The refrigerator kept drawing his attention. Finally, he left the kitchen to visit with the family and friends gathered in the living room.

He walked up to a heavy-set woman with gray hair who seemed to be in charge. She was busily filling everyone's coffee cups and tending to the group in general.

"Excuse me ma'am," began Glen.

"Oh, I'm sorry officer. Can I get you a cup of coffee?"

"No, but may I speak to you a moment?"

"Sure."

"Can you tell me who the first person was that came by the house here to help Lee?"

"Well, let's see. I wasn't the first one here. I think it was Opal, no, maybe it was Frances. I'm just not quite sure. Is it important?"

"It might be. Is there anyway you can look into that for me?"

"Sure, Opal is right over there."

Opal looked up when she heard them mention her name. She walked over to join them.

"This officer would like to know who the first person was that came by to help Lee Sunday morning."

"That would be Frances. I came just shortly after she did."

"Is Frances here?" asked Glen scanning the room.

"No she left a while ago," answered Opal. "Is there something I can help you with?"

"Lee said there was a piece of blueberry pie in the refrigerator and now it's gone. Any idea what may have happened to it?"

"Blueberry pie. Hmmm...No, I don't remember seeing any blueberry pie. We put some cream pies in there but no one brought a blueberry pie."

"No, this would have been just one slice on a paper plate," explained Glen.

"I didn't see any blueberry pie but I did see that paper plate on the top of the trash Sunday morning."

"Where's the trash now?" asked Glen.

"I burned it. That's okay isn't it? I mean, the wind wasn't blowing and it was in a wire burner."

"Sure, I'm sure that was fine. Thank you ladies."

Glen returned to the kitchen. Martin was finished with his questioning of Lee. The three of them returned to Dave's car.

When they were back inside of the car Glen said, "I don't know if this is significant or not but Sheri must've eaten that blueberry pie after Lee went to bed."

"How do you know that?" asked Dave.

"Well, Lee said she brought home a piece of cherry and a piece of blueberry. He said she was keeping hers for lunch Sunday. I didn't see it in the refrigerator so I checked with the ladies in the other room. One of them said she saw the paper plate from the blueberry pie on the

125

top of the trash. Since Lee didn't like blueberry pie, he wouldn't have eaten it."

"Isn't it possible one of the kids ate it or one of the people that came to help out?"

"There were two ladies here first thing Sunday morning. The second one to come said she saw the plate in the trash when she arrived and she arrived almost immediately after the first woman. I believe she said her name was Frances."

"You think there might have been something in that pie that made Sheri ill?" quizzed Martin. "Let's find out who this Frances person is. Right now we have no clues at all."

"Where's the trash from Sunday morning?" asked Dave hoping for their first lead.

"The bad news is it was burned this morning," reported Glen.

"Should one of us go back inside to find out who this Frances person is?" asked Martin.

"No need to do that. Her name is Frances Miller. She's Lee's sister. I'll give her a call," said Dave.

Glen silently had his hopes up that maybe there would be a connection.

Dave visited with Frances on the phone. He hung up and shook his head.

"Frances said when she arrived one of the kids was eating the pie for breakfast. The pie has nothing to do with Sheri's death."

Glen exhaled a long breath of disappointment.

"Let's go check out Jane's husband next," suggested Martin.

Dave called Jane's house. Her husband was not home. He called the mortuary just in case. That's where he was.

He asked John, from the mortuary, to keep him there until they had a chance to visit with him.

Dave drove them back into town to the mortuary.

Once inside he introduced Glen and Martin to Jane's husband.

Martin started his routine line of questioning. The results were the same. Jane was a perfectly healthy woman. No previous signs of heart trouble. Her husband had been away at a fertilizer seminar. He was called back early by family members. The last time he saw her was two days prior to her death.

They offered their condolences and thanked him for his time then left.

"Now what?" asked Dave.

"I suggest we go back to your office and hope the results of another autopsy might be in," said Martin.

It was getting late by the time they returned to the office. There was no news about Sheri's autopsy.

Martin looked through his notes.

"Guys, I'm sorry to say, but there's really nothing I can do here. There are no fresh crime scenes. We're not even sure if there are any crimes yet. We have nothing to connect any of the deaths. I'm going to head back to Denver. If I come up with any ideas I'll let you know. In the mean time when the reports come in please send me a copy."

Martin shook hands with both officers as he left Dave's office.

Dave was upset.

"See, this is why I wasn't in a big hurry to call them. There's just nothing here for them. I really hoped that damn piece of blueberry pie might have been our first shot at some evidence."

"Dave, don't worry about it. If something surfaces later or heaven forbid there's another death no one will question you as to why you didn't call for help. You did the right thing."

Glen looked at his watch.

"I guess you'll be heading back to Denver as well?"

"Nope, I told you I plan to stick around for awhile to help you figure this out. I told Debbie I'd buy her supper at the Chinese restaurant in Sterling if she brought my things to me. So I'd better get going. And by the way, consider this the ultimate show of friendship, I hate Chinese food, all those nasty vegetables."

Dave laughed his first laugh since Glen arrived yesterday morning.

Chapter 7

Early Wednesday morning, Glen was having coffee with Shelly before Dave appeared at the table.

"I'm surprised Dave's still sleeping," said Glen.

"He was up most of the night. I looked at the clock when he left our room to go to his office. I don't think he came back to bed until after four. I'm sure if he's sleeping at all, he'll only have had a couple of hours for the entire night."

Ann and Sean came in for breakfast. They ate fruit and cereal. Shelly offered to fix breakfast for Glen, but he wanted to wait for Dave. After the kids left Dave popped into the kitchen.

"Man, you look like hell in the morning!" teased Glen. "Is this what you have to look forward to every morning, Shelly?"

It was obvious Glen was trying to lighten the mood. He too was accustomed to his own sleepless nights, when a case wouldn't give his mind a moment's rest. The little Samantha case was a perfect example.

Dave kissed Shelly good morning. She got up to begin breakfast for the three of them.

"Shelly told me you stayed up all night. Did anything come to you?"

"Not really, I went over and over everything we told Martin. I double and triple checked my notes. It's the same thing over and over. The only link in the majority of deaths is that three happened on Saturday nights, that is if you consider the fact that Sheri started to die on a Saturday and was declared dead early Sunday morning. Jane and Lyle's being on a Wednesday and a Monday don't add into the equation. If you eliminate Lyle due to poor health, that tosses Jane out of the Saturday cycle."

"Would you like me to call on that toxicology report and see if they are gaining on it? That seems to be the only hope we have at the moment for evidence of foul play."

"Sure, if you have any favors due, please call them in."

Shelly set breakfast on the table and joined the men.

"I'm sorry, Shelly. Is there something I can help you with?" asked Glen.

"No, that's okay, just help Dave figure this mess out so we can all get some sleep at night."

Dave tried to include Shelly into the conversation. "What plans do you have for today?"

"Not much, I've got to pick up some groceries, clean a little and try to get a nap in. I don't have to work today. I'm thinking about canceling going to church tonight. I'm not up to the third degree."

"I don't blame you. That's what I'm expecting in town today. I think Glen and I might stop by here for lunch instead of going in to face the angry mob at the café. Don't plan anything; we'll make sandwiches when we get here. Is that okay with you, Glen?"

"Hey, I'm easy. I can eat almost anything."

"Except vegetables," teased Dave. "How'd dinner at the Chinese restaurant go last night with Debbie?"

"Actually, she noticed the Steak House at the interstate exit. She suggested we eat there. She said she would feel too guilty trying to enjoy her meal knowing I wasn't enjoying mine. So we had a great prime rib dinner. One of the best prime rib I've had in a long time."

"Debbie's so sweet. She spoils you way too much," said Shelly.

"Oh yeah, like you don't spoil this lunk sitting here feeding his face."

Glen slapped Dave across the back. They all tried their best to be sociable but it was obvious the case was haunting them.

Dave stood up, "Let's go face the music. The sooner we get it over with the better. Then maybe we can get some work done today."

131

Glen gulped the last of his coffee. He took his plates to the sink.

"Don't worry about that Glen, I'll handle it."

"Thanks for breakfast Shelly, it was great."

Glen had to practically jog after Dave who was already getting into his car.

They drove across town. Everything looked normal; nothing out of place. No one was acting differently.

"I'll bet none of those people lost sleep last night. No one knows how hard this is on me, but you can bet they will be quick to complain I'm not doing anything."

When Dave and Glen entered his office the dispatcher handed him a stack of phone messages. Dave glanced through them. They were all from the fine citizens of the town wondering if there were any leads yet.

Dave handed them back to the dispatcher.

"Call all of these people back and tell them we're working on it, but at the moment we have nothing to report. Don't put any of those calls through to me unless it's an emergency call. I don't want to be disturbed today. That goes for people walking in off of the street, just tell them I'm in conference with Detective Karst all day."

"Sure Dave. I understand."

Glen slipped away to use a phone that was not in Dave's office. He wanted to give him a few minutes of privacy to regain his composure after the pressure of the phone messages.

Glen found a phone. He dialed the number for the toxicology lab. He explained who he was and the name of the victim.

"I know the report is not due until Friday but I was wondering how things are going so far? Have you found anything we can use?"

Laura, on the other end of the phone, said, "We were about to call Sheriff Smith. We did find something in the tissue that should raise suspicion."

Glen could feel his heart rate increase. Finally, there might be a lead, one thread of evidence that could begin to explain this mystery.

"What is it?"

Glen scrambled to find a notepad and pen. He grabbed a sheet of paper from the printer thinking it would be faster.

"It appears this girl had an excessive amount of nicotine in her system."

"Nicotine? That's it? So she smoked a few cigarettes before she died. I need more than that."

Glen was hoping for some results showing a drug overdose or some other foreign chemical in her body, something that would either point the finger at a homicide, or totally rule out homicide. They needed something concrete to continue this investigation.

"Detective Karst, I said excessive amount; not the volume you'd get from smoking."

"What do you mean? What volume did you find?"

"A dose of say, seventy or eighty milligrams."

"Okay, I'm not familiar with the measurement of nicotine. How much would you get from one cigarette?"

"Well, if you were to smoke an entire cigarette you would ingest about one or two milligrams."

"That would mean this girl would've smoked forty to eighty cigarettes to raise the volume in her body to that level. Over how much time would she have had to do this for it to accumulate like that?"

"To raise her level and keep it there to kill herself she would have had to smoke them all at once. She would've become ill and passed out before she could have smoked that many cigarettes back to back."

"Okay, say she didn't smoke that many cigarettes. Could they have been crushed and put in food or something?"

"I wouldn't believe so. Think about the texture and the bad taste of eating crushed cigarettes. Again, she would've become sick and just vomited the whole mess up. Was there any sign of vomiting at the crime scene?"

"She was found in a bathroom, so I suppose she could've vomited into a toilet before she was found."

"Detective Karst, are you familiar with liquid nicotine?"

"No, not really."

"Liquid nicotine is used by some to replace smoking. For awhile there was an experiment to add

liquid nicotine to beer so you could smoke and drink in
one step."

"Oh that's brilliant. Who came up with that idea?"

"A brewery experimented with it for awhile, but
then dropped it."

"Tell me more about liquid nicotine."

"Liquid nicotine has an unpleasant taste, but
becomes nearly tasteless when added to a flavored
beverage. Using it in small doses allows the smoker to
decrease the amount of nicotine until he or she has kicked
the habit. It's much like using graduated patches and
gums. It does have its purpose. But if the level is
increased to the high levels we found in this girl's body the
result is fatal."

Glen was writing notes as quickly as Laura was
passing the information on to him. He didn't want to miss
one detail.

"What would the symptoms be?"

"Well, a smaller overdose would result in dizziness,
weakness, confusion, hypertension and then possibly
coma."

"What about a large overdose like in this case?"

"When you are talking about large doses, in
medical terms it would be intense vagal stimulation that
may cause transient cardiac standstill or paroxysmal
atrial fibrillation. Death is due to the paralysis of
respiratory muscles or central respiratory failure."

"So doing CPR on a person suffering from an overdose of liquid nicotine would be totally useless. Am I correct?"

"Yep, you hit that one right on."

"How much time would you say had to pass from the time of ingesting this until the symptoms and death would result?"

"It could take anywhere from five minutes to one hour depending upon the amount ingested and the person's body weight. Then, of course, you would decrease that time if it were injected directly into the bloodstream."

"Injected. I guess I assumed the vics would have ingested it in food. Were there any signs of needle usage on our girl?"

"I don't do that part of the workup. Hang on and let me grab my copy of her report."

Glen was feverishly writing the details down while she searched through her paperwork. The excitement mounting inside him set his own heart pounding so loud he could hear it in his head.

"According to the results of her autopsy there were no signs of needles anywhere on her body. I'd say it was safe to assume this girl ingested the stuff."

"Now we just have to decide if she did so voluntarily."

"Do you have any other questions for me? I really need to get back to work now."

"No, you've already helped tremendously. Would you fax a copy of your report to Sheriff Smith's office as soon as you have it typed up?"

"Sure thing, that's the plan. Good luck with your investigation. This is our first case of death by nicotine in our lab. When you get it all figured out stop by and let me know the whole story."

"Will do, and thanks again."

Glen finished his notes then ran out into the hallway to return to Dave's office. When he got to Dave's door there were people inside talking with him. Glen paced outside the door. He tried to get Dave's attention so he could break up the meeting, but he had no luck.

He paced more. His heart was still racing. Finally, he ran back to the office where he had made his phone call and called Dave's desk. The dispatcher intercepted the call. When Glen asked to speak to Dave she told him he would be in a meeting with Detective Karst all day. He explained to her that he was Detective Karst and that it was imperative that she put him through immediately.

"This is Dave."

"Dave get rid of those people. We have a lead!"

"Glen where are you?"

"I'm in the office down the hall. Can you get rid of those people so we can talk?"

"Yes, I need that information immediately. Could you please hold?"

Dave turned to the group from the town that came to visit with him about his progress. They had slipped past the dispatcher while she was on the phone.

"Excuse me, but this is a very important call. I must take it immediately in private, please. I'll let you know the minute we have something and thanks for stopping in."

He spoke into the phone.

"Okay, they're gone."

"I'll be right there."

Glen hung up the phone and raced down the hall to Dave's office. He stopped at the dispatcher's desk and asked her to not disturb them.

Dave was eagerly searching Glen's face when he walked in with papers in hand.

"What? Tell me what you've got!"

"I called the toxicology lab. They were just about to call you. They found liquid nicotine in Sheila's body tissue."

Dave wasn't quite sure what that meant as of yet, but he knew that by the excitement in Glen's voice it was the lead they were looking for.

"Somehow Sheila had a lethal dose of liquid nicotine in her system. It paralyzed her respiratory muscles and stopped her heart."

"No shit!"

Dave pounded his fist on his desk. He stood up and walked to the window, gazing out but not seeing anything, as his mind sorted through the data.

"Yes! We have a lead. Tell me more."

"The level of nicotine could only have come from liquid nicotine; not from cigarettes. She would've had to smoke like eighty cigarettes all at once to get that level in her bloodstream. The only way to do it would be by injection or ingestion. There were no needle tracks on her body so the stuff had to be ingested."

Dave was beside himself with excitement. "Do you think it was a suicide, or do you think we're dealing with a homicide here?"

"I suppose it could be one or the other, but now we have a cause of death. Let's see if we can push through the tox screen for the other two women. Now that we have a substance to look for, the testing should go more quickly."

"Right. Let me put in a call to the lab and have them run tests for the nicotine."

Glen could've made the request himself while he had Laura on the phone but he didn't want to take over the case. He felt Dave should handle it. He was very careful not to overstep his boundary as a friend coming to help.

Dave made the call.

"Let's go by the house and grab lunch. Then we'll stop by to visit with Doc to let him know what we've found."

"I'm sure he's gonna feel a hell of a lot better knowing there was nothing he could've done to help Sheila."

"Yeah, but she was not responding to the CPR administered by a nurse at the scene. When they got her to the hospital there wasn't much left for him to do, except to pronounce her dead. I think he feels worse about the others that were still alive when he was working on them."

"You know Glen, this is one damn mess. I find myself hoping these cases are related so we can get some answers. But have you given any thought to what will happen if they are? That would mean we have a killer among us in this quiet little town. How in the hell am I gonna find who it is, and what will happen once I do? As I said before, I don't think this town would ever be the same."

They drove to Dave's. Even though they told Shelly they would fix their own lunch she had a stack of sandwiches in the fridge waiting for them, along with a bowl of fruit and tortilla chips. She made a fresh pot of coffee and baked a cake.

"Boy Dave, I feel bad that Shelly put herself out like this. She said she wanted to take it easy today since she didn't get much more sleep than you did."

"Yeah, I know, but Shelly is not only the greatest wife a guy could have, but at times I think she's superwoman."

They ate their lunch in silence. They were friends long enough that every moment did not have to be filled with conversation to make them feel comfortable around each other.

Their keen minds were both working through the details and putting together a multitude of different crime scenarios. When the time was right they would share their thoughts and plan their next course of action.

Shelly returned home carrying a bag of groceries. Glen jumped up from the table to rush out to the car to carry the remaining bags into the kitchen. He made two trips with the bags. Dave was too deep in thought to even think about what was going on. By the time he realized what was happening Glen had carried all of the bags into the house.

"Gee, I'm sorry. I didn't mean for the two of you to carry in the bags by yourselves."

"And who do you think carries them in every other time I bring groceries home when you're not here?" teased Shelly.

She had just joined them, but was aware of a difference in the energy of the room. The tension had eased. She possessed a keen sense of negative and positive energy that surrounds people.

"Okay you two, what happened today?"

141

"Now how did you know something happened today?" asked Glen.

"Give it up old man, she's psychic or something. I can't hide anything from her."

"Psychic? I thought you didn't believe in such things? You gave me a pretty hard time about working with a psychic on my last case with the missing girl. Remember?"

"Yeah, well this is different. Shelly is just tuned in to my moods and me. She's not out trying to solve crimes or anything crazy like that."

"Psychic is psychic in my book," teased Glen back.

"You worked with a psychic in Denver on that little girl's case?" asked Shelly.

"Her name is Jennifer Parker. She's written some books on the stuff. Anyway, she volunteered her services and damned if she wasn't right on. It was the strangest thing. She says we all have some degree of psychic ability if we'd just learn how to use it."

"I'll stick with my brain and my gut feelings, thank you," piped in Dave.

"That's it exactly. Your gut feeling is really your psychic ability. The more of it you have, the better cop you make."

Shelly wanted to pursue the conversation more, but Dave butted in.

"I thought you wanted to hear about our morning."

"I do."

She sat down at the table to listen to their story.

Glen allowed Dave to tell the whole story. He was happy to see Dave with some direction in the case. The total frustration that had been written all over his face had been replaced with a new look of determination.

Dave explained to Shelly everything they learned about liquid nicotine.

"So where would a kid like Sheila get her hands on something like that?"

"I guess you can buy it to stop smoking," answered Glen.

Dave wiped his mouth and stood up.

"We'd better get going. I'm anxious to talk to Doc."

Glen cleared the table.

Dave kissed Shelly good-bye.

"Get some sleep will ya. Don't overdo today. I'll pick up something in town to bring home for supper so you won't have to cook. Tonight's church, right?"

"Thanks, it'd be nice not to fix supper tonight. I'm gonna cancel on church tonight. Remember?"

"Oh yeah. See ya later."

When they arrived at the clinic Doc was absent. The receptionist told them he was at the hospital delivering a baby.

"Amazing isn't it? Life just keeps going. Someone dies and a baby is born. The old human race keeps perpetuating itself," contemplated Glen.

143

They walked next door to the hospital. Dave stopped a nurse in the hall to ask if Doc was available.

"Not at the moment, but give him about fifteen minutes and he'll be finished up with the new mom. She had a boy. Doc's stitching her up."

"You know God must've known what he was doing when he picked women to have babies. I think if it was up to men the world would just stop. Can you imagine intentionally being sick, overweight, and then the pain of childbirth?" shuddered Dave.

Glen poured himself a cup of coffee while they sat in the waiting room for Doc.

Dave called his office to tell the dispatcher where he was and not to call him on his cell phone, but to use the radio instead, if he got any messages from the lab.

Doc stepped out into the waiting room with a smile on his face. He so enjoyed the excitement of childbirth. Seeing the parents beaming with pride was exhilarating.

"I hope you two gents aren't here to rain on my parade. Today's a happy day around here."

"Well, we have some news that's both good and bad," answered Dave.

"Let's go someplace more private," suggested Doc.

They followed him to a waiting area in the back corner of the hospital that was vacant. He pulled off his cap and put his feet up on the coffee table.

"So what's this news you have for me?"

"We heard from toxicology today about Sheila," started Dave.

Doc pulled his feet back off the table and sat straight up.

"What'd they find?"

His interest was obviously peaked.

"Her cause of death was central respiratory failure. Glen, read the medical terms to Doc, will ya?"

Glen opened his notebook where he had transposed his notes.

"Paraxysmal atrial fibrillation and paralysis of the respiratory muscles, caused by a high dose of nicotine. Probably liquid nicotine."

"What? Where would she get something like that and why would she be using it?"

"That's what we were wondering. Do you know if they carry it at the drugstore in the pharmacy?" asked Dave.

"Let's give Ron a call and find out." Doc picked up the phone on the table next to him.

"Ron, this is Doc Foster. Do you carry liquid nicotine?"

"No. Why?"

"Can you order it in?"

"I suppose so. Do you have a patient that needs it?"

"No, just wondered how easy it is to get your hands on it. Have you ever ordered it for anyone?"

"No, I'd remember if I had. Why?"

"I'll talk to you about it some other time. I've got to go now."

"He says he doesn't carry it and he's never had it, nor has he ever ordered it for anyone. So it didn't come from this town. Since that's the only place in town to order drugs of any type."

"Legal drugs," Glen pointed out.

"Yeah, legal drugs," agreed Doc.

Dave got a call on his radio. It was his dispatcher. The lab called about Sheri's toxicology test.

"Thanks, I'll give them a call."

Glen looked anxiously at Dave's face.

"The lab called, they might have something on Sheri."

"So soon?" How could they have all the tests in?" asked Doc.

"I asked them to run the nicotine test right away," explained Dave.

Dave took his address book out of his uniform shirt pocket to look up the number.

Glen and Doc had their eyes glued to him.

"Laura, this is Sheriff Smith. I'm returning your call."

"Hi. Just thought you needed this ASAP. The nicotine test on Sheri Foreman came back positive. That makes two in one day. What are you guys up to there?"

"Positive? You're sure? Was the level high enough to be lethal?"

Glen and Doc were nearly falling off the edges of their seats leaning in to listen to the conversation.

"It sure was. The level was the same as the girl we told Detective Karst about this morning. Oh, and just as a favor, I had them check right away for needle marks, and she was clean. My guess would be she also ingested this stuff."

"Thanks Laura, you've been a big help. I need you to call me as soon as you get the results on the third body."

"That's the plan. Bye."

"Bingo! There's a match. Both deaths were caused by liquid nicotine. It's time to go to work."

Dave and Glen rose from their seats to leave.

Doc rose slowly from his seat. He appeared to be very uncomfortable with the knowledge.

"Are you okay?" asked Dave.

"Huh? Yeah, I'm fine. I'm glad we know, but that's not very good news about two healthy people dying needlessly."

Glen and Dave left to return to Dave's office.

On the way there, Glen said, "Doctor Foster sure took the news badly. I guess I was a bit surprised. I thought he'd be relieved getting some answers." Glen had his suspicions aroused about any and all medical people at this point.

"Maybe he's thinking the same thing I am. Who's passing out liquid nicotine and why."

Back at the office Glen read through the fax from Sheila's case that the toxicology lab sent over. The report from Sheri had not yet been prepared.

Dave called Martin Harmon.

"This is Martin Harmon."

"Martin, this is Sheriff Dave Smith from Holyoke. We've got some news for you on those deaths."

"Great. Did you finally find your elusive lead?"

"Yep, turns out two of the five vics died from an overdose of liquid nicotine. We're waiting for the lab screen to be finished on the fifth body to see if it's connected."

"What's your plan on the first two if the last one comes up positive?"

"I'm not quite sure at this point. I guess we'll cross that bridge when we get there. We'd probably have to get the bodies exhumed. I'm sure the families will fight us on that one. I won't mention it until we have to."

"Keep me informed and we'll be here to help if you need us."

"Thanks. Bye."

"Well Dave, your gut instincts were right all along. These deaths are connected. It's going to be agonizing waiting for that last test to be called in."

"I know Glen. I hate to start any formal investigation at this point, at least not formal enough for the town to know about it. Let's go back to my place and scour the Internet to learn all we can about liquid nicotine."

"If Ron at the pharmacy is right about never having ordered it then someone purchased it elsewhere and brought it into town. Are there any new people in town that moved in recently? How about the hunters?"

Dave picked up the phone and called the post office.

Pam answered the phone.

"Pam, I need a list of any new families that have moved into the area in say the last six months, no make that a year. Just fax the list over when you have it ready. Thanks."

Next he called the electric company for the same information in case someone moved in that was not registered with the post office at least they'd need electricity.

Dave and Glen left to do their Internet search.

Chapter 8

The house was locked when Dave and Glen arrived at Dave's home.

"Wow! Shelly must really be spooked. Our house is never locked, not even when we leave town."

Glen's adrenaline rushed, he hoped Shelly was okay and nothing dangerous had happened inside the house. He kept his thoughts to himself while he anxiously waited for the door to be unlocked by Dave.

Dave stepped into the house quietly. All of the lights were off and the shades were drawn. He glanced a curious look at Glen. He continued through the house to the bedroom. The door was closed. He attempted to open it, but it was locked from the inside.

"That's odd. I didn't even know the door had a lock. We've never used it since we moved in," whispered Dave.

Glen's first reaction was to break the door down in an attempt to rescue Shelly from the dangers within. He stood motionless waiting for Dave to make the first move.

"Dave? Is that you?" called Shelly from the other side of the door.

"Yes, Shelly. It's me. Why is the door locked?"

Click

Shelly unlocked the door to let Dave in. Glen stood in the hall not wanting to intrude into their private space. He chuckled to himself about how he nearly burst into the room to save Shelly, sending splinters of wood flying. He would've been the one creating the danger by hitting her with the door had she been on her way to open it.

Dave repeated himself, "Why did you lock the door? Is something wrong?"

Blush rose over Shelly's face as she answered, "I guess with all that's going on. I mean you know the deaths and all... Oh, I don't know. I was scared. Okay?"

Dave embraced Shelly to ease her fear.

"Next time you're frightened you call me immediately. Do you understand? I'll be here in minutes. There is no need for my wife to be frightened when I'm the sheriff of this town. Now did something happen to frighten you?"

"The phone rang a couple of times. When I went to answer it no one was there. I guess I just let myself get jumpy about it. It was probably nothing, just a wrong number."

"Is everything okay in there?" asked Glen.

Shelly and Dave walked into the hall where Glen waited impatiently.

151

"Shelly's a little nervous about what's been happening. Someone called and hung up on her. I'm glad she went through the extra measures to secure the house. I am upset with her that she didn't call us when she was frightened."

"I would've been embarrassed to call you guys. You have too much on your plates already."

Glen put his arm around Shelly.

"Next time no matter what, you call us, most of the time a little diversion is good for us anyway. Don't ever be embarrassed when you're feeling uneasy. Remember what I told you. We all have some psychic abilities buried deep within us. You have to follow through on those feelings."

"Oh shit! You've gone whacko over this psychic crap," whined Dave as he left the hall to go into his office.

"Do you really believe in all of that stuff?" asked Shelly.

"If you would've asked me a couple months ago I would've denied any belief at all. Now, after working with that psychic, I feel I need to remain open minded until I can reach a definite decision, one way or the other. Now tell me about those phone calls."

"There's really not much to tell. The phone rang and I was in the bathroom so I didn't get to it very quickly. When I finally did get to it whoever it was hung up. Then it rang again. That time I answered it on the second ring. I heard the person hang up again."

152

"Do you think the caller waited until he or she heard your voice before hanging up?"

"The first time I was unsure, but the second time he or she waited for me to say hello a number of times before hanging up. I guess that's what made me feel uneasy."

"Next time give us a call. I'm sure it's probably nothing, but it's best to be extra careful at a time like this."

"What do you mean a time like this? Have you guys learned something new?"

"Well, I should let Dave tell you."

"Tell me what? Oh come on Glen, what do you have?"

"The report came back from Sheri. She also died from a lethal dose of liquid nicotine."

Shelly gasped and fell back against the wall in the hall for support.

Glen reached for her. He thought she was going to drop.

"Oh my God. The cases are related. You guys are dealing with a homicide here aren't you?"

"Well, we're not quite sure."

"Don't sugar coat it for me, Glen. I can understand how Sheila, a kid, could've been experimenting with something she shouldn't have. My God, Sheri would never have done such a thing. What's really going on?"

"Maybe we should go in and talk to Dave. I've probably already told you too much."

Shelly marched down the hall to Dave's office with determination in her steps.

"Are you going to tell me what's going on?"

Dave looked up from his computer. He could tell by the tone of Shelly's voice that she was angry with him. He shot a glance for help to Glen.

"I'm afraid I told her about Sheri's test results. She's concerned we may be dealing with a homicide."

"I don't believe it *may* be a homicide. I believe it *is* a homicide. I need to know exactly what's going on. Dave, we have Sean and Ann to consider. Are they in any danger?" cried Shelley.

"I wish I could say without a shadow of a doubt they're safe, but I really don't have enough pieces of the puzzle to see a clear picture. We know the nicotine connected two of the deaths. We're waiting to hear about Jane's results. If they come back positive to nicotine then we may definitely say we are dealing with homicide."

"What about the kids? Are they safe?" she asked.

"I honestly don't know if anyone is safe. We don't know how or when the liquid nicotine entered the bodies of our victims."

"We know the time had to be from within five minutes to one hour after ingestion. We need to retrace the last day for each of our victims," stated Glen.

He was interrupted when Dave's cell phone rang.

154

"Dave, we've got another death," said the dispatcher.

"Who? Where?"

"Cynthia, one of the teacher's aids at the school."

"We'll be right there."

Glen and Shelly knew by the look on Dave's face that someone else had succumbed to a mysterious death.

"Dave?" questioned Shelly.

"Go get the kids. Don't tell them anything. Just bring them home and don't let them go out."

"Who?"

Cynthia Mullerschallen, a teacher's aid.

"Did it happen at the school?"

"Yes."

Shelly began to cry. Fear for the safety of Sean and Ann overwhelmed her.

Glen handed her his handkerchief.

Dave gathered her into his arms.

"I know this is hard honey, but try to pull yourself together. We don't want to cause a panic. Just go to the school, and pull the kids out. Come up with some lame excuse about a dentist appointment, or something so you don't raise suspicion. It's best right now if whoever is doing this does not know that we have any leads at all. We need to catch this son of a bitch before he hurts someone else."

Shelly felt safe in Dave's arms. She was able to gather her composure. She knew what she had to do and how she needed to proceed.

"I'll be okay. I think I can pull this off."

She blew her nose and wiped her eyes.

Glen's heart broke watching the fear well up in the faces of his two dearest friends. He was glad he offered his services to his friend in need and could be there for them. Not having kids of his own he could only imagine how he would feel to discover Debbie was in danger. He made a mental note to give her a call as soon as the appropriate moment arrived.

"Okay buddy, are you ready for this?"

"As ready as I'll ever be. Let's head over to the hospital first, then go by the school to ask questions."

Dave turned to Shelly. He kissed her on the forehead.

"Okay, go pick up the kids. Do not let them leave, no matter how hard they beg. Tell them I want them to clean their rooms, or the garage, or anything. Tell them whatever it takes to keep them here and off of their phones. Blame me. I'll deal with them when I get home."

They walked Shelly to her car. As soon as she was out of sight the guys drove in the opposite direction to the hospital.

When they arrived at the hospital they went immediately to the emergency room. They saw Cynthia's family gathered in the waiting room. Dave and Glen

156

turned around to avoid the confrontation. They went to Doc's office in the hospital to page him.

He picked up the phone in the emergency room.

"Doc, this is Dave. I'm avoiding the family for the moment. Can you tell us anything?"

"Where are you?"

"We're in your office here at the hospital."

"I'll be right there."

Cynthia's family knew she was DOA. Doc, as he was leaving the room, gave them permission to go in with her body. He had already informed them an autopsy must be performed.

He slipped into his office to visit with Dave and Glen.

"Well?" asked Dave.

"The same as the others. I've already informed the family about the autopsy. They didn't seem to have a problem with it."

"What did you tell them was the cause of death?" asked Glen

"I told them her heart stopped."

"Good," responded Dave. "Good thinking. We can't let the town know just yet what we're dealing with. Glen and I are going over to the school now to ask some questions."

Dave and Glen started to leave the room.

"Dave," started Doc. "Please put an end to this."

"We're sure as hell gonna try."

157

When Dave and Glen arrived at the school there was utter chaos. Students were everywhere. Classes were halted. The panic was beginning. Parents were arriving at the scene. The faculty was gathered in a conference room.

Dave and Glen pushed their way through the crowd of students. Some were glad to be out of classes. Others were crying. Elementary school kids are never quite sure how to handle death. Especially when it happens to someone they know, but worse yet, at their school.

A small group of parents were heading for Dave and Glen.

"Uh oh, here we go," whispered Dave.

"Dave," called one of the mothers. "Can we have a word with you?"

"I'll deal with crowd control. You go interview the faculty for me, will ya?" instructed Dave.

Glen pushed his way through the crowd past the parents on their way towards Dave. He found the door marked faculty lounge and let himself in.

"I'm sorry this is a private meeting," said the principal as he rose to his feet.

"It's okay. I'm Detective Glen Karst." He flashed his badge. "I'd like to ask you a few questions. Is the entire faculty present here?"

"Yes, Detective Karst. We're all here," responded the principal. He was actually relieved to turn the floor over to Glen, as he had no answers for the staff.

158

"Can anyone tell me exactly what happened?"

"Cynthia helps out in Mrs. Atkins room," said one of the teachers pointing to Mrs. Atkins who sat at the table sobbing, unable to speak.

Glen turned his attention to Mrs. Atkins. He walked to her chair and put his hand on her shoulder. He knelt down at her side.

"I'm so sorry for your loss, Mrs. Atkins, but I do need to talk to you about what happened."

She nodded through her sobs.

Glen looked towards the principal. "I need to speak to Mrs. Atkins in private. Is there somewhere we can go?"

"You may use my office. Mrs. Atkins can show you the way."

Mrs. Atkins rose from her chair to go with Detective Karst.

"Wait," interrupted the principal. "Go out the faculty door through the hall this way. There'll be fewer people." He held the door open for them.

"Thanks," replied Glen as he guided Mrs. Atkins out the door.

She led him down the long corridor to the principal's office. His secretary looked up about to stop them from entering the principal's private office.

Mrs. Atkins returned her glance, "It's okay, he's a detective. He wants to talk about Cynthia."

The secretary watched them as they walked into the office and closed the door. Her phone had been ringing non-stop. Calls were coming in from concerned parents. It wouldn't be much longer before the town was in a full-blown panic.

There were glasses and a pitcher of water on the counter behind the principal's desk. Glen poured a glass of water for Mrs. Atkins. He tried to make her as comfortable as possible in an uncomfortable situation. He was well aware of the fact that having to speak with a detective is unnerving to many people, guilty or not. He hoped he was not making her unnecessarily uneasy. He knew she would probably prefer speaking with Dave.

"Are you ready to begin?"

She sipped her water then put the glass down. She looked up at Glen and nodded.

He took out his notebook and began.

"Just tell me as much as you can about today."

"Well," she cleared her throat. "Well, today was just like any other day. Cynthia came in this morning at her regular time. She helped with the kids. She left for a couple of hours at lunchtime. Then she came back to help with the afternoon classes. We were nearly finished for the day when she fell to the floor."

Mrs. Atkins began to cry again. She took another drink of the water.

"Okay, did Cynthia share with you that she wasn't feeling well today?"

"No, but her dog, Sadie, was ill and had to go to the vet. She ate one of her kid's toys and was in pain. She had to leave her at the vet's office. He said the dog would be fine once she passed the toy."

"Did she mention if she went anywhere else?"

"No, she went straight home to pick up Sadie, then directly to the vet clinic, then back here."

"What about lunch? You mentioned she left during lunchtime."

"What about lunch? She took a long lunch hour because she had so much to do."

"Where did she eat lunch?"

"Oh, she didn't eat lunch today. She was too busy with the dog and all."

"How do you know she didn't stop to grab a sandwich somewhere?"

"It's not like we have fast food here. It would've taken too much time to go into a restaurant. She was anxious to get back to school."

Glen felt a bit foolish. He forgot, once again, about the lack of city conveniences in a small town. There's not a fast food restaurant on every corner. There's not even one in the entire town. Unless you use the Taco John's Express at the gas station.

"What about after she returned to school? Did she eat something here?"

"No, I don't think so. Oh, wait a minute, she did grab a yogurt out of the refrigerator in the teacher's

161

lounge. She was eating it while the kids were working on their art projects. Why are you so concerned about whether or not she had anything to eat? I thought she died of a heart attack."

"Without an autopsy we don't know for sure, but Doctor Foster seemed pretty sure her heart stopped. I just have to ask routine questions to have a complete picture for our report."

"Why does she have to have a police report to have a heart attack?"

"Well, she died on school grounds, insurance and all, you know."

"Could you tell me at what time the students have their art class?"

Glen did not want to bring the food issue up again by asking what time she ate her yogurt.

"Art class is from two until three."

"Great, you're doing great. One last question, what time did you call 911."

"Two forty seven."

"How can you be so exact?"

"I looked at the clock when I was dialing the phone. I knew she would only have a few minutes for them to come and revive her before it was too late. Then I called the nurse and she came in to begin CPR. It didn't work though. She never came to."

"Before she collapsed, were there any outward signs she was in distress?"

"I thought that was your last question."

"I promise this will be my last question."

"No, she was fine. She left to go to the bathroom. When she came back she started to help the kids with their projects. She seemed fine, then I left the room to use the bathroom. When I returned I barely got to my desk when she collapsed."

"Thank you, Mrs. Atkins, I know this was difficult for you. You may go now."

Glen stayed behind in the principal's office to organize his notes. Glen's notes were always the most accurate, neatly written notes in the department. Although he could retain every detail in his head, his notes were a double check system for himself and his partner.

Suddenly, the door flew open, interrupting his silence. Dave slipped into the room closing the door quickly behind him.

"What'd you find out?"

"Mrs. Atkins told me Cynthia left during the lunch hour. She skipped her lunch to take her dog to the vet clinic. When she returned she went back to her duties. She did grab a yogurt from the fridge in the teacher's lounge. Some time between two and three she was eating it. She collapsed at two forty-seven."

"If she was fine all day, then ate yogurt..."

"I'm on it. The yogurt was probably laced with liquid nicotine.'

"Exactly."

"Let's go find that empty container and get it to the lab to check for liquid nicotine, as well as fingerprints."

"I'll give CBI a call and tell them to get a unit out here stat," said Glen.

"Great, if we can use them and their equipment we can move more quickly on this than having to send everything away. They should be able to get here by this evening. Now, let's go find that yogurt."

When the two officers stepped out into the hallway it was empty. Not a soul to be seen.

"What the hell's going on?" asked Dave, fearful of the panic.

Glen slapped him on the back laughing, "School's out for the day."

Dave looked at his watch, then gave a sigh of relief.

"Let's get to Mrs. Atkin's room."

Together they walked the corridors reading nameplates on the doors in an attempt to locate Mrs. Atkin's room. Along the way, they met the janitor. He gave them directions. Once inside the room the eyes of the two detectives scanned the room from top to bottom in search of the much needed yogurt container. Nothing. Neither of them saw it in plain sight. Next, they searched the room for the trash containers. There was one at the teacher's desk, and one at the back of the room near the sink. Dave walked to the desk while Glen walked to the back of the room. Both trash baskets were empty. Fresh plastic bags lined the containers.

"Damn, the janitor has already been here," complained Dave.

"Let's go back out and find him before he tosses those bags."

They stood outside the door looking up and down the hall. No one was there.

"You go that way, I'll go this way. Let's meet back here in a few minutes," suggested Glen.

Both men searched the rooms down the hallways hoping to find Mr. Brown, the janitor. Glen found him first. He was cleaning the boy's bathroom.

"Hi, my name is Glen Karst," he showed his badge to Mr. Brown. "Can I speak with you for a minute."

"Sure, boy that was a terrible thing that happened today. Poor Cynthia. She was such a nice, happy, lady."

"Did you clean Mrs. Atkin's room tonight?"

"Sure, I cleaned her room. Was I not supposed to touch anything? There was no yellow tape across the door or anything so I thought it was okay. It did give me the creeps though knowing Cynthia dropped dead in that room. Right in front of those poor kids."

"Where is the trash from Mrs. Atkin's room?"

"Why do you want the trash from her room?"

"I need to find something that may have been thrown away. Where is the trash from her room?"

"I guess it would be by the door at the end of the hall, in one of those black trash bags."

Glen looked down the hall; there, near the door to the back of the school building, were a dozen or so trash bags.

"Thanks."

Glen left Mr. Brown to find Dave. Dave was already returning to Mrs. Atkin's room.

"Any luck? I couldn't find him anywhere."

"Yeah, I found him. Are you ready to go dumpster diving like the old days? Only fortunately for us the bags haven't made it to the dumpster yet. They're piled by the back exit door."

"Great, let's go get dirty."

The two men walked to the stack of trash bags. One by one they tore them open exposing the contents. Most of the bags had papers in them revealing a teacher's name thus allowing them to determine whose room it came from without having to examine every piece of trash within.

They were in luck, the fourth bag to be opened came from Mrs. Atkin's room. The digging began. Slowly each piece of trash was removed from the bag. Since it was near the end of the school day that Cynthia had eaten the yogurt, her container was near the top.

Glen saw it first, the red and white container of strawberry banana yogurt. The search ended. He reached into his pocket for a small plastic evidence bag. He

166

retrieved the container by using the end of his pen to pick it up, dropping it into the bag. He then continued to search the bag for another yogurt container. He came up empty.

"That's it. Let's get out of here. We need to start connecting the dots," suggested Dave.

They drove first to Dave's house to be sure all was fine with his kids and Shelly before going to the office to wait for CBI.

Two angry teenagers met Dave at the door.

"What's going on? Why did you have Mom take us out of school just to clean our rooms? You guys are hiding something from us," whined Ann.

Sean stood behind her, letting her do all of the talking. The way he figured it, she was going to get the answer or be punished for her attitude. Thus releasing him from the wrath of Dave, if he was in a bad mood.

"Okay, calm down a bit Missy. Let's all go into the kitchen and we'll tell you the whole story," responded Dave.

Shelly began, "But Dave, I thought we weren't going to say anything just yet."

"I've changed my mind."

The kids followed their mom and dad into the kitchen. Glen followed the kids.

Once everyone was seated at the table, Dave began.

"Look, you know we've had a few deaths in the town recently. Two of who were students. Well, today we had another, Cynthia Mullerschallen, a teacher's aid from the elementary school."

"So what does that have to do with us? We go to the high school," quizzed Ann.

"Okay, let me back up a minute. When the autopsy report came back on Sheila, it stated her cause of death as nicotine poisoning. She had ingested a lethal dose of nicotine that killed her."

"Whoa! That's weird, what an idiot," commented Sean.

"Not exactly, when the autopsy report came in on Sheri, the findings were identical. We all know Sheri would not have intentionally ingested nicotine. The person at the lab said it was probably liquid nicotine. We are waiting for the report to come in on Jane. We should have those results in the morning."

"Wait a minute, Daddy, what are you saying?" asked Ann.

"What do you think he's saying? Someone's knocking these people off," answered Sean.

Ann looked into her dad's face. Tears began to well in her eyes.

"Daddy, that's not true is it? We don't really have someone trying to kill people do we?"

"Honey, I wish I could tell you that it's not true, but I'm forced to believe it is true. That's why I had Mom get you guys out of the school building and off of the school grounds. Most of the deaths seem to have occurred on school grounds, either at the high school or the elementary school. I just need to know you guys are safe so I can focus totally on finding whoever is responsible."

"Kids, for what it's worth, it is imperative that no one learn about this. We can't tip off our killer, and like your dad fears, we don't want to incite a panic in the town. No matter what, do not tell any of your friends. Okay?" said Glen.

They both nodded their heads in silence.

"So what do we do now?" asked Shelly.

"Tomorrow, I want you to call the school and tell them the kids have the flu or something. That'll take care of Thursday and Friday then the weekend will be here. CBI should arrive tonight. We're going to stay up day and night working our butts off until we solve this. Surely, in such a small town this investigation should move quickly.

Glen and I found our first piece of physical evidence today at the school. The best case scenario would be to find fingerprints linking the killer to the evidence, so we can pick him up and put a stop to this."

"What's the worst case scenario?" asked Sean.

"That he'll strike again, or that we won't find him and he'll move on to another town to continue his killing spree. Which reminds me, Glen, put in a call to search the national data base to see if there have been other cases of multiple deaths by liquid nicotine in any other states."

Glen left the room to make the call.

"You guys can have your phone privileges back, but under no circumstances can you tell any of this to your friends," warned Dave.

"Oh, come on Daddy, we've been kids of a cop long enough to have learned to keep our mouths shut when you are working on a case," reminded Ann.

"I know, I know, but things are different here. This is a small town. Everyone you meet, everyone you talk with, will be discussing the deaths with their own ideas and twists on it. Just listen to what they have to say and don't add any of your own comments. Remember, the kids know your dad's the sheriff. They're going to assume you have more knowledge about the cases than they do. It's only natural for them to pump you for the information."

"Does this mean you and Glen are going to be up all night?" asked Shelly once the kids left the room.

"There's not a lot we can do during the night except discuss things between ourselves. We can't exactly interview people, but you're right, even if we want to get some sleep, we probably won't. CBI will be here tonight. We'll at least be spending late hours with them."

Glen returned to the room.

"All set. The data search has begun. We'll know something as soon as they find it, if there's anything to be found at all."

"I'll start making sandwiches and coffee for tonight. How many guys do you think they'll be sending from CBI?" asked Shelly.

Glen shrugged his shoulders, "Oh, I don't know. Just one or two, I doubt if they would send more at this point, we just don't have enough for them yet. But really, don't put yourself out. We'll be fine, if someone gets hungry we'll just go grab a bite somewhere during the night."

Dave smiled.

Shelly grinned, "Yeah Glen, and where might that place be?"

"Huh? Oh yeah, forgot the town rolls up their sidewalks early evening. I'll help with those sandwiches and coffee."

Dave went into his office to retrieve his notes. He learned to never leave confidential stuff at the sheriff's office. One bit of classified information read by a cleaning person or deputy could be spread through the town in a matter of hours.

Dave returned to the kitchen.

"Are you ready Glen?"

"I guess so. Shelly is the fastest sandwich maker I've ever seen. We should have enough food in this cooler to feed the entire staff at CBI."

Dave kissed Shelly.

"Remember, the kids must stay home, no friends over either. Keep the doors locked, and this time call us if there are any prank calls or if someone shows up at the door."

Glen and Dave armed with food and their notes returned to his office to wait for CBI to arrive.

Chapter 9

With only the dispatcher, Dave, and Glen present, quiet resided over the station. Dave wanted his on duty deputies to keep an eye on the town and stay out of the office. The cold, snowy, weather took the appeal out of that task. The town was exceptionally still. There were no ballgames, or church events; the few things that were scheduled were cancelled due to the weather.

Dave checked his watch.

"I sure hope the guys from CBI are not having a bad time with the roads."

Glen poured coffee for the two of them. He looked at the clock on the wall. It was nearly ten o'clock. They expected CBI to arrive before nine o'clock. Dave paced looking out the window every few minutes.

"Why don't we just call and see what the delay is?" suggested Glen.

"They'll be here when they get here. I don't want to appear impatient."

Headlights shone on the window nearest Dave. He parted the blinds.

"I think help has arrived."

Glen glanced out the window over his shoulder.

"Looks like there's two of them."

Dave and Glen grabbed their coats to help unload the van.

Once the four men were back inside the warm office, Dave began to fill them in.

"Gentlemen, what we have so far are six suspicious deaths in the past eighteen days. The most common cause of death in this town is ill health or death of the elderly. Most of our victims have been young and in good health.

Test results from a tox screen on two of the vics showed death by lethal limits of liquid nicotine in their systems. We're waiting for the tox report on the fifth vic and will soon be running one on the sixth."

"What about the first and the second victims? Did they not test positive to liquid nicotine?"

"Don't know," stated Glen, "at the families' requests, there were no autopsies run on them."

"Do they realize we are going to have to check those bodies?" asked Martin Harmon.

"No, we haven't told them yet. That's on the agenda for tomorrow as soon as we receive the report on that fifth victim. If she comes back positive it would give us more reason to push the families into allowing us to exhume the bodies," answered Dave.

"We don't need their permission," explained Eric Peters from CBI.

"I know, I know, but anything we can do locally to get the cooperation of the families is best. This is a small town and things operate a little differently than in Denver. The people here are more sensitive to being pushed into anything. They stick together pretty well when they feel one of them is being treated unjustly. I need to do much more PR work to keep my job here secure. I promise by the end of the day tomorrow we'll be ready to move ahead with the plan to exhume the bodies," said Dave.

Martin interrupted, "Let's keep going. What do you have for us?"

"Not too much yet," explained Glen. "The last woman that died today had just finished eating yogurt. She appeared to be fine until shortly after she consumed the yogurt, then she dropped to the floor, dying nearly instantly. She did not respond to CPR."

"That seems to be consistent with all the victims," added Dave.

"I'm sure you guys have that container for us to start doing our job," said Eric.

"Yep, Glen has put it in my office refrigerator here. We took it out of the trash from the classroom where she died."

Eric took the container from Glen to check for fingerprints. Then they would check the contents for traces of liquid nicotine.

The dispatcher called, "Dave, Doctor Foster's on the line. I told him you were not taking calls, but he insisted I put him through. How do you want me to handle this?"

"Go ahead and put him through."

The dispatcher put Doc's call through.

"Doc, what's up?"

"Dave, we've got a situation here. I've had people piling into my office all afternoon worried about some epidemic causing heart attacks. It hasn't let up. I'm at the hospital. The emergency room's been a mad house. I've got people lining the halls thinking they're having symptoms of heat failure. Some of them want me to call the CDC. I feel guilty knowing about the liquid nicotine. When can I tell them something?"

"Don't tell them anything until I give you the go ahead. I'll get back to you in a few minutes. We need to brainstorm here to come up with a solution. We don't want people driving in this storm to get to the hospital with imaginary symptoms."

"Okay, but hurry. This is really getting out of hand here."

Dave hung up the phone.

"Men, we have a real problem."

He explained how anxiety was rising about a possible contagious disease plaguing the community. Doc's been examining people and fielding phone calls all day. The hospital corridors are lined with people afraid they may have contracted it. There was mention of calling the CDC.

"How should we approach this?"

"You could tell them the truth," suggested Eric.

"That's not a good idea," responded Martin. "I agree with Dave on this one. We have to keep it quiet. We can't let the residents know there is a killer among them. We also have to squelch this rumor about some deadly disease running rampart in the community before someone does get hurt on the roads tonight."

The four men stared at each other hoping the perfect answer would come to one of them. They could not make a radio broadcast telling everyone to stay home. Anything serious enough to be brought to their attention on the radio would increase the fear. The phone calls would only escalate. There's no local television news channel and the newspaper is only printed weekly.

There was no perfect answer coming to any of them.

"This is insane," said Glen, pacing and running his hands through his hair. The feeling of total helplessness does not come easy for him.

"Wait!" he said. "Those people calling into the hospital are calling with symptoms. We know there's pretty much no time for symptoms before death hits. Maybe, if Doctor Foster told them if they are having symptoms, they should assume they're safe. No, that's no good."

Glen was thinking out loud, and was not happy with his thoughts.

"Maybe you're on to something there. Maybe the nurses can take the calls and ask for symptoms. Maybe they can halt the traffic of patients to the hospital and narrow it down to the few that should really come in because they are experiencing a true medical problem," agreed Martin.

"That puts quite the load on the nursing staff. What if they encourage everyone to stay home? What if someone dies because the staff is growing weary of taking those calls and doesn't take someone seriously that really needs the help?" asked Eric.

"I've got to start planning some damage control, and fast. Once we get the test results in the morning, and we begin talking to families about exhuming bodies, the word will spread like a prairie fire. In the meantime, we need to help Doc out. He's carrying the bulk of our load on this because we won't let him talk," complained Dave.

"I've got it. We know that the nicotine had to be ingested. We know that in order to ingest the foul tasting stuff it had to be in food or a drink. Can't we just tell everyone we're dealing with food poisoning?" asked Glen.

"Not a bad idea," agreed Eric. "If your doctor could tell everyone that the cases seem to be food related then it will put people's minds at ease about something contagious going around. People will sleep better. It's late, most people will have finished eating for tonight, so the town can get a good night's rest buying us some time."

"Great! That's what we'll tell Doc. That should work for the time being. I'll tell my dispatcher to handle her phone calls the same way."

Dave returned Doc's call. They discussed his answer to the community. He agreed it was the safest answer for now.

Just as the men were about to get back to work the sound of a railroad train whistle filled the room. Dave and Glen looked up.

"What the hell?" said Glen.

Martin turned to Eric, "I can't believe you wore that damned watch here. At least shut off the hourly alarm."

Eric's face flushed red as he lifted his sleeve to disable his watch.

"Let me see that thing," laughed Dave.

Eric proudly showed off his watch that his wife and kids had gotten him for Christmas. Although Christmas is still a few weeks away, they couldn't wait to give it to him. Of course, it didn't help when his son had forgotten to shut off the alarm and his Christmas package under the tree was whistling like a train. They had to open it to turn it off.

Eric is a train buff. He has one room in his basement dedicated to his miniature world with a train running the distance of the room.

A sense of relief filled the room as the first hurdle was cleared in dealing with Doc's problem.

Glen poured coffee for everyone.

"Is anyone hungry?" he asked.

"I say we order in Chinese or a pizza and keep working," suggested Eric.

This time it was Glen's face that broke into a broad smile, "this town is closed up tighter than a drum. Have a sandwich."

Dave opened the cooler that Glen and Shelly had packed exposing a stack of sandwiches, fruit, cupcakes as well as paper plates and other eating utensils. The four men devoured the welcomed food.

"What time can we expect to hear our results in the morning?" asked Dave.

"My guess is the lab will have your answer around seven, said Martin. "Eric, as soon as you've finished eating, why don't you run those prints and check our yogurt sample for liquid nicotine."

"I'm finished," said Eric as he scooted his chair back and wiped his face with his napkin. He left to find a room with a sink where he could do his work. He had to settle for the men's bathroom.

"So you guys are relatively certain food is the agent by which the drug entered the bodies of our vics?" asked Martin.

"We're sure. We just don't know how or why the food was contaminated," replied Dave.

"Or where it was contaminated," added Glen.

"What do you mean where?" quizzed Martin.

"I've been giving it some thought. We're expecting to find a positive test result in the yogurt. If we do then we have to ask ourselves where was it contaminated? Did it happen at the factory? Did it happen during storage? Did it happen in the local grocery store? How about at the home of this Cynthia woman, or at the school? We've got a long trail to cover."

"You're right, just knowing it was contaminated doesn't put us a lot closer to a solution. I sure hope Eric can find a clean set of prints that will lead us somewhere."

"Do you have any suspects in mind yet?" asked Martin.

Dave remembered his requests from the post office and the electric company. He went to the fax machine. Both offices had sent answers to him. Dave looked at the names on the list. He handed it to Martin.

"These are the names and addresses of the newest members of the community. You can see by the dates when they arrived. No one stands out and the list is small."

"So this is it? How often do you get strangers hanging out in town?" asked Martin.

"This time of the year we get lots of hunters, but they are here primarily on weekends," Dave reported.

"According to your notes here most of the deaths have been weekend related."

"Oh hell, there's no way of knowing how many hunters have been through here, or if any of them have returned every weekend, or even who they are."

"Have you had any trouble with any of them this year?" asked Martin.

"No, as a rule hunters are a pretty tame bunch."

"Wait, what about that team that you ran off?" reminded Glen.

"Tell me what happened," said Martin.

"Not much to tell. They were told they couldn't hunt a farmer's trees. There was a no hunting sign posted. They chose to ignore both, and the farmer's wife called me. I had a talk with the guys. They were a little upset, so I sent them packing. Told them to hunt some other county and that I'd haul them in if I saw them again."

"Did you get their license number?"

"Yeah, I think Glen jotted it down."

Martin looked at Glen. "Boy, for a Denver cop you sure hang around here quite a bit. Have you been here for all the murders?"

Dave felt the anger rising within him. He knew the angle this CBI guy was after.

"I invited Glen to hunt. He was here when the first kid died, but he was back in Denver for the next two. He was kind enough to take some of his personal time to help me as a sounding board," Dave informed him with anger in his voice.

Glen knew being without sleep and the pressure of unusual circumstances in the town would be causing frayed nerves. Fortunately, Eric returned from his task changing the subject.

"I found a couple of partials; nothing great. The yogurt did test positive to the nicotine. But then, we were pretty sure it would."

"Let's run the partials to see if we can find a match," said Martin.

"Which computer would you like me to use?" he asked Dave.

"Here use mine."

Dave got up from his chair to allow Eric to sit down.

"What's your plan for tomorrow?" asked Martin.

"Well, let's meet back here at six o'clock. By that time we should have a match on the partials. Glen is checking other states for the same M.O. We'll hear the results from the third victim, then talk to the families about exhuming bodies," said Dave.

"We stopped by the motel on the highway before we came by here. We've got our rooms already. So, I guess we'll call it a night and meet here at six o'clock," said Eric.

The men bundled up for their trip outdoors to their cars. Fortunately, the drive across town on the icy roads was a short one.

Silence filled the car as Dave and Glen drove home.

"I'll see you in the morning," said Dave.

The two friends parted ways in the kitchen. Glen knew tomorrow would be a tough day for Dave. He would be surprised if he managed to get any sleep at all.

Glen woke before his alarm went off. He had been dreaming about Jennifer Parker, the psychic who helped him. She was trying to tell him something, but he could not understand anything she was saying. It was as if she was speaking a foreign language. He was aware that her message was important, but try as he might, in his dream he could not understand what she was saying. It was as if the communication portion of his brain had shut down.

He stayed in bed wishfully attempting to bring the dream into his consciousness. The feeling of frustration he experienced in the dream stayed with him in his wakened state. He focused as hard as he could on the dream, but still the message eluded him.

His thoughts were broken by the sound of his alarm. He turned it off as he climbed out of bed. Today was going to be a big day for Dave and he hoped he could offer his support both, moral and professional.

When Dave and Glen arrived at his office before six o'clock, the men from CBI were there waiting.

"Gentlemen," Dave greeted them, "let's get some breakfast at the café, by then we should have word back about the fifth vic. But before we go, let's check to see if anything came in on Glen's request for similar incidents in other areas."

Glen went to the computer to check for an email with the results. The answer was negative. No similar cases of multiple deaths by liquid nicotine were listed anywhere on the national database.

"Well, whoever we're dealing with here has either just begun his killing spree or has changed MO," said Glen.

Eric took his turn at the computer to check the results of his partial prints. He had asked for it to be both broad and narrow. The narrow search was limited first to just the town of Holyoke, with the search for matches broadening from there. There were a number of possibilities, but only one from the Holyoke area. That seemed almost too easy. He jotted the name down on a sheet of paper, then handed it to Glen. The name meant nothing to him. He handed it to Dave, hoping he knew the name. He did. Jonathon Duell.

Dave looked up to find the other three staring at him wondering if the search could be over so quickly.

"Do you know this person?" asked Glen.

"Yeah, he's just a kid, a high school kid. Damn, I hate to see a kid so young throw away his life like this."

"Okay, give us the details on this kid," requested Eric, as he took out his notepad.

"He's a really bright kid, a senior I think. He's not one of the jocks, more intellectual, but likes to be different. He's a little shy, but not extremely. He keeps to himself, and to my knowledge, has never been in trouble with the law before," answered Dave.

"What do you mean by different?" asked Martin.

"Oh nothing drastic, well maybe drastic for this small town, but nothing too extreme. He likes to wear his hair in a Mohawk. But trust me, this is a really nice kid," Dave replied.

"Don't forget what we dealt with in Littleton, that Columbine thing. No one suspected those boys could do such a thing. Shall we head over to the school to visit with him?" suggested Martin.

"School is closed due to the snow. Let's get some breakfast, come back here to check the lab results, then go by this kid's house," said Glen.

The other three agreed.

The café was more quiet than usual. Was it the snow or the gossip flying that kept people home this morning? Either way, Dave was relieved not to have to visit with anyone that morning. His mind was on Jonathon. What would force such a nice kid like him to do something so desperately evil? Deep within his heart, he couldn't bring himself to believe it was Jonathon. He somehow felt this was not the lead they were looking for.

All through breakfast the discussion was about Jonathon and other kids who had gone off the deep end, going on killing sprees at schools across the nation. They talked about how it was becoming an epidemic. Dave did not contribute to the conversation. He ate his breakfast in silence, nodding occasionally.

Glen knew this was hitting Dave hard. He almost wished he could send him home so he and the other two men could take over, sparing him any more of the pain and discomfort he exhibited.

One by one, the men paid for their breakfast. When Dave reached the counter, he signed his name. In silence, he followed the three out into the cold to the car. They drove the few blocks back to the office.

The dispatcher handed Dave a message. It was from the lab. He called the number. When he put the receiver down he looked up at the others.

"It's positive to nicotine."

"Okay, let's go pay this Jonathon kid a visit," said Martin.

Dave looked up his address in the phone book. He lived in town, not in the country. That spared them a long treacherous drive on icy country roads that morning. Soon they were standing at the door ringing the bell. Jonathon's mother came to the door.

The sight of four men standing at her door so early in the morning startled her. Then she saw Dave. She feared for the worst.

"What's wrong? Did something happen to Jonathon? He wasn't in an accident because of the roads was he?"

She searched their faces intently.

187

"No, there was no accident, we just want to have a word with Jonathon. I guess he's not home?" asked Dave.

"No, he wanted to put in more hours at work since there was no school today."

"Where does he work?" asked Dave.

"At the grocery store. Is there something wrong?"

"We just need to visit with him, I'm sure you have nothing to worry about," answered Dave.

"Worry, why would I worry? What's going on? Is Jonathon in some kind of trouble?" she begged.

"We just need to ask him a few questions. If you would like you can meet us in my office, we'll take him there where we can have some privacy," said Dave.

They went to the grocery store. Jonathon was in the back opening boxes. Dave approached him.

"Jonathon, we'd like to ask you a few questions."

"Sure," answered Jonathon. He was not the least bit nervous.

"Can you take some time off and come to my office with us?"

"When?" asked Jonathon.

"Now," responded Dave.

Jonathon grabbed his coat. The four men escorted him through the store out to Dave's car. They drove off.

All eyes were upon them as they left. Chatter spread in the store. Customers flocked to the windows to watch them drive off with Jonathon.

188

One woman said, "You can tell by the way he wears his hair, that boy is trouble."

Others chimed in with similar comments. They had no idea why the police had come for Jonathon, but they had already tried and convicted him right there in the small town grocery store.

Shortly after they arrived at the office, Jonathon's parents appeared on the scene.

"Can someone please tell me what's going on?" asked his father.

Dave stumbled over his words. Glen took over.

"Sir, there have been a string of deaths in town recently. Unfortunately, the deaths have been related. We're convinced the cause was contaminated food. We picked up a partial set of prints. When we ran those prints they matched your son's. We just want to talk to him. You're welcome to sit in on this."

Jonathon was beginning to squirm.

"Why are my son's prints in your computer to begin with? There must be some kind of mistake," questioned Mr. Duell, with concern.

His mother answered that question.

"At school they fingerprint the kids in case of a kidnapping. The police can identify them by their fingerprints. We had Jonathon fingerprinted in elementary school."

Dave began his line of questioning. He asked Jonathon about school and how things were going there.

Jonathon assured him everything in his life was fine. He then asked him about each of the victims and his connection to them.

Glen withdrew from the conversation as he drifted deeply into thought. This kid doesn't seem the type at all. Then the obvious came to him. He works at the grocery store. Of course his prints would be on items in the store.

Glen butted into the conversation.

"Jonathon, what is your job at the store?"

"I do a little bit of everything, but mostly I work at the checkout."

"So you would be touching everything before it goes into the sacks."

"Yeah, I have to scan them in."

Glen looked at the other three. They were all thinking the same thing.

"Thanks, Jonathon, that will be all. Thanks for coming in. Sorry to take you away from your job," apologized Dave.

Dave shook hands with Jonathon's dad. "Sorry about this, but we have to follow every lead. His fingerprints were there, so we had to check it out. I hope we didn't shake him up too much."

"I guess you're just doing your job," answered his father.

They left together. Jonathon returned to the store.

After Jonathon and his family left, Dave said, "It's time to go to the families and request the bodies be exhumed so they can be tested."

First, they drove to Tim's house. Both of his parents were home.

His mother offered coffee to the four men, but they refused.

Dave approached the topic with caution, "I have a favor to ask of you. I know this will be difficult, but we need to do some lab work on Tim's body."

"What are you saying?" asked his father.

"It appears the deaths that have been happening lately may be related. The connection seems to be through food. We have tested three of the bodies already and they all tested positive. We need to test Tim's body as well."

"Why? If all of these people died of food poisoning then, what good would it be for you to know if Tim died from the same thing? You're not going to touch my son's body!" said his mother.

Dave looked back at the others.

Martin stepped forward, "I'm here to help Dave. I'm Martin and this is Eric. We're from CBI in Lakewood, Colorado. That's the Colorado Bureau of Investigation. If there is a connection between these deaths, we're here to find out what happened, and to stop further deaths if we can. It's imperative that we examine your son's body."

"No! I said, no. You're not going to disturb Tim's body."

Eric began, "I'm sorry, ma'am, but we can do this with your permission, or without. We are within our legal rights to exhume your son's body. Asking your permission is a formality out of respect for you and your husband."

Dave wished Eric had given him a little more time to talk to the parents and let the concept sink in. He felt confident they would eventually agree. There was really nothing more to say now.

Tim's mother was crying. His dad tried to comfort her. He was angry as well.

"I think we're going to call our lawyer," he said.

"That's fine, I understand," said Dave.

They let themselves out.

Dave was angry.

"Next time, let me handle the family. Something like this is new. There probably has never been a body exhumed in the town before. It's quite a shock."

Eric apologized for being so insensitive.

Next, they drove to the home Lyle and his wife shared before his death.

His wife took the news easier than Tim's parents. She was not a very strong woman. That came from years of Lyle telling her what to do and when to do it. Many countrywomen are submissive. City wives are much more

192

independent. She agreed to let them do whatever they thought was for the best.

"Boy, that went easy," said Eric.

Once in the car, Dave made the necessary phone calls to exhume the bodies.

Life was not as smooth for Jonathon. He spent the rest of the day watching people in the store whisper behind his back. It was very disturbing for him. When he told his parents that night. His father persuaded him to cut his hair for the time being.

"It's best to just blend in until this blows over."

That was easier said than done. The innocent until proven guilty did not work in a small town. Although no one knew exactly why Jonathon was taken in for questioning, they did know that he was guilty.

The snowstorm had fizzled out by Friday. There were so many snow days accumulated thus far; the school took advantage of the storm to use a couple of them.

Jonathon went to work on Friday. When he arrived his boss was shocked to see him looking less dramatic. He cut his hair according to his father's wishes. He no longer stood out in a crowd. This saddened him, but he had been hurt by the attitude the customers had towards him after he went in for questioning. He was a sensitive boy.

That night there was a ball game. He went with a few of his friends. Whispers and pointing followed him wherever he went.

"Notice he cut his hair. I think the police made him do that. They're trying to get him to clean up his act. His poor parents, they must be embarrassed having their son in trouble with the police. I wonder how they caught him?" said an elderly women to her friend.

Her friend asked, "Does anyone know yet what he did?"

"No, but I'm sure we'll all know soon enough. I can't believe he's here and not locked up."

Jonathon felt every eye upon him. His friends suggested they get something to eat. They felt sorry for him. His friends were true friends. They would stick with him to the bitter end.

They stood in line at the concession stand, deciding what they would like to eat and counting their money before it was their turn to order. It was teacher's night. The elementary school teachers and coaches were selling the food for that evening. Throughout this season food was donated, along with the standard concession food, in an attempt to raise funds for the new uniforms.

Coach Callister noticed the sad look on Jonathon's otherwise cheerful face.

"Hey, don't let the gossip get to ya," he encouraged.

They made their purchases and returned to their seats. The game was an exciting one. The crowd roared insults and cheers. All could feel the intensity of the crowd. The coaches looked stressed; the cheerleaders and players were feeding on the energy in the crowded gym.

Jonathon removed his jacket. He was warm from sitting on crowded bleachers. He finished his coke then chewed the ice in an attempt to keep cool. He turned to one of his friends.

"I don't feel very well. I think I'm going to be ..."

Before Jonathon could finish his sentence, he fell over landing on the people sitting in front of him. One of his friends felt for a pulse. He couldn't find one. The people ahead of him were irritated that he passed out on them. They were sure he'd been drinking. Someone called out for help. The crowds eyes left the court and focused on Jonathon's limp body slumped over the bleachers. Doctor Foster was in the crowd. He yelled for someone to call for an ambulance. He pushed his way through the crowded stairs and bleachers to reach Jonathon. When he arrived, he knew he was too late. He knew Jonathon was the latest victim.

Chapter 10

Jonathon's body was transported to the hospital. When the call went out for an ambulance, Dave was alerted as per his instructions to the dispatcher. He wanted knowledge of every emergency call the instant it came in. He and Glen rushed to the hospital; while on their way, they called Martin and Eric. Dave gave them directions. They would have been able to find it on their own with no problem. Most businesses in a small town are on either the main street, or only a block away on either side of it.

Doc looked up as Dave and Glen approached him. He nodded his head confirming what they already knew. The two officers went to wait for the CBI men. As they walked down the hall, they passed Mr. and Mrs. Duell rushing towards the emergency room to check on their son, Jonathon. Mrs. Duell's cry could be heard throughout the small hospital.

"Glen, we've got to stop this. It's tearing my heart out, all of these kids. It's just got to stop."

"I know, Dave, we're getting there, Buddy. We're getting there."

Eric and Martin stepped inside the small hospital. They looked anxiously at Dave for an answer.

"Doc confirmed it's the same as the others. Of course, we'll do an autopsy to be sure, but that's just a formality as far as I'm concerned," said Dave.

"Maybe we shouldn't wait until Monday to get those bodies exhumed. Tomorrow's Saturday, let's get it done and get those bodies to the lab for tests," suggested Martin.

Dave agreed. When the four of them went back to Dave's office for a discussion about the latest death, Dave called the cemetery staff, instructing them to begin in the morning. Reluctantly, they agreed to begin first thing in the morning. They were equipped to do the work, although the ground was frozen. This year they were exceptionally busy with so many deaths in such a short amount of time.

Dave started a pot of coffee. His goal was to stay in his office until they had devised some sort of plan that met with his approval. He needed to stop this immediately before someone else lost his or her life senselessly.

Glen took over for Dave knowing his friend was feeling overwhelmingly emotional.

He went to the whiteboard on the wall. He listed the deaths in the order that they occurred, the day of the week and the location.

Tim	Saturday	11/15	high school
Lyle	Wednesday	11/19	church
Sheila	Saturday	11/22	high school
Sheri	Saturday	11/29	home
Jane	Monday	12/1	grade school
Cynthia	Wednesday	12/3	grade school
Jonathon	Friday	12/5	high school

Studying the chart for patterns Eric began, "The perp has no preference to men or women, young or old."

"That's right," agreed Martin. "The day of the week shows no specific significance either."

"I can see no particular pattern in the spacing of days between hits, except the last four happened two days apart. Our person is getting impatient or bolder as time goes on because he or she is hitting more frequently," Glen pointed out.

Finally Dave pointed out the obvious, "The locations show the schools are his favorite spots to hit. But why?"

Glen asked, "Where should we go from here? I feel that the perp is local. If he was a hunter he probably wouldn't be here the entire week."

"That's right," agreed Dave. "Also, he wouldn't have the school ball schedule to know when the games are local, nor would he have gone to the church when Lyle died without being noticed as a stranger."

"Good point," said Martin.

"I'd say it's safe to drop the yogurt investigation. My guess is it was not contaminated at the factory or during shipment. I'd have to say it was tampered with here. Do we know if any of the others had consumed yogurt, just to rule it out?" asked Eric.

Dave looked at his watch. It was getting late. He decided to call some of the families anyway. He began with Tim's family.

Tim's dad answered the phone.

"Hello, this is Dave Smith. Could you answer a quick question for me?"

The angry voice came back over the phone, "Why in the hell should I answer any questions for you? Besides, you have your nerve calling so late at night. Monday you plan to disturb my son's resting place. I have nothing to say to you."

Before he could hang up the phone, Dave quickly added, "Another young boy died tonight. We need your help to try to figure out what's happening here. Please, just a moment of your time."

By that time Tim's mother picked up the other phone to listen in.

"I need to know if Tim consumed any yogurt on the day he died?"

"Why? What has yogurt got to do with his death? Do you think that's where the food poisoning came in?" she asked.

"We're not sure, it's the only lead we have so far."

"Well, I couldn't tell you for sure. We always keep yogurt in the refrigerator. Tim liked it, but I'm not sure if he ate any that day," she answered.

"How about the brand. Can you give me the brand name?"

"Oh, I don't know. I always buy the store brand, whatever that is."

"Thanks, you've been a big help. Sorry to have disturbed you. Goodbye."

When Dave hung up the phone all eyes were upon him waiting for his answers.

"She couldn't say if Tim had any yogurt that day. He did eat the stuff and the brand was the same brand that Cynthia ate."

"That's two out of seven," said Eric. "Let's keep going. We may have to follow up on the yogurt after all."

Next Dave called Lyle's wife.

"Hello" she answered in a sleepy voice.

"I'm so sorry to wake you. This is Dave Smith. We're in the middle of this investigation and we need to ask you a couple of questions. We had another death tonight and we are trying to connect them all."

"Who died?" she asked.

"I'm not at liberty to release that information yet. I'm sure you'll hear about it tomorrow. It was another young boy though."

"Oh dear. I wish this would end."

"So do we, ma'am, so do we. Now I need to know if Lyle ate yogurt."

"He ate it alright, but he sure didn't like it. I was trying to get him to lose weight, so I made him eat yogurt instead of dessert. He sure did complain. But then you know Lyle he sure liked his dessert. Yep, he sure liked his dessert. I think he liked pie the best. He used to like fruit pies, but the last few years he took a liking to cream pies. I think he liked the extra sugar in them or something."

"Me too, I like all kinds of pies. Now, I need to know if Lyle had any yogurt on the day he died."

"Well, let me think. That was the day of Tim's funeral. We were in a hurry to get to the church that day. I fixed bacon and eggs that morning. Yeah, I remember because the bacon spattered on my dress. I forgot to put my apron on. You know when you start to get older you forget things that you never forgot before."

"So Lyle had bacon and eggs. Did he have any yogurt with them?"

"I suppose he could have. He was complaining he was hungry while I was cooking. Then I had to change my clothes before I finished cooking. That was my favorite blue dress. I had to take it right to the laundry room to work on that stain. Bacon grease can set in you know, if you aren't careful. I told Lyle to quit complaining and grab some fruit from the refrigerator until I could finish breakfast. But I don't know if he took fruit or yogurt. Is it important that you know if he ate fruit instead of yogurt?

201

He kind of liked to eat those kiwis. He might have had a kiwi. He liked the kiwi-flavored yogurt sometimes, too. Let's see, I think we had some apples and oranges in there too."

"Can you tell me what brand of yogurt you buy?"

"Oh, I don't know. I guess I buy them all. I like to get all the different flavors. I don't pay any attention to the brand."

"Okay, thanks. That's all I need from you now. If I have any further questions I'll give you a call."

"You do that. I'll get up early tomorrow so I can find out who the boy was. Thanks for letting me know. Bye."

Dave turned on the speakerphone after the first call. The others in the room were chuckling after he hung up the phone.

"We can go either way on that one," said Martin.

Next Dave dialed Sheila's parents home.

Her mother answered the phone.

"Hello, this is Dave Smith." Dave repeated his introduction then went right into the yogurt question.

"Sheila did eat lots of yogurt. She thought she was too fat. You know high school girls. They can never be thin enough. They'll skip breakfast, eat yogurt for lunch then go out and eat pizza, chips and pop in the evening with their friends."

"Would you happen to know if she ate any the day she died?"

"Oh sure, she ate it every day. Why?"

"Can you tell me the brand you buy?"

"Doesn't matter. I just buy whatever sounds good. I don't pay any attention to the brand. I suppose we would have some of all of the brands in the refrigerator. Why the questions about yogurt?"

"Well, since we think we might be dealing with food poisoning of some sort we are trying to find out what foods the people that died had in common."

"And you think it could be the yogurt?"

"At this point we're still not sure; that's why the phone calls."

"Thanks for the warning. I'm going right into the kitchen to throw out all of the yogurt we have."

"Please don't do that just yet, we may need to check it out."

"Okay. Bye"

"Another one that could go either way," said Glen.

Dave looked at his watch again. He knew country people were early to bed.

Eric noticed him checking the time.

"Come on Dave, we really need to keep going," he said.

"You're right," agreed Dave.

He called Sheri's house next. When her husband answered the phone he repeated himself then got right to the question about the yogurt before her husband had a chance to say anything.

"Yogurt huh? Beats the hell out of me. I never used to even open the refrigerator. Sheri always did all of the cooking and the shopping. She always had the meal on the table when I came in. I've never eaten the stuff myself, don't think you could pay me enough to."

"So you don't recall seeing any in the refrigerator after she died. Maybe you threw out what was there since you don't eat it?"

"I didn't clean out the refrigerator. I told the church ladies to take everything home with them. I don't cook. I just go to the café now for all my meals. I really couldn't tell you what was in there. Hang on let me go look now."

He set the phone down while he went into his kitchen. He picked up the kitchen phone.

"Nope, the whole thing's empty. The ladies cleaned it out. They left a note inside for me to call one of them if I should decide to start using it again so they could help me stock it with food."

"Can you tell me who the ladies were?"

"Nope, I never went to church with Sheri. But there's a phone number on this note. It's 555-4321."

"Thanks."

The two men ended their conversation.

"Man, what kind of guy can't even stock food in his own fridge?" asked Eric.

"Some of the men out here are completely helpless when it comes to women's work. The younger guys are much better at it, but the older gents truly cannot shop, cook or clean. They just hire it done if they lose their spouse," explained Dave.

"This is like stepping back in time," said Martin, a little surprised that towns like this still exist.

Dave dialed the number. Doris answered the phone.

After his introduction Dave asked, " Who am I speaking to?"

"This is Doris Thomas. How can I help you?"

"When you and the other church ladies cleaned out Sheri's refrigerator after her death, was there any yogurt containers in it?"

"Well, let me think. There were so many things in there. Her husband didn't want any of it. You know, I'm not sure, but I think there may have been. If there was it went to the church basement for the kids snack time at their bible study."

"Would it still be there?" asked Dave.

The others sat up and took notice. There may be some left that they could check out.

"No, we fed all the food to the kids so we could empty the refrigerator, with the holiday coming. We like to have an empty refrigerator to hold all of the desserts that come in while we have more church activity going on. Why? What's going on? Is there a problem?"

"We're just trying to find out about all of the foods that Sheri could have eaten the night she died."

"Oh well, she'd been here earlier that evening. We had lots of food here. She took some pie and other food home for her and her husband."

"Do you know what she might have eaten?"

"That would be hard to say. We had a pretty big crowd here that night. Lots of food was carried in. She probably had a little bit of everything. All of us that stayed late to clean up took the leftovers home."

"Is there any way you could get a list of names for the people who attended?"

"Oh sure, we have a guest book. Most people who attend sign in when they come. That way we have a pretty good idea of how many to expect for the next year."

"Can I ask you to bring a copy of those pages to my office in the morning?"

"Sure, but I don't understand."

"It's just all part of the investigation. Since we know the deaths have been food related we're trying to trace the steps of each person on the day he or she died."

"Okay, I'll see you in the morning. Do you need anything else?"

"No, that should be all. Thanks. Bye."

"You know what seems odd to me," started Glen. "Is that it appears only one of the yogurt containers at any given home was contaminated. You would think if it was factory related, some family would've gotten their hands on more than one contaminated container, causing someone else in the family to die."

206

"Hmm..." said Martin stroking his chin. "You do have a point there. If the yogurt was the method for getting the nicotine into the body, it also appears to be a little less random than we thought."

Dave called Jane's husband. There was no answer.

They sat there for a moment.

Dave broke the silence, "That just leaves Jonathon. Man, do I hate to bother his parents tonight. Their son just died. Should we wait until tomorrow?"

Martin said, "If Glen is right and the perp is moving more quickly hitting every two days we can't let any time go by. You know they're not sleeping tonight, that's for sure.'

Dave slowly dialed their number.

Mr. Duell answered the phone.

"Hi, this is Dave Smith. I'm so sorry about Jonathon. I feel really bad about calling you tonight, but we need to ask you a couple of questions. I'll try to be brief."

"Okay, what can I help you with?"

"Did Jonathon eat yogurt at any time today?"

"I doubt it, he has an allergy to all dairy products. But let me ask my wife."

He set the phone down while he went to her. He returned to the phone, "No, he was allergic to it. Dairy products gave him severe stomachaches. There's no way he would eat it, he was very careful about such things."

207

"Okay, thanks for your time."

"Wait. Why did you want to know about yogurt? Did this have anything to do with the yogurt you were asking him about yesterday?"

"Well yes, we were concerned about food poisoning so we are eliminating the possibility of contaminated yogurt from the factory. Since Jonathon didn't consume any yogurt we can put that theory to rest. Once again, thanks for your help."

"Glad to help. Bye."

"Bye."

Glen crumpled up the paper he used to keep track of the phone calls and the yogurt consumption. He tossed it across the room into the trashcan sinking it as though he was playing basketball.

"That shot the yogurt theory all to hell. I thought we might be getting a break here. Even if yogurt was the avenue to carry the poison something different was obviously used on Jonathon. That means those other yogurt eaters didn't necessarily get their dose of nicotine in yogurt. It could have been added to any food. We're going to have to contact all of these families again tomorrow to try to retrace the steps of all of our vics for the 24 hours or so before their deaths."

"We're back to square one. Damn," said Dave pounding his fist on his desk. He buried his face into his hands.

Glen's heart ached for his buddy.

208

Eric walked over to the chart to examine it again.

"According to this our perp might hit again on Sunday. He or she seems to hit only at schools or churches. That doesn't look good for Sunday services."

Martin agreed, "Even the death that happened at home was connected to a church activity earlier that evening."

"It's getting late. There's nothing more we can do tonight. We can't make any more calls. We'll have to pick up where we left off in the morning."

Eric stretched and yawned. "You're right. Meet back here at the same time in the morning?"

"I guess so," said Dave in a defeated voice. After the men left his office he locked the door behind him. He stopped by the dispatcher's desk.

"I don't want the cleaning crew in my office until I say so. Is that understood?"

"Sure Dave," she answered. By the look on her face you could tell she was puzzled, but she also knew by the tone of Dave's voice not to question him.

Early the next morning, the group met in Dave's office. That morning the bodies were to be exhumed. They planned to be at the graveside when that occurred. Dave informed the crew to notify his office when the graves were ready to have the caskets removed.

When he walked past the dispatcher's desk, for the first time in weeks, there were no messages for him. The story about food poisoning must have appeased the crowds for the time being.

He quickly checked for faxes and emails. Nothing.

"Let's go eat then we can split up and interview the families to trace the steps of the vics," suggested Dave.

It was seven o'clock when they walked into the café.

The waitress came to take their order.

Before anyone could place an order Larry called out from his place at the counter, "I'd order the yogurt. I hear it's to die for!"

His buddy, Tom, joined him in laughter.

The waitress shot Larry and Tom dirty looks then continued to take the order for Dave and his group.

"How in the hell did that get out already?" asked Martin.

"I'm telling ya, this is a small town. Nothing remains a secret very long. I'm sure the grocery store is not going to make any yogurt sales for a while," said Dave.

"Amazing. Totally amazing," remarked Eric.

Martin asked, "With the people so alert about what's happening in town, how could anyone even consider committing a crime here?"

"They typically don't, that's why Dave has it so easy," teased Glen trying to lighten the mood.

"Until now," reminded Dave.

Just as they were about to eat their breakfast Dave's cell phone rang.

"Hello," he said.

"Dave, you need to call the sheriff's office in Julesburg, immediately," said the dispatcher. She gave him the number.

Dave quickly dialed the number.

"This is Sheriff Smith from Holyoke, I was asked to give you guys a call?" said Dave with question in his voice.

"Could you hold please?"

"Sheriff Smith, this is Sheriff Adams. It seems we have a coincidence going on here."

"A coincidence?" asked Dave.

"It might be nothing, but I need to follow up on something that happened here last night."

"Okay, what can I help you with?"

"Local talk in the coffee shop is that there have been some unexplained deaths in your area."

"Yes, go on."

"I heard that a couple of them have been kids. Any idea what they died from?"

"We have our theories. Why?"

"Last night we had a young boy die after the ballgame in your town."

"What did he die from?"

"That's just it, we're not quite sure. He collapsed in the car with his parents on their way back home. They called for help and rushed him to meet the ambulance, but it was too late. Since we heard of a similar case or two in Holyoke we thought maybe you could shed some light on the subject."

"Tell you what. I'm in the café now. Can I call you back when I can speak in a more private setting?"

"Sure, that'll be fine. I'll be waiting for your call. Bye."

"Bye."

Dave sat back in his chair. His face told it all.

"What?" asked Glen.

Martin and Eric looked up from their meal. Glen's tone caught their attention. They were curious to hear Dave's response.

"That was the sheriff from Julesburg. Seems they lost a kid last night with the same symptoms. He was at last night's game with his parents. He collapsed on their way home. The sheriff wanted to know if we could shed any light on this mystery for them. He heard the talk in his coffee shop about our sudden wave of deaths here."

"What'd you tell him?" asked Eric.

"Nothing yet. I told him I'd call him back when I could talk more privately."

Silence fell at their table. The temperature of the room must've raised a degree or two from the intenseness of their thoughts. This was the first death outside of their community. Was it random? Was their killer moving on?

Dave looked at the men.

"Do you want to finish breakfast or go talk this out?"

They were quick to jump up without taking another bite. Dave called to the waitress, "Just put all of these on my tab."

Rushing out of the café caused the few customers inside to follow their every movement as they ran to Dave's car.

Sitting around Dave's desk he began the conversation.

"A new death in a new town. What's your take on it?"

"Well," began Eric. "My first thought would have gone back to the yogurt thing and the same batch hitting a nearby town. Jonathon's death put an end to that theory."

"Ah, but it could still very much be food related," added Martin. "There can't be too many delivery trucks in this area. I'm sure all of these towns are serviced by the same few trucks carrying food to all the stores and restaurants."

"True," agreed Glen. "But wouldn't you think we would've heard through the grapevine about similar deaths in nearby towns?"

"Glen has a point," said Martin. "Why, up until this death, have they all centered around Holyoke?"

"I think I can answer that one," reported Dave. "The boy and his family were here last night. They were at the ballgame. The boy died on his way home. Whoever is responsible for the liquid nicotine in the food killed that boy as well."

"So are we talking randomness here?" asked Eric.

"Sure looks that way," said Glen. "One more thing to note is that our killer or bad food hit two victims in one night. That's never happened before."

"So guys, how much should we tell the Julesburg sheriff?"

Martin suggested, "Why don't you tell him our vics have died from liquid nicotine in contaminated food. Tell him to be sure to perform an autopsy and make sure we get the results here. Tell him we are working on it and not to alert his local community until we have more to give him."

Dave looked at Glen for reassurance.

"I think Martin is right on this one, Dave. We need more information before we start a two-town riot."

Dave called the sheriff back giving him only the information the four of them had agreed upon.

The new boy's name was added to the chart on the wall with the date, and they used the school as the most probable location for poisoning.

"Okay, let's start again at the beginning," suggested Glen. "We're sure the nicotine is in food or drink, all of the deaths were caused by consuming the stuff. When you look at this chart you can see food was present at each of the locations. Now, we have to decide where the food came from and who had access to the food."

"Backing up from the moment of consumption then," said Martin. "The food was probably consumed on the school or church premises. Except for Sheri, who most likely ate hers at home."

"Yes, but Doris told me that those that stayed to clean up took the leftover food home with them. So she could have taken the contaminated food into her home where she consumed it," Dave pointed out.

Martin started again, "What strikes me as odd though is until last night only one person died from the food. That tells me only one person was meant to die. Otherwise, we'd have multiple deaths at one location on the same day. They've all been single deaths until last night."

"That leads us to believe the killer only intended to kill one victim at a time," said Glen.

"Okay, let's get back onto the food," said Dave. "Where did the food come from?"

He added another column to Glen's list for food source.

Tim	Saturday	11/15	high school	concession
Lyle	Wednesday	11/19	church	ladies group
Sheila	Saturday	11/22	high school	concession
Sheri	Saturday	11/29	home	ladies group
Jane	Monday	12/1	grade school	soup supper
Cynthia	Wednesday	12/3	grade school	yogurt??
Jonathon	Friday	12/5	high school	concession
Julesburg	Friday	12/5	high school	concession

"Each time our perp hit there were lots of people around and the food was either concession or brought by a ladies group. Cynthia's is still a puzzle," Martin said.

"All of these times and places gave anyone an opportunity to tamper with the food. The food's not protected. There are many people in and out. When I went to school, the concession stand was manned by volunteers or kids appointed to work rotating hours," said Eric.

"Yep, that's the way they do it here too," added Dave.

"Do you guys want some additional information to complicate things?" he added.

"Sure, why not?" said Glen.

"At the last few games additional food has been donated, already prepared, to help raise money for new uniforms," said Dave.

"So, that means *all* of the food in question could have been prepared in someone's home," said Martin.

"Hell, this could be anyone," said Glen. "The food could have been tampered with before or after it reached its destination."

"We need to contact the school and get a list of all the servers at the concession stand on each night in question. We still need to visit with the victims' families to be sure that's where the food was consumed. And, we need to find out which families donated food, and if possible, what food they donated," directed Martin. His CBI authority was coming out now. He felt helpless with murders happening right under his nose.

"I personally don't think we should waste our precious time right now on interviewing the families. I think we should get right on the server and donation list, then if we come up empty, go back to the families. Knowing how little time you have between consumption and death, my bet is all of the vics were poisoned at these locations," commented Glen.

"This is Saturday. There won't be anyone at the schools today. Let's divide and conquer. I'll get all the necessary phone numbers and you call about the elementary school, Martin. Eric, you take the high school and Glen and I will take the churches. I'm pretty sure we are talking about two different churches. I'll soon find out," said Dave as he saw Doris walking up the sidewalk with her list of guests from the church the night Sheri died.

He quickly called his dispatcher, instructing her to take the list from Doris without letting her into his office. While she had him on the phone she had more news for him. She put him on hold while she handled Doris.

"Dave, we have another death. Doc called and he wants you to call him at the hospital."

"Thanks."

Dave immediately called Doc.

When he heard Doc's voice he said, "Don't tell me another?"

"I'm afraid so, Dave."

"Can you give me any details?"

"Nope, just more of the same. It's Larry Olsen. He was shopping in the drugstore and he just fell over same as the others. He was with Tom when it happened. Tom snatched him up and drove him here. Thought it would be faster than the ambulance."

"Thanks Doc. I'll get back to you."

Dave walked over to the chart. He added Larry's name, date and location. The location was the café where they had just eaten their breakfast.

Chapter 11

The four men stared at the chart on the wall, followed by deep concentration, with each of them staring into space. No one moved a muscle, they appeared to be frozen into position. It was apparent that each of them, remaining still without breathing for a few seconds, was taking stock of his condition at the moment. Each wanted to make sure there was not the slightest symptom rising within the cells of their body to reflect the invasion of liquid nicotine into their systems.

Glen broke the silence, "Oh hell, looks like we're gonna live after all."

One by one, they looked at each other, realizing all shared the same fear.

"I feel fine. What about you guys?" asked Dave.

"My blood pressure is up, my heart is racing, but other than that I feel fine," responded Martin.

"Yeah, me too. Now that we know we're not dying, I can feel mine slowing back to normal," added Eric.

They all chuckled, cracking jokes and teasing each other about the look on their faces. Not one wanted to admit how scared he was for a few moments. Making light of the situation helped each of them to calm down, so they could return to work.

"I'll tell you one thing, I'm not gonna let Martin too far out of my sight since he's the one carrying the antidote," laughed Glen.

"In light of what just happened, I think all of our meals should be at my house," suggested Dave.

"You won't hear any complaints from us on that one," agreed Eric.

"You know this guy, whoever he is, has become one bold son of a bitch," said Glen. "He struck right under our noses at the café this morning. He's playing with us now."

"Do you really think so?" asked Eric.

"Yeah, I do. I don't think it's a coincidence," answered Glen.

"Then, why didn't he target one of us directly? That certainly would've had a greater impact on spooking us?" asked Eric.

"I'm not ruling that out. I think each of us is at risk for becoming the next victim depending upon how long this guy wants to play the cat and mouse game," said Glen.

Dave did not get involved in their conversation. He was on the telephone with Shelly. He told her what happened and cautioned her to keep the kids home, and not to eat out until this was settled. He told her to expect the four of them for all of their meals at the house from now on. He went so far as to suggest she drive to Sterling for groceries and to stock heavily.

"Do you think he's going to tamper with the food in the grocery store?" asked Glen.

"I'm not sure, but I'm not taking any chances where my family is involved," admitted Dave.

"What about the rest of the town? When are we going to warn them?" asked Eric.

"I don't know, I just don't know," said Dave with distress in his voice. He was in such turmoil. He should tell everyone to spare more lives, but on the other hand, exposing what they know could tip off their killer. He might stop killing, which is good; he might leave town and continue his killing spree elsewhere, which is bad. Either way, they might never catch him and that is their ultimate goal. They need to stop the killings, catch this guy, and lock him up where he won't hurt any more innocent people.

Dave went back to his chart on the wall. After Larry's name and the café, he wrote café for source of where the food came from.

"This means that someone contaminated the food in the café. Now, do we have it contaminated before it was delivered, after it was prepared, or during the preparation? It might actually be a little easier to track down the number of people involved with handling the café food. There had to be fewer people with the opportunity to get their hands on the food," explained Glen.

"Hey, I've gotta call the sheriff from Julesburg back. What do we tell him? Do we stick with our plan to tell him as little as possible?" asked Dave.

"I think that's the best we can do for now," suggested Martin. "I've seen first hand how fast news travels around here. So far only the four of us, and Doc know about the liquid nicotine. If that gets out, our guy will surely find out. If he's local, he's probably already got his thumb on the rumor mill to keep current about what we're doing."

Dave picked up the phone to call Sheriff Adams. His dispatcher put the sheriff on the line.

"Adams here."

"This is Sheriff Smith. You're right, we're having a rash of unexplained deaths around here. Actually, they have become food related. We're deep into an investigation here to discover the source of contamination. Since the boy in question probably ate something from the concession stand here at a ballgame, it's probably safe to assume that's where he was exposed to the toxin."

"So, are we talking botulism?" asked Sheriff Adams.

"No, not exactly. Seems a foreign substance has found it's way into some food and we're trying to determine what foods were consumed by our vics, and where the food originated from. Do us a favor will ya? Make sure there is an autopsy done on that boy, and have the lab check for liquid nicotine. We need a copy of the lab results sent here. Do not, I repeat, do not tell anyone about the liquid nicotine. We're trying desperately to keep this under wraps for a while longer."

"But why? If the food was contaminated at some factory shouldn't we be warning people? I don't want to take the blame for something happening to anyone in Julesburg, if it can be avoided. I'd think you'd feel the same way about Holyoke."

"Until we can find which food was contaminated, we're trying to avoid a panic. Our plan for today is to visit with each family to learn what the vics consumed during their last twenty four hours. Then once we have a connection we can go from there."

"Tell me about this liquid nicotine."

"There's not a lot to tell. It has a foul taste, but can easily be masked in food or drink. Once consumed in large doses it is fatal within the hour. There are no real warning signs until it's too late. The victim doesn't respond to CPR, and unless an antidote is given as soon as you realize you've consumed it, it's too late."

"Damn, that's some powerful stuff. Where in the hell is it coming from?"

"That's what we're trying to find out. So, can you do us a favor, and just give us a little more time before you spread the word? We'd really appreciate it. We'll contact you as soon as we have something concrete that you can go to your people with."

"Sure, I'll keep things quiet at this end. I'll call the lab myself to request the body be tested for liquid nicotine. I won't mention it to the family or any of my staff here. Just don't leave me out of the loop. I want to be kept informed."

"Thanks, and I promise the moment we have a break through, we'll contact you."

Dave hung up the phone, "Whew! He almost didn't want to work with us on this one. He felt it was his duty to inform the people of Julesburg about the possibility of contaminated food."

"Can we trust him to keep quiet?" asked Martin.

"I know you've discovered how quickly gossip flies in a small town, but I'd like to think that among sheriffs working on a case, confidentiality would be respected. I think he should be okay as long as we keep feeding him more information as it becomes available to us," Dave reassured them.

"Okay, what's next?" asked Eric.

Dave called his dispatcher. "I need the contact names from the high school and the elementary schools. I also need you to find out the names of the church ladies that prepared the food for Tim's funeral. Along with those names, I need phone numbers, and we need them quickly."

While they waited for the information from Dave's dispatcher, the four men planned their questions for the parties they were about to interview. They wanted to be thorough so they would not have to return to them for further questioning. They also knew they needed to word their questions in such a way to avoid raising suspicion among the people being interviewed. That would be the most difficult task of all.

The dispatcher gave Dave the names and numbers he requested. Dave looked up the addresses of the people on the list. He gave directions to each of the men so they could find their way as quickly as possible to each location.

They agreed their first stop, as a team, would be back at the café. That could cut down tremendously on their investigation time.

It was now ten-thirty on a Saturday morning. The caskets would soon be exhumed. Time was slipping away from them. They agreed to wait until after lunch to visit the people on their lists.

They bundled up to leave the building. The winter weather was harsh. The crew working on the graves had their work cut out for them. Something about the bleak coldness of the weather matched the cold heart of the killer.

The café was filled to capacity. Talk was buzzing about Larry's death. Everyone assumed a heart attack took his life. If anyone had any idea his death might have been caused by something he ate, at the very café they were currently eating in, the café would be empty in moments.

225

Dave quietly motioned to the waitress to join them in the back of the café. An empty table in the entire two rooms could not be found. The weather was bad, schools were closed, and everyone knows the best place to learn gossip is at the cafés and coffee shops, so all were filled to capacity.

Once she joined the men in the back of the café, they huddled around her to prevent others from listening to what they were asking.

Dave started, "Say, did you notice Larry having any problems while he was here this morning?"

"No, what do you mean?"

"You know, was he acting his normal, obnoxious self, or was he more quiet than usual?"

"Oh no, he was his same obnoxious self," she chuckled. "I can't believe he was in here this morning, and I served him. Now he's dead."

"Do you remember what he had to eat this morning?"

"Well, he had breakfast at home. I served him a cup of coffee."

She had to think for minute. They waited.

"Oh yeah, he had a slice of cherry pie."

"Where is that pie now?"

"Well, he ate it."

"No, I mean where's the rest of the pie? Did you serve it to anyone else?"

She thought again for a minute. "No, there was only one piece, and Larry ate it. He said it didn't taste as good as our pies. He said next time to be sure I only serve him our pie."

"What did he mean by that? Where did the pie come from?"

"Well, it came from the school game last night. Normally, the left over food from one of those donation nights goes to the school for the kids to eat at lunchtime. Since the school is closed, we bought all of the left over homemade desserts to serve here. We thought it would be a shame to let all of that food go to waste, and this way we could donate to the school uniform fund at the same time."

Disappointment covered the faces of the four officers. The lead they were hoping for didn't pan out. They are back to square one, once again. The food was prepared in someone's home. It could have been tampered with at the preparation site, or at the school. Chances that the food was tampered with at the café were nearly zero.

"So, the pie came from the game last night? How busy was the café this morning?"

"Yes, the pie came from the game. How busy were we this morning? Oh, I don't know, no more or less than usual. I guess it depended on what time of the morning you're talking about."

227

"What about before or during the time that Larry was here?"

"It was pretty quiet then. Well, you know that. You guys were here when Larry was here."

"Any strangers in here at that time?" asked Eric.

"Strangers? You mean hunters? Oh yeah, there were a few in to buy coffee for their thermoses. Why? What do strangers have to do with the pie, and what does what Larry ate have to do with him having his heart attack? What's going on?"

"Nothing really, I mean, we're just trying to help Doc figure out where Larry had been, you know, everything he did. Also, if anyone talked to him that noticed anything wrong with him," lied Dave.

"Maybe you should ask Tom those questions. He was with Larry the whole time. I heard it was Tom that took him to the hospital."

"We do plan to visit with Tom. We just wanted to know from you if there was anyone else we should visit with."

That made her feel important.

"Thanks for all of your help."

"You're welcome," she answered.

Before the men had an opportunity to leave the cafe, she had a group of people swarming around her like bees gathering nectar. They were trying to gather gossip. Dave felt confident he hadn't left her with any information that she shouldn't have. He also knew that the information that she did have would soon be embellished with each time it was repeated.

Dave looked at his watch. The time for the caskets was approaching. They drove to the cemetery to watch and wait. They wanted to be there to witness the removal of the caskets from the graves, and to ensure no one was there that shouldn't be until they were safely loaded in the hearses to be taken to the lab for testing.

Much to their surprise, Tim's parents were there as well. Dave walked to their car. "Good morning folks," he said. "I'm really sorry we have to do this. Our hands are tied. This information is important to our investigation."

Tim's mother and father would not answer Dave. They stared out the window pretending he wasn't there. The back window rolled down.

"Dave, I don't think this is a good time. Can't you see how distressed they are," said Coach Callister in his very quiet voice. "When they called me to tell me what was happening today, I offered to come along in case they were too distraught to drive home."

"Thanks Coach, I feel better knowing you're with them," Dave said in nearly a whisper.

"It's the least I can do. Tim was more than just a star player when I was coach, he was more like family." He wiped a tear from his eye.

Dave tipped his hat and walked back to his car.

"Who was that?" asked Martin.

"Those are the parents of one of the bodies we're removing. They're furious with us for disturbing his resting place. Coach Callister is with them. He was Tim's coach from his freshman year through his junior year. Before Coach Jones took over this year. A real nice guy, Coach Callister, he's retired now, but still a very active member around the kids' sports and their families. He never had kids of his own so his team sort of filled that void for him."

"Well, here we go," said Eric. Tim's casket was removed from the grave.

Dave walked over to the graveside to watch as the casket rose the last few inches. He walked along side of it as it was carried to the first hearse. Moments later the second casket was removed containing Lyle's body. He escorted it to the second hearse. The two hearses left the cemetery in single file, followed by Tim's parents.

Dave hoped that they were not going to follow the hearse all the way to Denver to the lab. He didn't think it would be a good idea for them to be there when Tim's body was removed from the casket. He also knew he had to keep his feelings to himself.

When the vehicles were out of sight, he joined the other three men. Instead of beginning their questioning of the people on their lists, they thought it would be in better taste to do so after lunch. No sense in disturbing those people during their mealtime. Dave drove them to his house.

As the men entered his house they stamped the snow from their boots and removed their heavy coats. There were wooden pegs lining the wall in their mud porch. The men hung their coats neatly on the pegs. The smell of chili simmering on the stove was impossible to miss.

Once inside the kitchen, Dave spotted a note from Shelly.

Dave,

I took the kids with me to Sterling. We should be back around three. Help yourself to the chili on the stove. There's sliced cheese in the fridge. The crackers are on the counter. There's iced-tea or hot tea, and the coffee was made fresh just before we left. There's cherry pie on the counter.

See ya later,

Shelly.

Dave busied himself getting the bowls and silverware. Glen knew his way around the kitchen pretty well, so he helped. Eric and Martin stood there, not knowing exactly how to help.

"The bathroom is down the hall," pointed Dave. "In case either of you need to use it."

"Thanks," said Martin as he headed in the direction pointed out by Dave.

The hot chili was a much-welcomed meal for the chilled men. The cherry pie, on the other hand, was not quite as inviting, knowing it was probably cherry pie that caused the death of Larry. They hesitated at first, but soon put their fears aside devouring the pie left by Shelly.

After the men finished eating their lunch, it was time to interview the list of people.

Dave drove them downtown so they could divide and conquer. The plan was to meet back at Dave's office when all of the interviews were completed.

Glen offered Eric his pick-up, while Martin drove the CBI vehicle. Glen and Dave left together. Dave dropped Glen off at the church where he was to meet with the people on his list. Then Dave went to visit with the women that were on the list that Doris had brought in. Those were the people that were at the church event the night Sheri died.

It turned out not to be as easy as planned. With each new person they spoke to, a new name was added to the list to interview. Fortunately, they were able to call those that were not free to stop by the schools or the churches.

Glen finished first. His was fairly easy. For Tim's funeral there were a handful of women that prepared the standard church menu for the after funeral dinner. Glen jotted down all of the names. The same women served and cleaned up afterwards. Glen had seven women on his list. Although he had the names of who were involved with the food preparation and serving, that did not cover the guest list, which was comprised of most of the town. Tim was a star athlete. He was a very pleasant, boy, loved by all who met him.

It was nearly four-thirty before the men were back together in Dave's office.

They compared notes and laid out the names.

"Who has the longest list of names?" asked Dave.

The men compared the length of the lists; Glen's was the shortest, followed by Martin's from the soup supper at the elementary school. Next was Dave from the church where Sheri had been on the eve of her death. Finally, the longest list, was Eric's from the high school concession stand.

"Okay, let's begin. My kids have this Boggle game where someone reads off their words and if you match you eliminate the word. We'll do it backwards. We'll only eliminate those names that appear only once. So, put a check mark next to the names that match the ones on Eric's list. Eric, let's have your names, please," requested Dave.

Eric began reading his list. One by one names were either checked or eliminated. He had nearly one hundred names on his list.

Once the first step was finished Dave said, "Now I'll read off my list of names skipping the ones that did not appear on Eric's list."

"Wait, what if the three of us have names that match, but they weren't on Eric's list?" asked Glen.

Dave thought about it for a moment.

"You're right. I suppose it's possible for our person to be listed on most, but not all of the lists. Let's go with my original plan and mark those first that appear on all four lists. We'll work out other combinations later."

Dave began to read from his list. Then Martin did the same. There was no need for Glen to read his since the matches should be complete.

All of the women on Glen's list were a match. When the others compared their lists they were surprised to find most of the names appeared on all of the lists. It seems the same group of women are the ones that did most of the volunteer work for the schools and churches.

The only group of names that appeared to be in their own little cluster was a group from one night on Eric's list. He had a list that contained the names of all of the teachers and coaches from the high school and elementary school. It was teacher's night to serve. A few of their names showed up on the other lists, but not many, especially the men.

"This sucks," said Dave. "It looks like we could have thirty suspects. I can't run around town accusing all of these women. I'd get strung up."

"No, you know what really sucks?" asked Glen. "The fact that we may or may not have thirty or more people that we can consider possible leads, but we have no motive. We have no connection between the victims. We still appear to have random deaths happening. And let's get real here. All of these deaths are taking place where so many people have access to the food. I don't feel like we're gaining on anything here."

"Glen's right. Nothing works. None of the pieces fit. We don't have enough information gathered to build any type of case. Think about it. We have all of these deaths. They're all with liquid nicotine. The yogurt theory is out the window. It can't be a food delivery situation with food that was tainted at a factory, because no other towns are affected. This is isolated to the Holyoke area. I would say it's safe to assume that no one is tampering with the food at the grocery store level, because all of our deaths can be traced back to one of these gatherings where food is served. The only common link is the food is homemade and access is easy," Martin pointed out.

"I know," said Dave. "Let's get with the lab results and check to see if they have stomach contents listed. Maybe we can narrow down the type of food these people ate or drank to narrow down our list of possible suspects."

"I'm on it," said Eric. He called the lab.

"Let's back up to Cynthia," said Glen. We know she ate the yogurt and we know the yogurt was contaminated. We need to know where that yogurt came from. That's the only lead we can follow in a straight line."

Dave opened his notebook. Mrs. Atkins was the teacher Cynthia was helping out. She was the last person to see Cynthia alive, other than the kids.

"Come on Glen, let's go find Mrs. Atkins. You two stay here to wait for the lab results. We'll stop by here to pick you up for supper at my house," Dave called to them as he was heading out the door. Glen was close at his heels, putting on his jacket on the run.

Dave had written down Mrs. Atkins address and phone number in his notebook during his interview with her.

"One thing about it, you don't have to waste hours in traffic when you have to find someone to interrogate. Everyone's right in your own backyard," remarked Glen.

They rang the bell. Snow was beginning to fall. The flakes were falling like large feathers. There was a gentleness about them that was comforting to Dave in his time of desperation. He noticed Glen reaching his hand out to watch the large flakes drop onto his glove before disappearing from the warmth of his hand.

Mrs. Atkins came to the door.

"Can I help you?" she asked.

Glen was in plain clothes, but Dave had his sheriff's jacket on. She was immediately comfortable knowing who they were. She was a widow not unaccustomed to men showing up at her door.

"May we come in to ask you a few more questions?" asked Dave.

"Sure. Come right in. Here, let me take your coats."

She kindly took their coats and hung them neatly in her hall closet. Her house was immaculate. The sight of it being so clean and tidy made Glen think of Debbie. He made a mental note to call her when they left Mrs. Atkins house. He had been so busy he wasn't being very good about calling her. He would get so wrapped up in his work he'd forget the time. He meant well, but he didn't always follow through with his intentions in a timely manner.

Debbie wants to understand, but it is harder for women. They can run multiple thoughts through their minds at one time while men seem to be able to focus on only one at a time. Sometimes, her feelings were hurt when he didn't call. He would try to convince her that she was really on his mind more than she thought. She would forgive him and he would always promise to be better next time, of course, he wasn't.

He brought his thoughts back to the interview they were working on. Mrs. Atkins left the room to retrieve coffee and cookies for the men.

She returned with a pot of piping hot coffee and freshly baked cookies.

"You're in luck," she said. "I just started a new pot of coffee before you arrived. And the cookies, well, cookies are something I rarely have time to bake with school and all. Now with the school being closed and the nasty weather outside, it was the perfect day to bake cookies."

She poured the coffee and placed two cookies on each plate on the table in front of the men as they sat on her sofa.

"Thank you," began Dave. "We need to speak with you about the day Cynthia died."

"I'm still in shock over that," she said. "How can such a young active mom, like Cynthia, just drop over from a heart attack?"

Glen asked, "Do you remember if Cynthia brought a lunch from home that day?"

"No, I don't believe she did. She had to run home, pick up her dog, and go to the vet clinic. Then take her dog home again and hurry back to school. But then I told you all of that already. She didn't have time to fix anything at home or stop to buy anything."

"So, as far as you know, her lunch was the yogurt she was eating?" asked Dave.

"Well, yes. That wouldn't be the first time Cynthia found herself too rushed for lunch."

"What has she done in the past when this happens?"

"She generally raids the refrigerator in the teacher's lounge. There's a cup in the refrigerator and a list on the door. We keep candy bars, drinks, fruit and yogurt in there. It's not uncommon, you know, for one of the teachers to get so busy they miss lunch, or skip it all together.   Sometimes, when they finally make it to the cafeteria for lunch the food is either gone, or being packed up.   It's not fair to the cooks to ask them to bring it back out, so the teachers decided to build their own little stash and store it in the fridge."

"Where does the food come from?" asked Glen.

"From the teachers," answered Mrs. Atkins. We all take turns going to the grocery store to stock it. We take inventory when it's our turn. Then we take the money from the cup and fill in what's missing."

"So, it was okay with the teachers that Cynthia, an aid, dipped into the stash?" asked Glen.

"Sure, as long as she paid, they were okay with it. They didn't put her on the list to go shopping. That was strictly for the teachers."

"All of the teachers? Including the men?" asked Dave.

"Well, yes. We do have a couple of men that join us with our little food pantry, but not all of them. They seem to rarely miss lunch."

Dave sipped the last of his coffee and popped the last bit of his second cookie into his mouth. He stood up to leave.

"Thank you so much for your time, and of course, the great cookies," he said.

"That's it? That's all you wanted to talk to me about, just the yogurt? I'm not sure I understand all of this hubbub about yogurt when she died of a heart attack. Is there something going on that we don't know about?"

"No, we're just following through on some questions. We'd better go. I have a meeting at my office."

Back in the car, Dave said, "Well, that didn't gain us much, except that she got the yogurt on school grounds just like all of the other food that contained liquid nicotine."

Glen's cell phone rang. It was Debbie.

"Hi Glen, I haven't heard from you in a while and was wondering if everything was okay?"

"Hi, I was just thinking about you. I was about to call you myself when my phone rang."

She wanted to believe him, but she had her doubts.

"How's the investigation going? Will you be coming home soon?" she asked.

"Boy, honey, I hope so. The investigation is still a dead end. We have people dropping like flies here. CBI is here and we don't have one solid lead to go on, other than the cause of death. I'm not sure how much longer I'll be here. But I promise you, as soon as this is wrapped up, I'll head home."

"I was hoping you'd help me pick out a Christmas tree soon. Then we've got to get started on some shopping. You will be home for Christmas, won't you?" she asked in a teasing voice, but half serious at the same time.

"Oh hell, yes. I can promise you I'll be home with you and the dogs for Christmas, even if this is not wrapped up by then," he promised.

"Oh, before I forget," she said. "Some woman, named Jennifer Parker, called for you. She said she felt you needed her? Isn't she that psychic you worked with?"

"Yeah, that's her. Weird, I had a dream about her the other night. I dreamed she was trying to tell me something, only I couldn't understand her. This psychic stuff is just too strange. Did she leave her phone number?"

"Yeah, let me see. Here it is. 722-554-7837."

"Wait, give that to me again."

"722-554-7837."

"Okay, it's 722-554-7837, right?"

"Yep, you got it."

"Debbie, I have to go. I'm in the parking lot in Dave's car. He's in his office with CBI. I need to get in there. I'll try to call you tomorrow. I love you."

"I love you too, and you'd better call tomorrow!!"

Chapter 12

Glen jogged across the parking lot to the door. He said hello to the dispatcher as he walked past her desk, on his way to Dave's office. The men were comparing notes when Glen walked in. Dave filled them in on the yogurt situation. The lab results were in with stomach contents. There was nothing conclusive there. Sheri had consumed a variety of foods at the church that evening. The food with the least amount of digestion was chocolate pudding. Chances were good that was the last thing she ate, and the most likely source of her poisoning.

Jane's stomach contents consisted of chili and cherry pie, along with iced tea. Sheila had nachos and coke in her stomach. Jonathon had popcorn and coke. The results were not in yet for the boy from Julesburg.

They were sure Cynthia's was going to be the yogurt and it was. There would be no way to discover the contents of the two bodies that were being exhumed. Those were long gone since an autopsy had not been performed on them.

"So here we go. We have, cherry pie, chili, iced tea, yogurt, chocolate pudding, coke, nachos, more coke, and popcorn," said Dave.

"Hmm... there doesn't seem to be a good connection here," started Eric. "I was really hoping to see only one or two similar items so we could figure out who made the food and narrow down our search. But looking at this list, it seems most of the food was prepackaged and not necessarily homemade."

Martin began, "We have a couple of cokes, we could maybe consider two cherry pies, if we count Larry. The nachos, popcorn, pudding and others are just not connected. Damn this is not getting any easier."

"Wait," said Glen. "Look at the list again. It's probably safe to assume both kids had the stuff put into their cokes. We know the cokes had to come from the fountain machine. It would be impossible to tamper with the popcorn since it's not liquid, the same with the nachos. I suppose it could have been in the cheese, but that's not as likely as the coke. I'd bet on the coke as the carrier. Next, I'd vote on the cherry pie, and finally the chocolate pudding. So, we have cokes that could only have been tampered with at the concession stand. The cherry pie had two victims, but on two separate nights. It wasn't the same pie. Now, if the pies were contaminated, it could only be at the point of serving. If the entire pies were contaminated at the preparation site then we would have more dead bodies. I think, fellas, it's safe to assume that the food was being contaminated at the point of serving. Someone had to be slipping the stuff into the food as it was being served."

"It's possible that the victims were being singled out. Or, that it's random and the food was tampered with, not knowing who was going to consume it," explained Dave.

"Damn, this is still not good enough for me. We still don't know if the victims were chosen or if they were random. We still have no motive," complained Martin.

"Yeah, but we now know the food was not contaminated from some factory. We know the food was not contaminated at someone's home, since the coke came from the fountain at the school. Our killer had onsite access to the food. We know he or she has been at every event. Hell, he might be standing right there getting his jollies watching his vics fall," said Glen.

"Yeah, and most of the time he was doing his dastardly deed right under our noses, since we, or at least I, was at most of the locations as the deaths happened," admitted Dave.

Martin, with his dry sense of humor asked, "Does that mean we should add you to our list of suspects? You were obviously there to contaminate the food."

Dave sneered at Martin.

Glen thought his humor was badly timed since Dave was already blaming himself for all the deaths, not being able to prevent them.

"Let's get back to our lists," suggested Dave. "Was there anyone serving at the concession stand, on all the game nights, when someone died?"

The lists were examined and the answer was no. Different servers were on for each of those occasions. No lead there.

"It has to be someone from the crowd. Someone that can just blend in and no one would suspect him. Hell, he could've even been sitting next to someone at one of these events slipping the stuff into their food without anyone noticing," said Glen.

"I find that more difficult to believe," said Martin. "The way everyone watches everything that goes on here, I think someone would've seen something."

"That's true. It's hard to believe this person could pull this off over and over without being seen," agreed Eric.

Dave looked at this watch.

"Hey, we'd better go. I'm sure Shelly's got supper ready. It's bad enough she has to cook for us, the least we can do is to not be late."

They gathered their notes and left.

Shelly had a great spaghetti dinner prepared for them when they walked in. Dave took Shelly aside to tell her about Larry and the cherry pie. She felt badly that her choice of desserts for them for lunch was cherry pie. She and Dave had their private little laugh.

"I hope no one died from spaghetti," she chuckled.

Dave gave her a big hug and a kiss.

"Thanks so much for helping us out like this. I hate to put the extra burden on you, but the guys agree we probably have targets on our backs."

"Oh Dave, you're not in any real danger are you? Is there something you're not telling me?"

"No, don't worry, we're not taking any chances. We're being extra careful."

"Maybe we should get the other guest room ready and you can have Martin and Eric stay here. Is there a chance someone can tamper with their things in their motel room when they're not there?"

"I doubt if we need to go that far, but it would sure be nice if we could stay together to keep working around the clock. If you're sure you don't mind the extra work, I'll put that idea past them."

"Dave, it would be easier on me if I knew you guys were working here. I wouldn't have to worry about you so much."

Shelly and Dave went back to the dining room to join the others.

"Say, guys, Shelly has a great idea. She's willing to set up the other guest room for you two so you can stay here with Glen and me. We can work around the clock if need be. We know the food here is safe."

"I'd hate to put you to any extra trouble, Shelly," said Martin.

"I'd feel better knowing Dave was safe, working at home, where I won't have to worry about him," she said.

"Dave? What about the rest of us? Don't you worry about whether or not we're safe?" teased Glen.

Shelly blushed a bright red.

"Of course, I mean, I would worry about all of you," she said stumbling over her words.

Glen walked over to her chair and gave her a big hug. "Hey, I'm just teasing. Gotta keep the mood light around these serious guys."

Shelly received extra compliments from the men for supper. They all agreed after supper to move Eric and Martin into the spare guest room.

Glen helped Shelly clear the table. She fed the kids before the men arrived. She knew sometimes they liked to work during their meal and having the kids at the table might hamper their ability to discuss confidential matters. Dave knew from past experience that Shelly could be trusted. This time, however, was the first time any of Dave's cases hit so close to home with friends and acquaintances of hers dying. He was surprised she was holding up so well.

Shelly had done a really good job of hiding her emotions from Dave. She wanted to be his support at home. Dave coming home from his office, to a nagging wife pressuring him to solve the case, was not what he needed. She did her share of crying while he was not around. She was indeed terrified. She was terrified for him, her kids, and herself. Each day when she woke she was praying the killings would end. She wondered if one of her close friends might be next.

After the table was cleared Shelly went to the refrigerator and removed a tray of dessert dishes. One by one she placed a dessert in front of each man. They all looked down at their desserts. Finally, Martin burst into laughter.

Soon the others joined him.

Shelly looked confused. She thought maybe there was a bug in one of the desserts.

"What?" she begged.

She looked at Dave for his support. He was wiping tears from his eyes. The men were releasing their tension with hysterical laughter.

"Honey, remember what I told you about the cherry pie?"

"Yes," she paused. Then she joined them with their laughter as well. "Don't tell me. Chocolate pudding?"

"Yep," answered Dave. Trying to get the words out between his gasps for air and the tears flowing down his cheeks.

Glen, for one, was happy to see Dave laughing. He had been suffering so over this case.

Martin turned to Eric, "You first."

They all laughed again.

"Dave, she's your wife, you start," teased Eric.

"Oh you guys!" complained Shelly. She took the first bite. Then she walked around the table and took a bite from each of their dessert dishes. "There are you satisfied? You might not be getting the nicotine, but you're all going to share my germs as punishment."

The guys ate their pudding, but not without a couple more hysterical bursts of laughter; much like when they were school kids when laughter would become contagious in the classroom.

After dessert, Shelly excused herself to prepare the guest room. Martin and Eric took that opportunity to go back to the motel to gather their things and check out.

While they were gone, Dave received a phone call from one of the residents of Holyoke.

"Dave, what in the hell is going on?" the voice on the phone asked.

"What do you mean?" asked Dave.

"This is Tom, I was with Larry this morning when he died. I thought it was a heart attack just like everyone else in this town thought. We just left our church service and my wife's sister lives in Julesburg. Her husband, a deputy, told her that there might be some nicotine stuff in food around here killing everybody. Is that true?"

Dave rolled his eyes as he looked across the table at Glen.

Glen immediately knew something was wrong. He raised his hand to the side of his face, mimicking a telephone, to ask permission to listen in.

Dave nodded.

Glen slipped away from the table to pick up the phone in Dave's den.

"Now, Tom, calm down. We're not quite sure what's going on just yet. We're trying to get to the bottom of this."

"Dave, just answer me one question. Was there or was there not something in the food that killed Larry?"

"I can honestly tell you, Tom, that we do not know. We won't know anything until an autopsy has been done."

"Then you do suspect something, don't you?"

"This is a routine autopsy and we can't suspect anything until the results are in?"

"I think you are being mighty evasive. I think you know something, and I think we have a right to know what's going on. Does Larry's death have anything to do with the other recent deaths?"

"Well, Tom, again, I can't say anything without the autopsy results."

"Fine, but you'd better come clean with us as soon as those results are in. When do you expect them?"

"We should have them by Monday."

"Okay, we'll give you until Monday, then we expect some answers."

He hung up the phone without saying good-bye.

Glen left Dave's den to join him in the dining room.

"Whew! I guess we knew this would hit sooner or later. I was just hoping it would be later," said Glen. "What's your plan for Monday?"

"I'm not sure. I guess we'll have to call a town meeting Monday night. I'll have to answer questions for the locals. Damn, that's not going to go over very well. I wish by some twist of fate that we could end this before Monday."

"I hear you," agreed Glen.

When Dave mentioned a twist of fate, he thought of Jennifer Parker and her call to him. He also thought of his dream with her in it. His thoughts were interrupted by the sound of the phone ringing. It was another concerned citizen. The prairie fire had started.

Dave fielded the second phone call, and then there was a third. He barely had the chance to hang up the phone when it would ring again.

Martin and Eric arrived back at Dave's house, Glen filled them in about the word being out and the constant stream of phone calls that Dave was receiving.

While Dave was on the phone with the seventeenth call, the doorbell rang. Shelly went to the door. She stepped into the dining room where all of the men were seated watching Dave and listening to him attempting to calm the town. He looked up at her.

She whispered, "Olga and Jeff are at the door. They want to talk to you about what's going on."

251

When Dave finished with his call, he took the receiver off of the hook, then went into his living room where Olga and Jeff were waiting. The other three men followed to observe how he was going to handle people face to face.

Jeff began, "Dave what's going on? There's been talk at church. Olga's sister came home and called her about someone eating poisoned food?"

Dave said, "Jeff, I'm planning to hold a talk on Monday night at the school. We're hoping by then to have something to tell people. We're still waiting for test results to come in. We really don't have any concrete answers yet."

"So there is something to this then, isn't there?" asked Olga. "Is there something wrong with our food from the store? What is it, so we don't buy it and feed it to our kids?"

"We don't have any answers for that either."

"I saw your wife in Sterling today stocking up on food. You do think there is something wrong with our food here and you're just not telling us. What kind of sheriff would let innocent people die. I think you should be honest and inform all of us about what you know."

"Olga, I would if I could, but we just don't know enough to tell anyone anything. Please, just give us until Monday. If you feel uncomfortable with the local food, I might suggest you eat in. Eat only canned goods, until we get some answers. I can't tell you any more than that. Now we really do need to get back to work."

She looked at Glen and the other two men.

"Who are your friends?" she asked.

"This is my friend, Glen, from Denver, and this is Martin and Eric."

"Are you guys cops?" she asked.

Dave took over. "Olga, Glen is a detective from Denver that I used to work with and Martin and Eric are from CBI. They're here to help with the investigation. You see we are taking this seriously and with their help we hope to find answers more quickly. But we really do need to get back to work."

Jeff asked, " What does CBI stand for?"

Martin answered, "We're from the Colorado Bureau of Investigation."

Panic covered the faces of both Jeff and Olga. They excused themselves from Dave's house. Dave watched from the window as they drove away.

"Hell, the words out now. Prepare for a riot."

Martin turned to Glen, "Did you bring your SWAT equipment?"

No one appreciated the timing on his joke.

Dave went to his computer. He typed up a notice for his front door. WE ARE NOT TAKING VISITORS. IF YOU HAVE QUESTIONS PLEASE WAIT UNTIL MONDAY NIGHT AT THE HIGH SCHOOL GYM AT 7 P.M. SHERIFF SMITH

He went to his telephone and recorded the same message on the answering machine. He and the other three men were going to have to stay put for a while. Going out in public would be saved only for reasons pertinent to the case. He knew they would be stopped and asked questions every time someone had a chance.

The phone continued to ring every few minutes throughout the night. Shelly even received a few calls on her cell phone. She didn't answer.

"Martin, what's your cell phone number?" asked Dave.

He gave the number to Dave who jotted it down on a slip of paper. He then called his dispatcher and told her to only put official calls through to him and to use Martin's cell phone. Before they hung up she told him she was receiving lots of calls and didn't know what to tell people. He explained the plan for Monday night.

They went to bed, but the phone continued to ring stopping everyone in the house from sleeping. Dave, angry, finally got up and shut the ringer off. The house returned to its normal, quiet, state and all slept to the best of their ability.

During his sleep Jennifer Parker came to Glen in a dream. He tried to understand what she was telling him. Once again, it was as if she was speaking to him in a foreign language. She was being so patient with him. It was as if she knew if he tried just a little harder, he would understand her. He never did.

The next morning the dream haunted his thoughts. He could not let it go. He looked at his watch. It was seven o'clock. He went into the kitchen. Dave was sipping coffee with Shelly.

Shelly offered to fix breakfast for Glen, but he refused.

"Dave, I have to go home for a while. I'll be back before seven on tomorrow night. I promise I won't let you go through that alone. Martin and Eric are here to help until I return."

"Why? What's up? Is Debbie okay?"

"Oh yeah, she's fine. I just have some business to attend to. If you need me, just call. If you learn anything new, let me know right away. You've got my cell number."

"Sure Glen. I've kept you here far too long already. I'm sorry about that. You don't have to come back if you don't want to, ya know."

"I know, and I want to come back. This case is getting a little personal now after the hit in the café. I'll be back tomorrow night."

He had already packed his bags. He stepped into the hall to pick them up.

He bumped into Martin while he was carrying them down the hall.

"What's up?" he asked.

Glen glanced at his watch again. He was anxious to leave.

"Dave will fill you in," he said. He squeezed past Martin, patted Dave on the back, and kissed Shelly on the cheek. "I'll see all of you tomorrow."

Glen rushed out of the door, warmed up his pick-up, then quickly left town.

His thoughts bounced back and forth between Debbie and Jennifer Parker. He was anxious to surprise Debbie. He planned to take her to lunch as soon as he got to Denver. Maybe the surprise would cheer her up and make up for the fact that he hasn't been very good about calling her lately.

He wondered what Jennifer wanted. He was hoping if she was for real that she might have some answers for the dilemma in Holyoke. With one hand carefully guiding the pick-up, he searched his duffle bag on the seat next to him for her phone number. He wasn't quite sure where he'd stashed it. Damn, he thought, I can't find it.

He drove a few miles further. He tried to concentrate on the phone number. The numbers were coming to him. His concentration would be broken when he would try to rationalize that he couldn't just start calling numbers on a hunch. He turned his thoughts back to Debbie. His subconscious mind kept drawing him back to the numbers that were materializing in his mind.

"Oh hell, what's a wrong number," he said to himself. He picked up his cell phone and carefully dialed the numbers that kept popping into his mind.

"Hello Glen," said the voice on the other end of the phone.

Silence ensued.

"Hello, is anyone there?" the voice asked again.

Glen cleared his throat. "Yes, this is Glen. Is this Jennifer?"

"Yes, this is Jennifer Parker. I've been waiting for your call."

"Oh, I was a bit startled when you knew who I was. You must have caller ID."

"No, I've never had a need for it."

"Then how'd you know, I mean, if you don't have caller ID...what do you mean you were waiting for my call?"

"Weren't we communicating in your dreams last night?"

"What?"

"I had a dream last night that we were together trying to talk. Didn't you have the same dream?"

"Yes I did, but how did you know?"

"Glen, think about it?"

"Oh, yeah. Sorry. I have to admit, though, this is way too strange for me."

"How many times have you called someone, only to have him say he was planning to call you, or he was just thinking of you?"

"I guess lots. It happened with Debbie, that's my wife, just last night. I was planning to call her and she called me first."

"Exactly. Our souls are connected. Your thoughts came to me in the form of energy. Some say when you have dreams that are so realistic you feel as though they really happened, they did. Your dream was so intense I felt you calling me. My energy mixed with your energy and I could view the same dream. So, in a sense we were together in your dream. Unfortunately, your conscious mind would keep interrupting so communication between us was weak."

"Uh, right," said Glen with doubt in his voice.

"I guess you're just not ready for all of this. How can I help you, Glen?"

"Well, Debbie said you called. I was wondering what you wanted."

"The first time you had the dream I thought you would try to reach me, and when you didn't, I thought I'd give you a call. So I did. Your wife said you were out of town working on a case. I knew then that you must need me."

"How did you know I had the same dream twice?"

"I was there, remember?"

Glen ignored that last comment. "So why did you call me really?"

"Because I knew you wanted to talk to me."

"Okay, let's just say this is one big coincidence."

"We will if that makes you feel better."

Glen was thoroughly confused. His common sense told him this whole conversation was insane, but there was a small, part within him that felt comfortable with what she was saying. This only added to his confusion.

"Let's just say for the sake of curiosity if what you are trying to tell me is true, what message did you have for me in the dream?"

"If you had just relaxed and not tried to analyze the situation in the dream, we could've connected and discussed your question."

"But, I was dreaming. How could my conscious mind have any control over my dream?"

"Glen, with a little practice, anyone can choose what they would like to dream about. They can also direct their actions within the dream. Why do you suppose we wake ourselves up from a nightmare? It's because we can. When the dream gets too frightening we choose to leave it. The same ability holds true for dreams that are not frightening. We do have control over our dreams."

"I'm wide awake now and we're communicating in a way I'm more comfortable with, the cell phone. So, what is it you were trying to tell me in my dreams?"

"What is it you wanted to ask me?"

"We're working on this case. It's a real stumper. I had you on my mind. I didn't know if you could shed any light on what we were experiencing on the case."

"Would you like me to?"

"Do you mean you can?"

"I'm not sure. Just as with little Samantha I have to feel something. Did you bring anything that can help me connect with your victim?"

"Did I bring you anything? How'd you know I was heading home? Never mind, forget I asked that one. I'm just not used to having someone wandering around in my mind."

"Oh, I'm sure your wife has been able to read your thoughts occasionally. You don't think that's so strange do you?"

"I guess you're right. That does happen once in a while."

"It happens to everyone. I've just been blessed with the ability to hone that skill and bring it forward at will. I'm anxious for the day when I can do it one hundred percent of the time, and I do feel myself getting stronger."

"No, I didn't bring you anything. Is that necessary for you to help?"

"It makes things easier. Perhaps if we can get together in person I can read your energy better, and allow myself to delve deeper into your case. How can we get together?"

"I should be home in a little more than an hour. I plan to surprise Debbie and take her to lunch. Would you like to join us?"

"I'd rather not. I hate to interrupt the lunch you plan with your wife, besides it's more difficult to concentrate in an area where there are a lot of people, too much energy in the room.

"Where then?"

"Would it be alright if we met at your home? The house will be comfortable to you and your energy will be present very strongly there. I think it would work best."

"If that's what you want, sure, here's my address. Do you need directions?"

Jennifer chuckled.

"Scratch that last comment," Glen laughed with her.

"Shall we say four o'clock?"

"That'll be great, I'll tell Debbie as soon as I get home."

"Bye, until then."

"Bye."

Glen was very anxious to get home to see Debbie. He wanted to fill her in on the conversation he just had with Jennifer. He wanted her viewpoint on it. She was always so open-minded and he trusted her opinion.

He tried to listen to his radio for the remainder of the trip home. He couldn't tell you what songs had played. His mind kept replaying the conversation he had with Jennifer. He thought about all she tried to teach him. He wondered why he wasn't more resistant to it. There truly was comfort in the things she was telling him. Maybe it's the way she told it with such confidence. Maybe if she told him the sky was green in the same convincing tone, he'd be tempted to believe her. He always trusted his instincts and judgments, but this had him questioning the ease with which he was accepting her comments.

He pulled his pickup into the driveway. A wave of fear rushed through his body. He realized he had no idea how he'd gotten home. The last thing he remembered was dialing Jennifer's number then talking with her. The next thing he knew he was home. He understood he was deep in thought, but wondered how he maneuvered through traffic with his mind on automatic. He truly had no memories of the remainder of the drive. He'd experienced it before while he was deep in thought, for a few moments. This time he lost the entire last hour.

When he opened the door he was surprised to be greeted by one of his German Shepherds. Debbie preferred they stay outdoors. He was always the one to spoil them and bring them inside where they could fill the house with dog hair in record time.

Debbie walked from the bedroom and jumped when she realized someone else was in the house. Glen laughed at her, then she threw a sofa pillow at him. He went to her. He held her in his arms apologizing for laughing. He looked into her eyes and stroked her hair. Then he kissed her a long, passionate kiss.

"Wow, if I didn't know any better, I'd think you missed me or something," she teased.

He reached down and swatted her.

"Ouch!" she whined. "What are you doing home? Surely, the case didn't break since last night?"

"No, I just had this overwhelming urge to come home to see you. I have to go back tomorrow afternoon. Things are really in bad shape there. I excused myself until then. What's the dog doing in the house? Are you turning into a softy?"

"No, I just had a feeling of uneasiness. I usually don't get nervous staying alone...let's just say having her in the house made me feel better. But, now that you're home, she can go back out."

"I thought I'd surprise you and take you to lunch. Are you up to it?"

"Sure, but I started a pot of soup earlier this morning. I guess it'll keep. Where do you want to eat?"

"You pick. Oh, I talked to Jennifer Parker on the phone on the way home. She's going to stop by here at four o'clock to see if she can help us with the case in Holyoke. Is that alright with you?"

"Sure, but let's skip going out to eat. If we're going to have company this afternoon, I have other plans for you."

She unbuttoned his shirt. He scooped her up kissing her and carried her off to the bedroom.

Chapter 13

At exactly four o'clock the doorbell rang. Glen answered it. Debbie was a little nervous. She'd never met a psychic before. It was quite unnerving to have someone enter your home that you know can enter your mind just as easily.

"Jennifer, it's nice to see you again. Please come in," invited Glen.

"You have a lovely house Detective Karst." She looked across the room at Debbie as she was approaching the two of them, "And a lovely wife."

"Thank you," said Debbie. "Can I get you something to drink?"

"She'd like herbal tea, hon. Red if you have it."

Debbie looked surprisingly at Glen.

"He's not showing you his psychic abilities, my dear, he's got a great memory for details," said Jennifer. "Someday though he will accept the powers within him that are stronger than he thinks. He is correct, a nice red herbal tea of any flavor if you have it."

Debbie went to prepare the tea, grateful she had an excuse to leave the two of them alone. The connection between the two of them made her uneasy.

She returned with tea for Jennifer and coffee for Glen.

"I'm sure you two would like to be alone to discuss the case," said Debbie.

"You can stay if you like," said Glen.

He was sitting in his chair near the fireplace. Jennifer took a spot on the sofa and Debbie placed herself in a chair across from Glen.

"Where would you like to begin?" asked Glen.

"Let's start at the beginning," said Jennifer. "Just tell me the story with as many details as you can remember. If I have any questions along the way, I'll stop you."

Glen began. He told her about the ballgame he attended with Dave and the circumstances surrounding the death of Tim, the star athlete. One by one, he told her of the deaths, until finally he ended with the latest victim, Larry. She allowed him to tell his story uninterrupted.

"My, my, that's a terrible situation you men are dealing with. Someone is definitely a very troubled individual."

"Can you help us? Do you have any idea if we are dealing with a man or a woman?" asked Glen with hope in his voice.

"I'm so sorry Glen, I'm not getting anything except your feelings of frustration and anxiety. I feel strong vibes of panic and fear, but I can't say that I have anything that can help you. If you would like, I can return to Holyoke with you to see if I can pick up something from the community."

"I couldn't ask you to do that," responded Glen.

"You didn't ask me, I offered. I only offer when I feel like it. Now would you like me to return to Holyoke with you or not? If you would like me to go, I need to go home to prepare for the trip."

"If you think you can help, then please *do* come. I will warn you though, you may meet with some opposition. Sheriff Smith does not have much faith in psychics."

"And you do?" she teased.

Glen's face flushed. "Let's say you're slowly making a believer out of me."

"What time would you like me to be back here tomorrow?" she asked.

"I'd like to leave shortly after lunch, say about two o'clock."

"I'll be here."

"Would you like me to meet you somewhere else so you won't have to drive all the way here to my house then follow me to Holyoke. I could save you some miles if we met closer to the east side of Denver."

"No, that is quite all right. I have no intentions of driving my own car. I will be riding with you."

That took Glen off guard.

"I'm not sure how long I'll be staying there. I'm not sure how you will get back home when you need to leave. I could be there another week or two."

"I understand. I also know it must be this way and the reason will unfold at a later date. Trust me."

Glen shot a glance at Debbie.

Looking back she raised her eyebrow and smiled.

Jennifer stood up to leave.

"I will be back here at two o'clock sharp. Might I suggest you contact Sheriff Smith and prepare him for my arrival."

"Sure, yeah, I'll give him a call."

Glen and Debbie walked Jennifer to the door.

"It was delightful meeting you Mrs. Karst. Please use the remainder of your hours together to the best. Create a memory you will never forget. Memories give us strength during a time of turmoil and sadness."

She walked out of the door to her car without looking back. They watched as her car left their view.

"Whoa, what'd she mean by that?" asked Debbie.

"I'm not quite sure. She sure has an air of mystery around her doesn't she?"

"Glen, I have to tell you she made me feel uncomfortable. I really wish you didn't have to go back. Can't you get out of it?"

"Debbie, I really don't want to leave you either. I can't walk out on Dave. This is a big deal now. Too many people are dying and we have to put a stop to it. Don't worry, I told you we're being extra careful. We're only eating the food that Shelly prepares for us. It's not like someone's running around with a gun or a bomb. I'm actually safer on this case than on most of the others I work on."

"I guess you're right. I just hope this is all behind us by Christmas. We need to do something very special this year for Christmas. Jennifer has me thinking we need to make more memories that we can hold on to in our old age."

Glen picked her up, "Let's go make more memories right now," and he carried her off to the bedroom again.

At Dave's house no one was answering the door or the phone. The town steadily grew impatient. The dispatcher was being bombarded with calls and people lining the hall wanting some answers. Things became noticeably worse after all the church services had concluded for the day. Large groups of people gathered in one area before and after the services, aided in spreading the word. Some of the ministers and pastors were incorporating the news into their sermons. Dave was quickly losing popularity in the town.

Martin and Eric were not accustomed to such intense interest by such a large number of people. Generally, they were free to conduct their business of

268

investigations without having to face the public. They pitied Dave for having to be in this situation.

Together, they continued to search the few facts they had for a missing clue. They looked for any lead that they might be able to pursue. Nothing, absolutely nothing, jumped out at them. They were sure they were not missing anything.

Martin and Eric both came to the realization that there was really nothing more they could do. There was no need for their ability to run fingerprints or lab tests. There was nothing they could use their national database for. There was just nothing to go on. They knew they needed to return to Denver with the promise to return if anything came up that required their assistance.

Martin took Eric aside. "What do you think? How much longer should we stay?"

"Why don't we leave first thing Tuesday morning? Glen will be back and Dave won't have to face the mob alone. We'll be at that town meeting with him. I think it would look bad if we left before then," answered Eric.

"I'll tell Dave after the meeting tomorrow night," said Martin.

Debbie called her place of employment to take a sick day. She wanted to be with Glen until he left at two o'clock. He wasn't working at his office that day; his sergeant didn't even know he was back in Denver. There wasn't enough time to jump into any of his construction projects he had going around their house. So they planned to spend every free minute together until Jennifer arrived.

She did so just as promptly as the day before. The doorbell rang at the same time their clock chimed. She arrived, not one minute before nor one minute after, but precisely at two o'clock.

"What does she do stand outside the door watching her wristwatch?" asked Debbie.

"Shhh..." said Glen as he went to the door. Knowing that Jennifer could get inside his mind made him uneasy about what thoughts he or Debbie might have about her.

Glen opened the door.

"Good afternoon Detective Karst, Mrs. Karst. Are we ready to depart?"

"Yes, I have my bag already packed in my truck. May I carry your bag out for you?"

"That would be lovely. It's in my trunk." She pressed the trunk release on her keyring, her trunk slowly opened.

Glen first went to his truck to start it. He wanted to warm it up since the day was so cold. Debbie started to go out with him.

"No, you wait in here where it's warm. I'll be back in a second," he said.

Jennifer remained standing on the step at the door.

"Would you like to come in?" asked Debbie.

"No, thank you, Mrs. Karst. I will wait in the pick-up truck so the two of you can say your proper good-byes in private."

Once Glen had her bag loaded she climbed into the truck.

Debbie closed the door after she left the step.

Glen came back inside. He held Debbie in his arms one last time. He kissed her a long, passionate kiss. They both wanted to stop this trip from happening. He could feel Debbie sob through the kiss. He stood back and looked into her eyes. Tears were streaming down her face.

"What's the matter?" he asked.

"I don't know, I just really don't want you to go. But I understand you have to, really I do. Now just go." She pushed him gently towards the door. "I'll be fine. Just come home to me as soon as you can, safe and sound."

"Hey, I promise. We've got that tree to pick out and shopping to do. Remember Christmas will be special this year. We'll make sure of that," he told her as he stepped out of the door.

Instead of going to the window to wave good-bye as he drove away she went into the bedroom, and threw herself down on the bed sobbing. The pillows still had the scent of Glen's aftershave on them. She buried her face into his pillow.

Glen was quiet as they began their journey. He was concerned about Debbie's emotional state.

"She'll be fine. She's stronger than she thinks," said Jennifer.

Glen was not sure how well he was going to like having his thoughts read all the way back to Holyoke.

"Yeah, I know. She's a pretty great lady. She's just having a pretty rough time with me being away. I think part of it is the holiday season and all," said Glen.

The remainder of the drive to Holyoke was filled with idle chitchat about the weather, family, travels or whatever else popped into Glen's mind not requiring deep, emotional thoughts that could be invaded by Jennifer. If she could invade his dream state from miles away surely she could do the same with his every thought sitting just inches apart.

A couple of hours into the trip Glen wondered if they should stop for a bite to eat. He didn't want to impose on Shelly, but was also aware that it might not be safe for Jennifer to eat anywhere in town.

"Would you like to stop for a quick bite to eat before we arrive at Holyoke. I'm not sure how safe the food is considering the circumstances going on there."

"That would be splendid. I have a favorite little restaurant in Sterling that would work," she answered.

When they arrived in Sterling she gave Glen directions away from the downtown area. They were walking up to the door when Glen realized that the restaurant they were approaching, the Wonderful House, was oriental food.

He hesitated in the parking lot.

"So this is your favorite place, huh? Have you eaten here a lot?" he asked, hoping to find a way out of going inside to eat.

"Don't worry Glen, you will enjoy the meal, I promise. I sense your reluctance to enter, but you will be pleasantly surprised," she said, with a smile of confidence on her face.

The restaurant was quiet that time of day. It was too late for the lunch crowd and too early for the supper crowd.

"Allow me to order for you," she said.

At first Glen was going to refuse, then thought this could be another test for her. He had not yet found a Chinese dish that really appealed to him. He was a steak and potatoes kind of guy.

She ordered the vegetarian delight, egg drop soup, and herbal tea for herself. A feeling of discomfort came over Glen. There was just no way he was going to choke down some vegetarian delight. She ordered General Tso chicken for Glen, along with hot and sour soup, and a beer.

He looked quickly at the menu trying to figure out what in the hell General Tso chicken was. The waitress was waiting for the menu so he had to give it up without answering his question. At least he'd enjoy the beer, he thought.

More small talk continued at the table while they waited for their supper. The soup arrived first. Jennifer dove right into her eggdrop soup. Glen played with his soup without tasting it.

"Go ahead. Take a risk," teased Jennifer.

He was slightly embarrassed that she had noticed his behavior. He slowly raised the spoon to his lips. He sipped the soup. Not bad he thought. He tried a whole spoonful. He was surprised at the spices in the soup. He actually enjoyed the flavor and the warm sensation it created as he swallowed it. The cold weather made this kind of soup a perfect choice for the day.

He finished his bowl before Jennifer finished hers. The waitress brought their main courses. Glen was pleased to find that there were no vegetables on his plate. He didn't mind rice so maybe this meal would not be a total loss after all.

Jennifer's dinner was just the opposite. She had nothing but vegetables in some sort of white sauce. It did not look appealing to Glen in the least.

"I've traveled to and eaten in many places in my day, but none can compare with this dish, at this restaurant," she admitted.

Glen slowly tasted a small bite of the chicken. Again, much to his surprise, it was a dish he could actually eat without being repulsed by it. He relaxed and enjoyed the meal. When they were finished Jennifer insisted that she pay.

"You see Glen, I knew you did not want to come here. I knew that you had yourself convinced that there would be no Chinese food that could possibly appeal to you. I had to show you how to open yourself up to new experiences. That is the only way you will grow and learn your purpose. In the future, you must open yourself up whenever possible. There are many lessons you must learn in this life."

"Thank you for the meal and thank you for the lesson. You were right. I did enjoy the meal. I'll be able to take Debbie to eat Chinese more often now, since there is something on the menu I can look forward to eating," he said.

"You're very welcome," she responded happy with the lesson she taught.

The last hour of the trip flew by. Glen felt better about being with Jennifer. He no longer felt threatened by her abilities, but rather curious as to how much she could teach him about himself that he was unaware of.

He introduced Jennifer to everyone at Dave's house. He took Shelly aside, "I hate to do this to you, Shelly, but would it be alright if Jennifer stayed here with us. I'll give her my room and I'll sack out on the sofa, if it's okay with you."

"Sure Glen, it's fine, but I can have one of the kids take the sofa and you can have one of their rooms," she suggested.

"No, I'll be fine on the sofa, trust me. I want to do it this way."

"If you insist, it's fine with me then."

"One more thing," he started, "Jennifer is a vegetarian."

"Oh Glen, how could you?" teased Shelly half serious and half teasing. She was accustomed to cooking for the meat and potato type of guest. This indeed presented a challenge.

When all of the introductions were complete, Dave took Glen aside. "Remember, no one is to know that Jennifer is a psychic. My butt's already in a sling in this town; I don't need any more friction from the people."

Glen agreed.

"Well, are we ready to head over to the school?" asked Dave.

They all agreed. Shelly followed the men to the school in her car. She took Jennifer with her. While she was alone with her she mentioned to her, at Dave's request, that it would be best if no one knew she was a psychic.

She understood and agreed to keep that to herself.

Dave and his men entered the school building with all of the deputies prepared for crowd control. The scene was much like one you might see in Washington D.C.,

276

when the President of the United States is preparing for a press conference. Most of the people were anxiously waiting to hear what Dave had to tell them, while others were calling out for answers to their questions before he was ready to begin. The crowd was actively visiting among themselves, passing bits of gossip back and forth.

It was half past six when Dave entered the gymnasium. He was astonished to see the large number of people already assembled on the bleachers. The superintendent was setting up a microphone so all could hear Dave's voice. This was the biggest event to ever hit Holyoke. Soon the gymnasium was filled. There was standing room only as more people continued to shuffle inside.

Glen touched Dave's shoulder as a show of confidence.

"If you aren't up to this, I can take over for you if you'd like," offered Glen hoping Dave wouldn't take him up on the offer.

"I'll be fine. It's my job, I have to do this," he answered.

The microphones were tested; the superintendent introduced Dave to the crowd.

Dave, clearing his throat began, "Good evening ladies and gentlemen. I'm here to answer your questions about what's been going on here. I would like to start with the fact that we do not have any conclusive answers for you at this time. We are working around the clock to try to find those answers. Along with myself, I have a close friend, Detective Glen Karst, from Denver PD here. Also, Officers Martin Thomas and Eric Miller, from CBI. That stands for the Colorado Bureau of Investigation. If anyone here has any information he or she feels could aid in our investigation, could you please come forward with that as quickly as possible, no matter how insignificant you may feel the information is."

The crowd silently listened to what Dave had to say, "Let me begin by saying we do have a connection to the recent deaths. It appears that nearly all of the deaths were by ingestion of a foreign toxic substance. The autopsy reports that have come in thus far have confirmed the existence of this substance in all of the cases they've examined. We're trying desperately to learn the point of entry into the food source. At this point, we have no clues or leads to go on. We're hoping that if anyone here has seen or heard of anything, please come forward. You can remain anonymous if you so desire."

Martin's cell phone rang. He stepped into the hall to take the call. When he returned to the room he handed Dave a sheet of paper. Dave halted his talk to read the paper.

"Ladies and gentlemen, the final reports are in. I'm afraid all of the cases involved are connected. The substance was confirmed in Tim, Lyle and now Larry's autopsy reports. I'm sure many of you know that we had to exhume the bodies of Tim and Lyle on Saturday morning. We sincerely apologize to the family members, but the information from their autopsy reports was imperative to the case."

"It appears all of the contaminated food has been consumed at public gatherings, at either church events or at one of the schools. That should not be a surprise to any of you. I'm sure by now, you are all aware of each death and the location. Our advice to you, until we can find out the source of contamination, is to be aware of the food you consume. It might be best to stick to canned foods until we have more answers. Dry foods such as noodles, chips etc. are fine. The food itself must be a wet or liquid type of food to hold the substance. As soon as we have any more details, we will let you know."

"We're aware of your concerns, but please refrain from contacting my office or my home with your questions. That takes precious time away from our investigation. We need to keep the lines open at the office for emergencies as well as information pertinent to the case. I promise that we will let you know when we learn more. I apologize for taking so long to have this talk, but until very recently we did not have anything to tell you. Does anyone have any questions?"

Hands flew into the air. Dave shot a glance at his three men standing to his left. He motioned for them to step closer to aid in answering the questions.

Dave began pointing to people in the crowd one by one.

"How is this substance getting into the food? Is it from the manufacturer?"

"Good question," responded Dave. "To the best of our ability to answer that question we would have to say no. We've found that the victims have all eaten a variety of foods containing it."

"You keep calling it a toxic substance. Does it have a name?"

"Yes, we've determined that it is liquid nicotine."

"Is that something available locally?"

"No."

"You refer to the dead people as victims. Do you feel a crime has been committed?"

"At this point we are unsure."

"So, that means you are considering it? Does that mean this might not be an accident?"

"Once again, at this point, we are unsure."

Someone yelled from the crowd, "Are you telling us there could be a killer among us?"

"At this point, we are unsure."

The room burst into conversation. The voices were angry and the crowd was frightened. For the first time it was confirmed in public that there might be cause for real concern.

"What are you doing to protect us?"

"We are investigating. At this time that is all we can do. We have no way of knowing which foods might be contaminated."

"Can you tell us which foods so far have been confirmed to hold this liquid nicotine?"

Dave turned to Eric. He took out his notebook then stepped up to the microphone. Dave wiped the sweat from his brow.

"Thus far we have this list of foods as suspect. We have two bodies that contained coke from the fountain machine at the high school, we have two cases of cherry pie that were homemade, we have one case of chocolate pudding and one of yogurt. We have not yet been informed of the case from Julesburg. We cannot guarantee all of the foods I have listed. That is the list we have narrowed it down to based on stomach contents from the autopsy reports."

"Is this spreading to other communities since there was a death of a Julesburg boy?"

"Not exactly, he had attended the same ballgame where Jonathon collapsed. This boy collapsed in the car on his way home with his parents."

"Is it safe then to assume that the only community involved is Holyoke?"

"To our knowledge, yes."

"Does this have anything to do with why you took Jonathon to your office for questioning? Was he somehow involved?"

"That was routine questioning. His fingerprints were on the yogurt container that tested positive to liquid nicotine. When we learned that Jonathon worked at the

281

checkout stand it was obvious to all of us that he had to touch all of the food that went through his checkout stand. We do not think that Jonathon is connected in any way, to the cases we are working on. I repeat, that was strictly routine questioning. We are striving to be extremely thorough with our investigation."

"I'll take just one more question then we have to close and return to our work."

"Is it true you've brought a psychic in on this investigation?"

Dave and the others were floored. How could anyone possibly know about Jennifer Parker? He was at a loss for words.

Glen stepped up to the microphone.

"Jennifer Parker is a friend of mine. She helped me with a case about a missing child in Denver. She was curious about this case so I brought her along with me. We did not officially call in a psychic."

The crowd went crazy. Holyoke is a strong Christian community. The work of a psychic is considered the work of the devil by some. In any event, it was not a welcomed idea.

Questions continued to fly in Dave's direction. He refused to answer any more. He felt he gave them the most information he had available to him. There was nothing more he could share with them.

He and the three men left the gymnasium. Shelly was thinking ahead and slipped out with Jennifer before anyone noticed who she was. She wanted to spare her questions or harsh statements from those that did not understand the work of a true psychic. The exposure most people have to psychics consists of telephone psychics and fortunetellers at fairs, carnivals, and circuses.

"My, the crowd of people surprised me. I didn't expect your entire town to appear for your husband's talk tonight," said Jennifer.

Shelly looked at her, "I guess I'm surprised that anyone or anything can still surprise you. Glen has spoken highly of your abilities."

"My abilities do not allow me to know the future in great detail. I'm stronger at reading the present or sensing the needs and feelings of others. Sometimes, I can bring the two worlds together when the message is strong enough and the time is right."

"What two worlds?"

"The worlds of those in body and those no longer in body. The soul lives eternally, the body is just a temporary home for the soul."

The drive home was short. Jennifer and Shelly went into the house. Shelly needed some time to digest what Jennifer had told her. She was not sure she understood or believed what she was hearing.

Inside the house the men were sitting around the dining room table discussing the town meeting.

Martin took this time to make his announcement, "Dave, I think Eric and I are going to head home in the morning. There doesn't seem to be any work for us here. We'll remain just a phone call away if you need anything, but frankly we have no leads to follow. I hope you understand."

"Of course I do. You both have families in Denver that miss you. Trust me when I say I'm glad you two were here and you were a great help. I have the utmost respect for the work you do and how you handle yourselves. I appreciate that you worked with me, not above me. I'd like to say I hope I can work with you again in the future, but I really hope to see you in the future for a personal reason, not to share something as sad as the work we are facing here."

"Thanks for understanding," said Eric. "We'll leave first thing in the morning. Jennifer, it was a pleasure to meet you. Maybe we'll have an opportunity to work together someday. We can always use a good mind at CBI."

"Oh, and Mrs. Smith..." started Martin.

"Call me Shelly," she interrupted.

"Okay, Shelly, you were a very gracious hostess under the circumstances. I hope we weren't too great of a burden on you."

"No, not at all. I told you having you work here so I knew Dave was safe comforted me. Now how about that dessert that you all turned down before we went to the town meeting?"

Glen smiled.

Shelly looked at him, "No it's not cherry pie or chocolate pudding. It's ice-cream floats made with coke!!!"

She had the last laugh. Then she went to the kitchen and returned with a chocolate cake and a stack of dishes. Glen went back to the kitchen to help her with the coffee.

"You wouldn't have some herbal tea for Jennifer would you?" he asked.

"Open that drawer and help yourself."

Glen opened the drawer, and to his surprise, Shelly had an assortment of over twenty herbal teas. He then had to wonder if maybe he was the only person on earth who refused to drink herbal tea. He chose a few that sounded red by the description. He joined the rest for dessert and coffee.

"Jennifer, what did you think of the residents of our fine town?" asked Dave.

"They are frightened, that's for sure, but rightfully so. How sad to have a killer among you. To know one of your neighbors could be so cold and callused to kill men, women and children. It must be heart wrenching."

"Do you feel they have a killer among them?" asked Dave.

"What do you mean? You don't?" asked Jennifer.

"What I mean is we haven't ruled out a stranger, say a hunter or a houseguest of someone," answered Dave.

"Oh no, I just assumed you knew he was among the residents of the town," she answered.

Martin asked, "Are you saying our killer is a man?"
"Oh yes, and he was there tonight at your meeting," she responded.

Jennifer's bold statement took them by surprise. Dave was not impressed. Martin and Eric wanted to hear her out. Glen was hopeful.

Martin asked, "How did you know he was there?"

"That's easy," answered Dave before Jennifer had a chance to respond. "If we're talking about a local standing around watching his victims drop, of course he would want to be at the town meeting to see just how much we've learned about him."

"To answer your question, I could feel the energy of all those within the room. Most of the energy was nervous, frightened, energy. I would have a flash from time to time of contentment. Someone in that room was very happy with the fear he had caused in the community."

"How do you know it's a man?" asked Dave.

"When I would try to focus as the feeling of contentment would come to me. I would have glimpses of a hand with a syringe. At first I thought it could be a doctor or a nurse. Then as it happened over and over I could tell it was a man's hand, eliminating that of a nurse. Unless you have a male nurse here, but I assumed most small towns are not ready for male nurses."

Glen asked, "Can you tell us any more about this man?"

"Give me a break," said Dave as he got up to leave the room.

"I'm sorry," said Glen. "Don't say I didn't warn you."

"I know, that's okay. I'm not surprised," admitted Jennifer. "I'm afraid I can't tell you any more about this man at this time, and maybe never, unless I can be in the same room with him again. Maybe if I could visit the homes of the victims, I might be able to get in touch with their souls from the other side, to see what they experienced during their last hour."

Martin and Eric stepped out of the room leaving Glen, Jennifer and Shelly alone. They decided to stay at the motel one last night to free the spare guest room for Jennifer. While they were packing Shelly went to look for Dave.

He was in his office.

"Dave, what's going on? Why did you walk out like that? Don't you think that was a bit rude?" she scolded.

"Shelly, as if I don't have enough on my plate now, I have to open my home to some quack psychic. I can't believe Glen brought her here. I wonder if that was his intention all along when he tore out of here in such a hurry yesterday."

"I can't speak for Glen, and I surely don't know what his intentions were, but I do know that as long as she is our house guest she deserves the same respect as any other guest in our home."

"Okay, okay, I'll try to keep a civil tongue, but Glen had better not let her presence jeopardize this investigation."

Together they returned to the room with Glen and Jennifer. Glen knew that Jennifer was totally aware of Dave's feelings even before he mentioned them to her.

Martin and Eric appeared shortly after Dave and Shelly returned to the room. They were packed and ready to go. Dave walked them to the door. Glen excused himself from Jennifer to go along to say good-bye and to thank them for their help.

"Be sure to call us if you need us," reminded Martin.

"You'll be the first we call in for help. I promise," said Dave.

"Please call us with any new information, even if you don't need us. We're anxious to see how this case unfolds," suggested Eric.

They shook hands, then left for the motel.

"I wish they were leaving because the case was solved, not because it's a dead end," lamented Dave.

"We'll get there, Dave. This is not going to become an unsolved mystery. I can feel it," insisted Glen.

"Don't tell me you're getting in touch with your psychic side. I have to admit, Glen, I'm disappointed that you brought her here. I really can't deal with that psychic shit on one of my cases. Please keep her out of my way."

"I'll handle Jennifer," promised Glen. "She's very aware of your feelings and she won't do anything to embarrass you, or jeopardize this case. I can guarantee that."

Chapter 14

The next morning was Tuesday. As the kids were getting ready for school, there was a notice of school closing for the Holyoke schools on the radio. They were the only school closed.

It was obvious after the town meeting last night that the school board decided to close the school until further notice. Dave called them to be sure he was correct and he was. They felt in order to protect their kids there would be no more classes, or games until this was solved.

Sean and Anne whined with cabin fever. They didn't want to remain at home another day. Shelly suggested she take them to Fort Collins for a couple of days. Dave agreed. No sense keeping them prisoner in their own home. Besides, he didn't want any of this psychic stuff to rub off on them.

Glen assured Shelly he could handle the meals in her absence. Dave was not much of a cook. In the past, while she was away he ate all of his meals at the local café. Since Larry's death, the café's business was suffering. With the fear of targets on their backs, home with Glen's cooking it would be. Jennifer graciously offered to assist Glen.

Glen was right about Jennifer; she did not push herself or her abilities on Dave. She quietly absorbed their discussion about the case. As the hours passed, Dave's attitude towards Jennifer lightened. He relaxed enough to crack a couple of jokes in her presence.

To ease the mood even more, she told a few psychic jokes to show Dave she was able to laugh at herself.

"So, boss, how shall we use today?" asked Glen.

"I'm not quite sure. It's been pretty quiet around here lately. Have you noticed that since last Friday night there have been no more deaths?"

"Yeah, I was thinking the same thing. But then, there hasn't been the opportunity. All of the community dinners have been cancelled. Sounds like the games have been cancelled. The café is about ready to close their doors and the schools are closed. Not much of a chance for our killer to strike at a public setting with food available," said Glen.

"Is this going to present a problem for you two?" asked Jennifer.

"What do you mean?" asked Dave.

"How will you flush him out?" she asked.

"I'm not sure, I was having the same thought. What if town closes down like this for a few weeks. What's to stop him from striking again once things return to normal? Without any new attempts we can't catch him in

291

the act. He might not surface for a long time. I'm not sure how long the town can go on in hibernation mode."

Glen and Dave took Jennifer downtown to show her Holyoke's main street. It was quiet. The weather was warming up. The snow was melting on the streets. Typically, on a day like today the town would be buzzing with people. Most of the street was empty similar to a Sunday morning.

The grocery store parking lot was empty. Dave and Glen walked through the store with Jennifer in case there was something special she wanted to purchase, since she would not be joining them with their meat dinners.

The store's owner walked up to Dave.

"Sure hope you can solve this, and fast. I have no customers. Everyone's going to Wal Mart in Sterling to buy their groceries; they feel it's safer. I thought my shelves of canned goods would be selling out first thing this morning, but people are even worried about those. After what you said last night I thought I'd be selling dry goods as well, but no such luck. I'm just not selling anything."

"I'm sorry, I wish I could say we're close to putting an end to this, but we're not," said Dave sadly.

"Where are your CBI guys?"

"They headed back this morning, their work here was done. Until something new happens there's nothing more they can accomplish here."

"Ain't that like a couple of city cops. A person dying isn't enough to keep them interested. They want some big crime or they're disappointed and go home."

"Well, it's not really that way. They were here to assist me with whatever lab equipment and crime scene help I needed. I couldn't give them any work, so they went home. If I need them, they'll be back."

Jennifer and Glen browsed the store shelves for ingredients for her meals. She filled her cart mostly with the produce. Small town inventory for fruits and vegetables did not compare to the larger organic stores that she was accustomed to in Denver.

Dave followed them through the checkout stand. His thoughts went back to Jonathon. If they could've caught this guy, maybe Jonathon would still be alive. He'd be the one checking out the groceries this very moment.

Jennifer turned to Dave, "I'm sure Jonathon is aware of the way you're feeling. He'd want you not to blame yourself."

Dave looked at her, stunned.

She finished her business at the checkout, grabbed a bag, while Glen grabbed the others. Dave stayed behind staring at her as she walked to his car.

Before Dave went to join them he saw Tim's mother approaching his car. She walked behind Jennifer. Jennifer turned to her.

"Are you the psychic everyone's talking about?" she asked.

'Well, I suppose so," Jennifer answered.

"I need to know, is Tim okay?" she asked.

"Was Tim your son?"

"Yes, please let me know if he's okay."

"Ma'am, I'm not sure I can do that. Do you have anything that belonged to Tim with you, or perhaps a picture?"

Tim's mother opened her purse. She took out a photo of Tim. She looked at her son with sadness then handed the photo to Jennifer.

Jennifer felt the mother's anguish. She held the photograph firmly between her hands. Nothing. She felt nothing.

"I'm sorry, I'm just not getting anything." She handed the photograph back.

"Wait, wait here," begged Tim's mother. She ran back to her car. She opened the trunk. Inside were boxes of Tim's clothes. She was on her way to donate them to the needy. She took out his favorite letter jacket. She rushed back to Jennifer with the jacket.

Jennifer took the jacket from her. She held it then handed it to Glen. She removed her own coat, trading that for Tim's jacket. Wearing Tim's jacket she could feel his energy. She could feel Tim. Tim was with them. She could see him standing near his mother. A smile came across her face. Jennifer watched as Tim brushed the hair from his mother's forehead. Tim's mom reached up and touched the hair that moved on her forehead thinking it was the wind.

Jennifer wanted Tim to show her his last moments. He died rather quickly. He struggled for air, he was frightened, and then suddenly there was a peaceful passing. He was gone before he dropped to the floor. Jennifer's body jerked as she experienced Tim hitting the floor.

"Are you alright?" asked Glen. He'd seen first hand when Jennifer has the ability to connect, sometimes it is very draining for her.

The sound of Glen's voice brought her back.

"Ma'am your son was here with us. He spends a good deal of time with you. He knows you are not yet ready to let him go completely. When he feels the time is right, he'll move on. I watched him gently caress your forehead, moving your hair. His passing was quick. He was afraid at first, because he could not breathe, but death came quickly and his passing turned peaceful moments before the end."

Dave walked up to the car to witness the event. He wasn't quite sure what to say. He knew Tim's family was still angry with him, so he prepared to be reprimanded, in one way or another.

Tim's mother turned to him, she took his hands in hers, "Thank you Dave for bringing this woman to us. She says Tim is fine. I know he's with me and he's fine. That's the best any mother could hope for. Had you not brought her here I would forever be wondering about my son. Thank you." She squeezed his hands.

Jennifer removed the jacket and returned it to her. Glen noticed she was trembling. He quickly helped her into her own coat and rubbed her shoulders in an attempt to remove the chill from her body. Her body was not responding to the weather; it was trembling from the experience.

Inside the car, Dave turned to Jennifer seated in the back. "Thanks for telling her that. I'm sure you know it made her feel better. I only wish I could've made them feel better sooner."

"You're welcome, but I only told her the truth. Her son is with her. I saw him."

Dave could not respond. He started the engine, and then they drove home to put away the groceries.

When they pulled into Dave's driveway there was a boy sitting on their step waiting for them. He approached them as they left the car.

"If you're here to see Sean or Anne, they went to Sterling today, with their mother," said Dave.

"No sir, I'd like to talk to you," he said.

"Oh sure, come on in out of the cold," said Dave curious about this boy.

He followed them into the house.

"Can I get you something to drink?" asked Glen.

"No thank you," answered the nervous boy.

"What can I help you with?" asked Dave.

"Well sir, you said if anyone had any information that he should come forward, and I'm well...I'm not sure... Maybe I shouldn't bother you." He turned to walk away.

"No, wait, sit down. Start by telling us your name," encouraged Dave.

Glen piped in, "You can remain anonymous if you choose."

"Oh yeah," agreed Dave. "We can keep your name out of this if you want."

"I'd like that," he started. "My name is Robert, but I'd prefer you didn't tell anyone about today or that I ever talked to you."

Dave's curiosity was aroused. "Sure, Robert, you've got it. We won't say a word. Tell us what you've got."

Robert stammered, he couldn't find the words to begin.

Glen started for him.

"Robert, did you know any of the victims?"

"Yes, I knew all of them. Well, not very well, I mean, I guess I didn't really know them. I just knew who they were. Except for Jonathon, we were pretty good friends. I was with him when he died."

Glen continued, "Are you here to tell us something about Jonathon's death?"

"I'm not sure. I think maybe Jonathon committed suicide or something."

Now their interests were really peaked.

"Let's start back at the beginning here, okay Robert?" asked Dave.

Robert, even more nervous than before, started again, "Jonathon was feeling really bad the day he died. He was upset with the way everyone in the town was treating him after you took him in for questioning. I think he was too upset to handle it and killed himself."

Dave and Glen exchanged glances. Could this be the lead they've been hoping for?

Robert, you are aware that Jonathon died from liquid nicotine aren't you?" asked Dave.

"Yes, sir, I am."

"Well then, Robert, do you know if Jonathon had access to liquid nicotine?"

"Yes, sir, he did."

Dave wiped his mouth. He paced around the room, wringing his hands. This kid, this mere boy sitting in his kitchen, at this very moment, might hold the key to crack this case wide open. He wanted to approach this very carefully.

"Do your parents know you're here?"

"No sir."

"Would you like to have them here?" asked Dave.

"No, sir, I'd rather not. You said I could remain anonymous. You aren't going to call them are you?" he asked in a panic, standing to leave.

"No, no Robert, I won't call them if you don't want me to. I do want to record this talk if that's okay with you. I won't use your name I just want to get all of the facts. Miss Parker and Glen here will be witnesses that you gave this information voluntarily. Is all of this still okay with you?" asked Dave.

"Sure I guess, as long as you don't call my parents and you don't use my name," agreed Robert.

Dave went to his office for his tape recorder. Jennifer went to the refrigerator for iced tea. She poured a glass for the nervous young man. His hand trembled as he took the glass from her. Glen stood behind him rubbing his shoulders trying to relax and reassure him.

With the tape recorder on Dave began, "Tell us how Jonathon had access to liquid nicotine."

"A few weeks ago I went to his house. We had plans for the day. He said he couldn't go until he finished what he was working on. He was searching on the Internet. I asked what he was searching for; I thought I could help him. At first, he didn't want to tell me. Then he told me he was doing a search for liquid nicotine. When I asked him for what, he didn't answer. So I sat there watching him do a search. When he found a number of places that sold it he tried to buy some. Most of the places wouldn't sell to him because he wasn't a doctor or pharmacist, they wanted a license number before they'd let him place an order. Finally, he found a spot from some other country. I don't remember where.

299

Anyway, he could buy it from them. He filled out the form to place the order. He gave them his credit card number. That part surprised me. I didn't even know he had a credit card. Just the week before we wanted to buy a software program from Ebay and he had to ask his parents to do it because it required a credit card. So he placed the order, then we left."

"Did he tell you when it arrived?" asked Glen.

"Nope."

"Did you two ever discuss it again?" asked Dave.

"Nope. I never thought about it again until my parents came home from that meeting last night talking about liquid nicotine in the food."

"Did you say anything to your parents about what you just told us?" asked Dave.

"Nope, I thought maybe they'd think I had something to do with it or something. You know how parents are. They complained about me hanging around with Jonathon because of his Mohawk. But he was really cool. He was smart, and funny. He was the best friend I ever had."

"Is there anything else you have to tell us?"

"Nope. Do you think Jonathon had anything to do with the nicotine stuff getting into the other food?"

"I'm not sure at this point, do you think he could've done that?"

"Nope, I think he could've hurt himself, but I don't think he'd ever hurt anyone else. Not Jonathon, he was the nicest guy I knew. He'd even stop on the street to move a baby bird into a bush to give it a chance. He was friendly to everyone. He was a little shy sometimes, but no, I don't think he could. Can I go now?"

"Sure Robert, but one last thing. We will need a phone number where you can be reached," requested Dave.

"Here's my cell number." He had it on a card in his pocket for his small computer website business.

Dave walked him to the door.

"Whew! What do you think of that?" he asked.

"I can't believe we might have our first lead. I just hope the boy was being honest and that he's not covering for someone," said Glen.

"Oh, he's being honest alright," said Jennifer.

They both wanted to believe her.

"Where do you want to go from here?" asked Glen.

"We need to get into Jonathon's computer without causing too much suspicion to check out this story. No offense Jennifer," he said.

"None taken," she smiled.

Dave called Jonathon's home; there was no answer.

"Let's take a drive over to see if they might be shoveling snow or something," suggested Dave.

Glen knew it was wishful thinking, but agreed sitting around waiting would be too difficult. Together the three of them climbed back into the car to drive to

Jonathon's house. There was no sign of his parents anywhere. Dave walked around behind the house just to be sure. His impatience was showing.

A neighbor, looking through the window, came to her door. "They've left town," she informed them.

"Do you know when they'll be back?" asked Dave.

"About a week or so. They went back to her parent's house for the holidays. They go every year when school gets out. This year they went early. Since...well...you know, Jonathon and all."

"Great, just great. We get our first solid lead then we run into this snag," complained Dave.

"So how do you handle a matter like this in a small town. Do you need to get a warrant and a locksmith?" asked Glen.

"Well, I was hoping to have the cooperation of the parents. I really wanted to keep this quiet. I didn't want to include others in this computer search," moaned Dave.

Dave looked at his watch. It was too late in the day to get a warrant. He glanced hopefully at the house. Chances are someone has a key besides the family that lives there. Maybe even the neighbor that seems to know their business. He had to play by the rules even if it meant waiting until morning.

Reluctantly they drove back to Dave's house to wait until morning. Glen and Jennifer prepared supper, while Dave went into his office to do an Internet search for liquid nicotine to see if he could find the same link that Jonathon may have found.

Glen asked Jennifer, "Any vibes I should know about?"

She smiled at him; she knew he wanted to believe in her. She could feel he did, more and more as time went on.

"While we were at that boy's house I could sense the sadness that his parents had been feeling. The house radiated with love. That boy and his parents had a good relationship. I couldn't feel his presence there. I'd have to say he's with his parents."

"But, could you tell if we were on the right track?"

"I feel the end is near, so I guess if you go with that feeling, then yes. I'd have to say you are probably on the right track."

"Do you see any more deaths?"

"Glen, you are asking a lot of me. I told you I'm not into fortune telling. Sometimes, it's not good to see what life holds in its future, it is better to play it out as planned."

"Does that mean you believe in fate or predestination?"

"Not exactly, we have free will. I believe we're born with the knowledge of our past and future within us. The problem lies in retrieving the information. Sometimes it's not clear to us until death."

"What good is it then?"

"Life is a learning center. You take with you the knowledge of life's experience, then when you choose to come back again, you will be more aware than the previous time."

"What do you mean, when we come back? Are you saying you believe in re-incarnation?"

"Glen, it doesn't matter what I believe in or what I know, it matters only what *you* believe in, know, and learn in this lifetime. Search for answers within yourself."

Jennifer continued to prepare the salad while Glen warmed up the spaghetti leftovers for Dave and himself. Glen stopped asking Jennifer questions. He needed time to absorb and process what she was telling him. He was glad that Dave was not there with them.

Jennifer knew that Glen was processing. She smiled to herself. She knew her work with Glen was helpful in a way he could not and would not understand now, but that it would become clearer to him in the future.

The table was set. The spaghetti was ready. Jennifer took the hot rolls from the oven. Glen poured iced tea for all three of them. When all was finished, he left the kitchen to tell Dave dinner was served.

"Hey Dave, let's eat."

"Glen, check this out. Look how many places sell this stuff. Look how many hits I got. Fortunately, not one of them will sell to me without some sort of medical license. I wonder how many links Jonathon had to go through before he found one that would allow illegal sales?"

Glen stepped behind Dave to read the screen over his shoulder.

"Scary as hell, isn't it?"

He slapped Dave across the back, "Let's eat."

Dave rose from his chair slowly, forcing his eyes to leave the screen. This was the closest they'd come to cracking this case. Food was not foremost in his thoughts.

Jennifer was seated waiting for them when they arrived in the kitchen. The salad Jennifer prepared was in itself a meal. She had a generous portion while the two men barely touched the salad. They consumed all the spaghetti that Shelly had left. The dinner rolls that Jennifer made were also gone as quickly as the main course.

Jennifer ate slowly. She watched both men. They barely spoke to each other. Dave had his mind on his Internet search while Glen had his mind on his soul search. Life is good when one is learning, thought Jennifer.

Dave's computer beckoned him to return to his office. He stood to begin clearing plates. Glen knew Dave was accustomed to getting up from the table and returning to work without clearing his place.

"We'll handle this," said Glen. "You go to your office, you have work to do."

Jennifer and Glen cleared the table and cleaned the kitchen.

"I think I'll excuse myself now to take a bath. Afterwards, I plan to go to bed early. I have some reading to do. I'll see the two of you in the morning. Good night."

"Good night Jennifer. Just yell if you need something. I'm sure between the two of us we can figure out where Shelly keeps most anything."

Glen went off to his room. He called Debbie. He was excited to tell her about their breakthrough in the case. She was happy for him. She was happy for herself. She hoped this would bring him home sooner. After they said their good-byes, Glen laid his head back onto his pillow to think.

The sun shining into the bedroom window woke Glen. He'd slept the entire night without being aware of being asleep. He woke tired. Jennifer and Dave were nearly finished with breakfast when he entered the kitchen.

"I was beginning to think you were our latest victim," teased Dave.

"Did you have a pleasant journey in your sleep?" asked Jennifer.

"Uh, yeah, I guess. I fell asleep so quickly and slept so soundly that I feel as though I just closed my eyes for a quick moment, then it was morning."

"Eat up quickly. I want to get to my office. I need that warrant today. I'm hoping that neighbor can let us in. I want some progress now," said Dave.

"I'll just have a cup of coffee. I'm not hungry. Just give me a couple of minutes to shave and brush my teeth and I'll be ready."

Glen kept his word. In record time he was clean-shaven and ready to go. They grabbed their coats wasting no time getting into the car.

Dave kept a close watch on the time. The moment he could get into the courthouse for a warrant, he'd be there. He busied himself with accumulated paperwork on his desk. The calls had nearly stopped. There were no more deaths. He was hoping to get his answers to the questions that had been haunting them soon. Maybe, just maybe, life could be back to normal in Holyoke, Colorado before Christmas.

Dave had his warrant; the three of them were standing outside at Jonathon's house. Dave knocked on the neighbor's door.

The same woman came to the door.

"Can I help you?" she asked.

"Yes, ma'am. Do you happen to have a key to your neighbor's house?"

"No, sir, I don't."

"Do you know where I can find a key to their house? Maybe the neighbors on the other side?"

"No, sir, I don't think they have one either."

"Do you know if they have one under a mat or flower pot or hidden somewhere else in the yard?"

"No, sir, I don't think so. They never lock their house."

"Okay, thank you."

Dave rushed back to Glen and Jennifer waiting patiently on the steps. "We're in!"

"Great. She must've had the key then?" asked Glen.

"Nope, she said they never lock their house."

He tried the door. She was right. They walked in.

Antique furniture filled the house. Jennifer busied herself picking up one small piece after another. Occasionally, she would get a glimpse of the past and the previous owner. Although amusing to her, she did not share what she was doing with the two men.

Dave and Glen found their way through the house to Jonathon's room. Swiftly the computer was turned on to reveal their first problem. Jonathon had a password.

"Damn," said Dave.

Jennifer heard him; following the sound of his voice she entered the room.

"What seems to be the problem?" she asked.

"Jonathon has his computer password protected," explained Glen.

"May I try?" she asked.

"Sure, have at it," said Dave as he disgustedly pushed off in the chair.

Jennifer sat at the computer. She touched many items on the desk. She ran her fingers over the keys. In total silence she sat with her fingers on the keys. She stared at the screen requesting the password. Finally, without looking at the keys, her fingers began to type. She was unaware of the letters she was striking, but whatever she typed worked. The computer was now accessible.

"How in the hell did you manage that?" asked Dave.

Glen smiled proudly. Had he not brought Jennifer back to Holyoke with him, they may never have gotten the password to enter Jonathon's computer. They would have had to turn it over to CBI to break the password, which could have taken days or weeks.

Dave noticed the grin on Glen's face and returned that look with a half smile, half smirk. He sat at the computer again. He immediately logged onto the Internet. As he typed the words for liquid nicotine, it came up before he had a chance to continue the spelling. That proved, without a shadow of a doubt, that what Robert had told them was the truth. Jonathon had done a search for liquid nicotine.

While Dave tried to follow the history of connections and links Glen searched the desk. He was not sure what he was looking for; he hoped to find something to link the purchase of liquid nicotine to Jonathon.

309

"Bingo!" said Glen.

"What? What did you find?" asked Dave with enthusiasm.

"Looks like we have a Visa number and expiration date scribbled on this sheet of paper."

Jennifer stood back watching the detectives do their work. She was pleased to see how they used their psychic abilities to draw them to the right spots, but sad they were unaware that they possessed such abilities beyond the average person. Having psychic ability is probably what drew them into police work to begin with. Among cops, though, it's called "gut instinct".

Dave pulled out his notebook and dialed Martin's cell phone.

"Hello," said Martin.

"Martin, Dave here. We've finally had a break. I need you to run a check on this Visa number. He gave Martin the number. How soon can we have the results on that?"

"I should be able to give you a call back in less than thirty minutes. What kind of breakthrough did you have?"

"After our town meeting, one of the kids in town came forward. He told us that his friend, one of the vics, was searching for liquid nicotine on his computer. He watched him do it. He also watched him place an order for it. We're sitting at the computer right now. There's evidence that the search indeed happened. Now, we need to find out who this credit card belongs to. The boy we spoke with said his friend didn't have a credit card."

"Good work, Dave, I'm happy for you. Sounds like the break you've needed all along. Have there been any more deaths?"

"Nope, not since the last two boys."

"Was one of the boys the owner of the computer you're using?"

"Yes, what are you getting at?"

"Wasn't he the same boy whose fingerprints were on the yogurt container?"

"Yes, my God. We had him in for questioning. Since he died there have been no more deaths. His friend said he thought he committed suicide."

"My guess is you guys may have found your killer. I'd say his conscience got the best of him after he'd killed so many people, he committed suicide."

"That's so hard to believe. He was such a great kid. I'd have been proud to have him as my son."

"One never knows what goes on inside the head of a depressed person. They're masters at showing the world what it wants to see on the outside, while living in torment on the inside."

"Let me know what you find out about that card number."

"Okay. Bye"

"I don't agree with your friend Martin," said Jennifer. "This boy was not your killer. This boy was a victim."

"I really do appreciate all of your help, Jennifer, but the evidence is growing against this kid. I hate to admit he's responsible, but for the moment it all points to him," said Dave.

Dave went back to the computer to see if he could find the company that filled the order for Jonathon. Glen continued to search the room, hoping to find a receipt or some other tangible piece of evidence to link Jonathon to the purchase of the substance.

Jennifer busied herself wandering around Jonathon's room getting to know him. She was more convinced than ever that she was right. She also knew that in time the two detectives would be forced to agree with her.

In less time than expected Dave's cell phone rang.

"I have your visa cardholder's name. Are you ready?"

With pen in hand Dave said, "Shoot."

"According to our search the man's name is Richard Callister. Do you know him? That name sounds familiar to me."

"Yeah, I know him. That's coach Callister. He's the one who was in the car with Tim's parents when his body was exhumed."

"Well, I guess you need to tell him this kid used his card to buy an illegal substance."

"Thanks Martin, we'll head right over to his house."

"Good luck, and keep us informed."

Chapter 15

Dave shut off the computer. Glen closed the drawers and tidied up the desk. Jennifer rearranged a few things on the desk to return them to their normal positions. She knew better than the men where they belonged.

On the drive to Coach Callister's house, Jennifer had an overwhelming urge to not go along. She was drawn back to Dave's house. Following her instincts, she requested they drop her off at Dave's on their way to Coach Callister's house. They did.

She paced inside the house not knowing why she was drawn back to it. She checked the phone for messages. Nothing. She went to her room and unpacked her cell phone. She checked it for messages, nothing. She was becoming more uneasy by the minute. She was losing focus. Back in her room, she unpacked an assortment of candles and her stash of herbal tea.

She warmed a cup of water in the microwave while she drew a bath. She arranged the candles around the tub, closing the shade on the window. She slipped into the tub with her tea and lighted candles close by. She needed to relax and focus. She was certain that police work was not her life's ambition. She was a teacher, a guide for the soul. This was too depressing for her.

Dave and Glen rang the bell at the coach's house. There was no answer, so Dave rang it again. Still no answer, so he rang once more.

"Come on, come on you have to be home," he said nervously, shaking his leg with impatience.

Glen paced back and forth across the sidewalk. He glanced at the garage. He saw a window and peered inside.

"Hey, there's a car in here. He must be home."

"Maybe he walked into town or left with someone," said Dave.

"Yeah, maybe."

Glen remained impatient. He walked around the house. He heard a radio playing. There were lights on when he looked into the window. Then he heard the start of running water in a shower.

He ran back to the front of the house.

"He's home, or at least someone is. There are lights on, the radio is playing and I can hear a shower."

"There's laws against being a peeping Tom," teased Dave trying to relax himself.

He tried the door. It wasn't locked. He looked at Glen hoping for a look of approval to enter the house.

"What if it's his wife? I'd hate to startle some woman taking a shower with two men walking in on her," worried Glen.

"He's not married, his wife left him a year ago."

"That's too bad."

"Let's go in."

The two men let themselves into the coach's living room. They tried not to snoop without a warrant, and without his permission. They sat on a couple of easy chairs in the living room. For a bachelor he kept his place pretty neat and tidy. He didn't have much furniture, but it looked nice.

"He must read a lot, living alone and all," said Glen as he thumbed through a computer magazine.

The water stopped. Dave stood up. He walked in the direction the sound of the water had come from.

"Coach, hey coach. It's Dave Smith. I tried the bell, but you didn't answer so I let myself in."

"Hi Dave, make yourself comfortable, I'll be right in."

After what seemed eternity, he walked into the living room still in his bathrobe.

"What can I do for you two gentlemen," he said as he looked at Glen.

"We need to talk to you, if you have a few minutes," said Dave.

"I have a doctor appointment in a few minutes. Can it wait until later?"

"This shouldn't take very long, it's really important," continued Dave.

"Well, if it's important. Can I get you two something to drink? A beer, or coffee, or tea, or something?"

"No thanks, we don't want to use up any more of your time than we have to. Don't want to make you too late for that appointment."

"Sure, right. Okay, what can I help you with?"

"We may have some bad news for you. Do you know Jonathon Duell?"

"Yes, I know who he is, or I mean was. The kid with the Mohawk."

"Do you have any idea why he would have your credit card number?"

"My credit card number?"

"Yes, seems he placed an Internet order using your credit card."

Glen remained silent watching and listening. His eyes continued to scan the room; more as a habit from being a detective than to really hope to find anything.

"Oh yes, on Ebay. I'm not very good with computers and I knew Jonathon was a whiz. You know the nerdy types can really be an asset when you need help with computer stuff."

"So you were aware that he had your credit card number?"

"Of course, I gave it to him myself. I jotted it down on a piece of colored paper from my little desk pad. Is that what you're talking about?"

"Yes, that's it. Why did you give him your credit card number?"

"I needed to make some purchases, I heard you could find things that are less expensive if you shop for them on Ebay. I asked him to search for a few items for me, and if he found them to bid on them. I really couldn't begin to figure that out. I can barely turn my computer on. I gave him the number and told him if he got the bid to make the purchase for me. Did he do something wrong with my number?"

"Well, that's what we're trying to figure out. Do you have your credit card statements so that we can look through them? Have you noticed any unusual charges?"

"Can't say that I pay any attention, I just pay the bill. My ex-wife still uses it. I agreed to help her get re-established so she makes an occasional purchase with it and I just pay. She's never abused the privilege."

"He looked at his watch, I really should get going. Can we finish this later?"

Glen finally joined the conversation. "I'm sorry, Mr. Callister, but this can't wait. Could you possibly postpone your appointment so we can get this matter cleared up as soon as possible? It's very important."

The coach looked angry.

"Of course, if you insist. I guess Doc will understand. It's too bad you don't put this same enthusiasm into figuring out how to stop people from dying in this town."

Dave was set back, first by Glen not wanting to work with the coach, and secondly by the coache's quick anger.

When the coach walked across the room to his desk to look for his statements Dave shot a curious glance at Glen.

Glen's return glare told Dave that something wasn't setting right with Glen.

"May I use your bathroom?" asked Glen.

"Sure, second door, down the hall on the right," directed the coach without looking up from his task of sorting papers.

Glen went down the hall. He didn't go into the bathroom, he opened all of the hall doors peering inside. One of the doors led to the coach's office containing his computer. The room was just as tidy as the other. There were rows and rows of computer games and software disks. There were manuals and computer magazines everywhere.

"For someone who doesn't know anything about computers he sure has a shitload of programs and games here," whispered Glen to himself.

He moved the mouse and the screen turned from black to his desktop. The desktop was covered with icons. He tried to do an Internet search. The sound of the computer logging on was loud. Glen closed the door to avoid the other men from hearing him. He wanted to see if the coach, by chance, had done a search for liquid nicotine. His hunch was right. An ill feeling came over Glen.

He sat in the chair, searching his emails. He couldn't find anything incriminating. Then he saw there was an email still in the draft folder that had not been sent out.

In the living room Coach was not having any luck finding his credit card statement.

"Maybe it's in my office. Do you mind if I get dressed? I'll call Doc's office from my bedroom, and then check my office. Make yourself at home, I'll be right back."

"Sure, take your time, I'm sorry we had to impose on you like this," Dave apologized.

Coach went into his bedroom. The bedroom was connected through the master bathroom to his office. Glen was supposed to be using the guest bathroom.

Inside his bedroom, the coach put on the clothes he had laid out on the bed. Then he searched through his drawers. He walked through the bathroom towards his office. He stopped to listen at the door. He could hear someone in his office. His desk chair had a distinct squeak to it. He slowly opened the door. He saw Glen reading his email.

With silent precision he raised his arm and fired. Glen dropped to the floor. Coach ran back into his bedroom.

"What the hell?" asked Dave as he drew his gun. He ran down the hall not sure which room to search first. He opened door after door approaching with caution. The third door he opened was to the coach's office. Glen lay on the floor with a gunshot wound to the head. He rushed to him to check for a pulse. He found a faint pulse.

"Hang in there, Buddy." His eyes scanned the room. He closed the door to the room so he could call for help before going after the coach. Bent over Glen, shaking, he raised his hand to his shoulder to key his radio. A second shot rang from the same direction as the first. Dave was unaware that the door leading to the bathroom was anything more than a closet door. He only needed a few seconds to call for help before pursuing the coach. Those seconds were ripped from him as the bullet from the coach's gun ripped through his chest. He fell over Glen. Coach entered the room to delete the email draft that Glen had been reading when Dave struggled to raise his gun, shooting the coach before he fell into unconsciousness.

All was quiet. Three men lay bleeding with gunshot wounds and no one had been alerted. The few precious seconds needed to make that radio call were lost.

Back at Dave's house Jennifer felt ill. Panic swept through her every cell. Something terrible has happened. She knew it, something terrible, but where and to whom?

She climbed from the tub feeling weak. Her head was spinning. She felt herself at the threshold of fainting. She gathered herself up enough to get to the sink. She turned on the cold water. She tried to chill her hands, then her face. She needed to bring herself out of the faint.

"Hello, we're home. Is anyone here?" called Shelly.

"In here," called Jennifer with a weak voice.

Shelly didn't hear her. She proceeded to put away the groceries. Anne went down the hall to use the bathroom. The door was closed so she knocked, not expecting a response, she opened the door without allowing enough time for a weakened Jennifer to respond. Just as Jennifer opened her mouth to speak to Anne, she collapsed.

"Mom! Hurry, come quick!" screamed Anne.

"What on earth are you screaming about?" she scolded as she ran down the hall.

When she got to the bathroom door she saw Jennifer crumpled on the floor. Shelly went to her. She felt for a pulse.

"Anne, go call 911."

She propped towels under Jennifer's head. She arranged the towel she was wearing to cover her. By that time, Sean was at the door.

"What happened? Mom, is she going to be alright?" he asked.

"I'm not sure," said Shelly frightened.

A moan came from Jennifer, quickly followed by another. She opened her eyes to see Shelly, Anne and Sean standing over her.

"Are you okay?" asked Shelly.

"Yes, I felt faint. I guess I passed out," she answered.

"Anne, go call 911 and cancel the call, I think she just fainted. By the look of the steam in this room, my guess is her water was too hot and she stayed in the tub too long. She should be fine once the room cools off."

Shelly helped Jennifer to her feet. They rearranged her towel again, then Shelly walked her to the guestroom. She guided her into the chair, then left to get a glass of cold water for her.

When she returned with the water Jennifer was more herself. She sipped the cool water then stood to dress herself. Shelly left the room to continue putting the groceries away. She called Dave at his office to let him know what happened. The dispatcher told her he left early this morning and hadn't returned.

Shelly glanced at the clock; it was nearly lunchtime. She knew Glen and Dave would be coming in any minute. She hurried herself to prepare lunch. She called for Anne to set the table.

After a few minutes Jennifer appeared in the kitchen. She was relieved to see them setting the table, that meant Dave and Glen were either in the house or on their way.

"Are you feeling better?" asked Shelly.

"Yes, I'm so sorry I frightened you. I had this terrible feeling come over me while I was in the tub. I panicked. I needed to find out what went wrong. Maybe you're right, maybe it was the hot water. Where are the men?"

"I'm expecting them any time now. I bought fruit and veggies for you while I was in Sterling, there's a larger selection there."

"Thanks," said Jennifer as she watched out the window for Dave's car to pull into the driveway.

She was returning to herself. She felt in total control again. This time she was not in a tub of hot water. While thinking about Glen and Dave, she became ill again. She reached for the table.

Shelly saw her. She went to her, seating her carefully at the table.

"Maybe you should just sit for a while longer until you feel better. Let me fix you something to eat."

"Have you spoken to Glen or Dave since you returned?"

"No, they weren't at the office. But don't worry, they should be here any minute. Dave hates to miss a meal."

"Please call them. I need you to call them."

Shelly looked at Jennifer. She realized she was seriously concerned about the men. Normally, Shelly might not have been as eager to jump to conclusions, but when you have a psychic sitting at your table telling you something might be wrong you listen.

She dialed Dave's cell phone. He didn't answer. She tried his office again, but the dispatcher still had not heard from him.

"Could you call him on his radio, please?"

She knew if he was at the hospital visiting with Doc about the case, he'd have his phone turned off.

"Sorry Shelly, I'm not getting a response. Would you like me to keep trying?"

"Yes, please do. Ask him to call me as soon as you reach him."

Jennifer listened to Shelly's conversation. Her feelings of uneasiness mounted. The men were in trouble; she could feel it.

"Do you know where Coach...umm....Coach...?"

"Coach Jones?" asked Shelly.

"No, that doesn't sound right, it was a different name. He's retired now." Jennifer told her.

"Oh, you mean Coach Callister?" she asked.

"Yes, yes, that's it Coach Callister. Do you know where he lives?"

"Sure he lives on the edge of town. Why?"

"When the guys dropped me off here, they were heading to his house to ask him some questions. Why don't you try calling them there."

"Okay." Shelly looked up his phone number.

Ring…ring…ring…there was no answer.

By that time Jennifer had grabbed her coat and Shelly's, "Let's drive over there."

"If there's no answer, then they most likely are not there," Shelly pointed out.

"Trust me on this, please Shelly. We have to go to the coach's house and fast."

Now Shelly was frightened. She ran to her car breathlessly with Jennifer at her heels. Once inside Shelly backed into the street as fast as she could turn the wheels on the wet pavement. The snow and ice packed roads were still melting.

She drove as if she were on a high-speed chase to the coach's house. Dave's car was in the driveway. She leaped out of the car running to the door. She paused to knock.

"Just go in, don't bother to knock," said Jennifer, climbing the stairs behind her.

Shelly opened the door. She called out, " Is anyone here?"

There was no answer. Jennifer had already begun opening doors checking rooms.

"Oh my God, Shelly call for an ambulance, quick!" yelled Jennifer.

Shelly could not help herself. She ran into the room with Jennifer. Dave, Glen and the Coach were piled on the floor in a large pool of blood. Jennifer pushed her out of the room.

"Call for an ambulance. Now!" she screamed.

One by one, Jennifer rolled back the bodies. The coach had no pulse. Dave was on top of Glen. She rolled him over gently. She felt for a pulse. At first she couldn't feel one. She noticed when she rolled him over he took a breath. He must still be hanging on by a thread. She examined Glen next. She was able to find a weak pulse, though his breathing was very shallow.

The amount of blood loss at the scene was staggering. Jennifer's clothes were saturated as she knelt next to the men. When she stood up to check for the ambulance, she had difficulty walking through the lake of blood on the floor without slipping.

She met a distraught Shelly coming back into the room.

"I called for an ambulance. Is Dave alive?"

"Yes, I believe so. I'm sure Glen is as well, but the coach didn't make it."

Shelly ran into the room to be with her husband. She slipped in the blood. She fell on the floor face to face with the coach. She closed her eyes as she raised her bloodstained body up off of the floor.

Jennifer went back into the room. She focused on the scene. She could see the coach shooting Dave. She

327

focused harder. Glen had been hit first. He must have found something on the computer. She could feel his adrenaline had risen. She looked at the screen. It was blank. She touched the mouse. A letter appeared as an email.

To whom it may concern,

If you are reading this I must be dead. Let me explain. First of all, I wish I could say I am sorry for the pain and suffering I caused the families in Holyoke, but I'm not.

Jennifer stopped reading the letter, she heard the ambulance and police cars outside. She quickly hit the print command. She knew once the police arrived this would be a crime scene and she wouldn't be part of it.

While the EMT's busied themselves with the victims, she took the sheet of paper from the printer, stuffing it into her shirt.

Shelly walked beside of the stretcher carrying Dave. Jennifer did the same for Glen. The body of the coach was zipped into a black bag before being carried out.

Doc came to Shelly while she sat frantically waiting with Jennifer, "Shelly, I have to be honest with you it looks bad, it looks really bad."

Jennifer held Shelly while she sobbed. Her kids were on their way.

"What about Glen? How bad is it for him?" asked Jennifer.

"I'm afraid he's not much better than Dave. He doesn't appear to have lost as much blood, but he has a head wound. Even if he recovers I'm not sure how much permanent damage has been done."

"Can I see him?" asked Shelly.

"Sure, you can sit with him if you'd like."

Jennifer thought it would be best to call Debbie now. She knew she would want to be with Glen. She didn't have her handbag with her to look up their home phone. Then she remembered they had cell phones and the numbers were very close together. She asked if she could have Glen's cell phone. She went outdoors. She dialed her own cell phone number from Glen's. That gave her his number on her caller ID. She focused and could then remember the change in the last two digits of Debbie's number.

She paced out in the cold without a coat. It was so blood-soaked she took it off at the house not wanting to wear it any longer. Just as she was about to hang up Debbie answered the phone.

"Debbie, this is Jennifer. Jennifer Parker," she began.

"Oh, hello Jennifer. How's the case going?"

"There's been some real progress on the case, but Debbie, Glen's been hurt. I think you should come."

"Oh my God, no! How bad is he?" she managed through the tears.

"He's been shot and they are doing everything they can."

"Can't they fly him here to a bigger hospital?"

"They don't want to move him until they can stabilize him. I really think you should try to get here right away. He's going to need you."

"I'm leaving right this minute," she sobbed hysterically. "Can I have a number to call?"

"Just leave. I'll call you every thirty minutes with an update or sooner if need be."

"Thanks, I'm running out to the car now. Bye"

Jennifer looked at her watch. She was sure Debbie was going to be clock watching as she drove waiting for her call. She didn't want to disappoint her. She wrapped her arms around her body as she ran back to the hospital door shivering. She heard the crinkle of the paper she had stashed in her shirt.

She went inside to check on the men. She was allowed to sit with Glen, even though she wasn't family, until Debbie could get there. There was no change with Glen, but Dave was slowly losing ground.

She left Glen's side to go down the hall to the bathroom to clean up. She knew it would be more frightening to Debbie if she greeted her covered with blood. She was able to wash the blood from her face and hands and shoes, but her pants were hopeless. She met Doc in the hall.

"How's he doing?"

"He's still hanging in there, but I don't think Dave can make it much longer."

"Say Doc, can I steal a pair of scrubs from the hospital? I'd hate to greet Glen's wife like this."

Doc looked at her pants. "You're right. Come this way."

Once Jennifer was more presentable in the scrubs, she went back to Glen's room. She touched his hand. She could feel his will to live was strong. She was hoping it was not yet his time.

"Glen, I know you can hear me. I found the letter you were reading when the coach discovered you. I'm going to read it to you now."

To whom it may concern,

If you are reading this I must be dead. Let me explain. First of all, I wish I could say I'm sorry for all of the pain and suffering I've caused the families of Holyoke, but I'm not. You deserve to feel the pain after the pain you caused to my family and me.

I was your coach for many years. I did a great job. Then, after two bad years in a row, I was finished. Just like that, you booted me out. Oh, I know the school board announced my retirement in the paper to save me the humiliation of the entire town knowing I was being asked to resign. I could not believe the lack of loyalty.

Tim had to be the first to go. He and his family totally betrayed me. I made Tim the star athlete that he became. How soon that was forgotten. How quickly he

became so close to my replacement whose name I cannot even bring myself to mention. I had to start there at a ballgame. I had to take out his best player.

The rest of them were strictly random. I would simply add the liquid nicotine to food and wait for someone to eat it. I was surprised how quickly the liquid nicotine was discovered. I did a lot of research to find the right poison to use. I applaud the law enforcement for that one.

Jonathon, poor Jonathon, I do feel bad about him. You see, I pretended to befriend him. I deceived him into buying the liquid nicotine for me. I convinced him that some of the athletes had a problem with smoking and they were afraid the new coach would have their heads if they couldn't stop. I told Jonathon I needed the liquid nicotine to help them stop. I lied and told him it was better and safer than those nicotine patches. I swore him to secrecy. I told him it was not yet approved in the U.S. but that I knew it would help the team. He bought my lies and my nicotine.

Once he was picked up for questioning I thought my goose was cooked. He kept our secret. No one had told him yet about the liquid nicotine. I knew that was just a matter of time. I had to remove the only other person that knew about my purchase.

I'm not sure what my plan is at the moment. I don't know if I'm going to continue to terrorize the town. It has become rather intriguing especially with the experts hanging around from Denver. The game of good and evil is so much better in real life than in my computer games.

I suppose, when I tire of the game, I'll either move on to another town and disappear, with the mystery of the Holyoke killer going unsolved forever, or it's possible I'll just decide I'm tired of life and send this email moments before I end it all.

The letter ended there. It was unfinished. Jennifer looked at her watch. It was time to step outside to call Debbie.

Debbie picked up the phone on the first ring.

"How's Glen?"

"No change."

Jennifer could hear her sobbing. "Debbie, Debbie, that's good for the moment. He's hanging in there. I told him you were coming. I'll call you again, soon."

She waited for a response from Debbie, but all she heard were sobs before she heard the sound of the phone hanging up.

Jennifer returned to Glen's side.

Shelly popped in for minute.

"How's Glen doing?"

"Doc says no change."

"I think Dave did it right this time. I don't think he's going to make it. She burst into tears, falling into Jennifer's arms."

She stepped back, wiping away the tears. She needed to regain her composure before the kids arrived. She went back to Dave's room.

Moments later, Jennifer heard the screams from the next room. Shelly and the kids were hysterically calling to Dave not to leave them, but he was gone. Jennifer knew his time on earth was finished. He had done his job and it was time to move on.

She monitored her watch closely to keep her promise to Debbie. It had been an hour already since her first call. She was less than two hours away now.

The ritual repeated itself. Debbie answered the phone on the first ring.

"How's Glen? Any change?"

"No, still no change.

"How's Dave doing?"

Jennifer hoped she wouldn't have asked that question.

"He didn't make it."

Debbie hung up the phone.

When Jennifer returned to Glen's room alarms were sounding, the staff was racing to his room with a crash cart.

"Hello, Glen," said Dave.

"Dave? What's going on?"

"We were shot, Glen. My time was up. I've gone home."

"What do you mean? Are you trying to tell me we're dead?"

"I am, but you're not, you're bouncing between the two worlds."

"What two worlds?"

"Human and the spirit world. Glen, this was all part of the plan we made. You are still too much alive to grasp it all."

"Explain it to me."

"When we were part of the spirit world we made a pact to become human again. We returned to earth to advance our knowledge and understanding of ourselves. We chose to do it together. We, along with the others we connected ourselves to, made the journey to live life in human form once again. We can return as many times as we like to experience life in many different ways. In our last lives together on earth, we were women. Actually, we were sisters."

Glen listened intently. He believed every word Dave was telling him. It was as if he already knew the story, and hearing it from Dave allowed him to remember.

"With each new life we gain so much awareness. We must learn true love to again be one with our God, to be one with the universe. Each lifetime brings us closer to fulfilling this ultimate goal."

Glen looked beyond Dave. He saw the coach, only this time he recognized him as a friend from the other side. The other victims were there as well. They were all friends that had planned the journey together. Beyond them Glen saw deceased family members. They did not come forward, they just stood in the distance watching and listening.

"Glen, you still have to grow in your human life. You have not finished the work you chose for yourself before you started this life. My death and the deaths of the others were part of the plan to help you with the knowledge you seek. Go back, finish your work, and we'll see you when you return. Then we will plan our next journey, my friend."

Glen wanted to speak to Dave, but he had the same helpless feeling he had when he dreamed of Jennifer and her message to him.

Jennifer watched the nurses file out of Glen's room one by one. Doc was the last one to leave. Jennifer looked into his face.

"We pulled him out of that one. His heart was about to give out. All we can do is continue to wait and pray."

Jennifer checked her watch. More time had passed than she was aware of. She was so involved with the work they were doing to save Glen.

She repeated the call process to Debbie. She decided maybe for Debbie's sake she would withhold the information about Glen crashing and being saved.

Soon Jennifer was waiting in the parking lot for Debbie to arrive. She was directing her to the hospital on the cell phone. Jennifer guided Debbie to Glen's room.

Debbie ran to his side, stroked his hair and kissed his lips.

Doctor Foster came in to introduce himself.

336

"Glen's showing promise this last hour, if his vitals continue to improve I think he's going to make it. The bullet passed through the skull just an inch or so behind his ear at an angle that allowed it to exit with the least amount of damage. There will be swelling in the brain, in time we will learn if any damage has been done. I'm so grateful that we did not have to remove the bullet. We're not staffed here for such surgery and I'm not sure he would've survived a flight. We'll know more in the next twenty-four hours."

Debbie stayed in the hospital room with Glen day and night. Jennifer helped whenever she could. She picked up clothes for Debbie at Schunneman's Department store so she could shower and have a few changes of clothes during her stay. They both attended Dave's funeral. Jennifer stayed on with Dave's family while Debbie was at the hospital.

Two weeks later Glen was doing fine. Doc thought he was strong enough to travel. Jennifer packed her bags and joined them at the hospital.

As they wheeled Glen out to the parking lot, he saw his pick-up next to Debbie's car.

"How will we get the pick-up home?"

"I guess that would be my job," smiled Jennifer. "I told you the reason for me not to drive my own vehicle would show itself."

"I wish you would've been able to see into my future to tell me when to duck?" teased Glen.

The three of them began the drive back to Denver. Jennifer helped Debbie get Glen into the house. She laid the keys on the table, and walked to the door.

"Merry Christmas," she said as she closed the door behind her.

Glen looked across the room, he saw the Christmas tree that Debbie had bought and decorated without him. His parents had kept it watered and had cared for the dogs while they were gone.

"See I told you. You just never trust me," teased Glen.

"What?" asked Debbie.

"I told you I'd be home with you and the dogs for Christmas! How could you ever doubt me?"

Now it's time to test "*your*" ability as a detective. Can you find the "Elusive Clue"?

It's a word puzzle hidden within the story.

The answer to the puzzle will spell out the name of the killer.

To solve the puzzle:

A. You must locate the page or pages containing the puzzle or puzzle pieces.

B. Locate the letters you will need to unscramble the name of the killer.

C. If the clue remains too elusive for you, visit www.windcallenterprises.com to ask for clues to help find the "elusive clue".

I hope you enjoyed the book. If you haven't already read them, try "Tryst with Dolphins" and the sequel "Dolphins' Echo" for more exciting mysteries and once again the challenge of finding that "elusive clue".

Patricia A. Bremmer